ONCE UPON A...

Caribbean Summer

*To Mom and Dad, for a lifetime of love and support
and for teaching me that a relationship with Christ
is the greatest treasure of all.*

PROLOGUE

The Gulf Coast
July 1627

Even above the high-pitched scream of the wind, Captain Esteban Ontario Alvarez thought he heard the wails of his passengers below. He cast aside concern for the overindulged Castilian merchants, feeling his ship shudder and groan beneath his boots as they crested another enormous wave. If this storm did not soon abate, they would all perish.

He squinted his eyes against the constant spray of the sea and struggled to maintain hold of the helm. His first mate stood to his left, a soldier to his right, all three of them giving their full weight against the seas that threatened to rip the wheel from their grasp and send them spinning.

The wind was relentless in its drive toward the coast. Soaked to the skin after battling the storm on deck for hours, the crew was clearly losing the war. *"Jesucristo,"* the captain grunted through clenched teeth, willing himself not to lose his strained hold on the wheel. *"Sálvanos, por favor."* Jesus

Christ, please save us.

"*Capitán! Capitán!*" Screaming over the wind, Alvarez's cabin boy struggled valiantly to make his way across the deck to his superior. He fell, was swept against the ship's starboard railing with the next big wave, then picked himself up and pushed forward once again. Esteban watched out of the corner of his eye, his heart in his throat, but was unable to leave the wheel. If he gave an inch, they'd lose control of *La Canción.*

La Canción, the grandest ship to ever exit Veracruz's port...

"*Capitán!*" The boy pointed frantically, seemingly unable to form another word as terror overwhelmed him.

"*Sí,*" Alvarez choked out in agitation. "*Qué...*" *Yes, what?*

But at last, he saw what had stricken the poor lad. Tierra. Land. They would break apart on the reef if he didn't slow them down or change course immediately. With a quick gauge of the wind, he knew changing course in time was fruitless. "*La ancla! La ancla!*" he yelled at the boy, wanting with everything in him to release the wheel and run for the anchors himself.

The boy clung, monkey-like, to the torn sails, railing, masts—anything he could grab—as he made his way forward to the one thing that might save them. The ship, a giant that weighed over three tons, rocked chaotically. So steep was the incline from starboard to port, the boy knew that even if they did manage to slow their rapid advance, they were in serious jeopardy.

But he could not release the weighty anchor alone. The boy heaved open a hatch and scowled at a frightened sailor clinging for his life belowdecks. "The anchor!" the boy screamed. "'Tis our only hope!"

The chagrined man hurriedly climbed the ladder-like stairs, and immediately set to helping the boy release the huge iron hook with wet, desperate hands.

The six-hundred-pound weight sank quickly, pulling with it leagues of chain. They could feel when it struck the ocean floor a minute later, dragged across sand and loose rocks for a moment, then sank its teeth into a massive coral reef.

The ship lurched at the force of the anchor's braking power, throwing every loose object and body aboard.

Captain Alvarez and his men were thrown from the helm. As Alvarez dug his fingers into the cracks of the boards, trying to climb back toward the wildly spinning wheel, he wondered what might be happening belowdecks. Was the hasty building schedule telling? He knew the mahogany ribs, weaker than oak, were likely straining under the burden of heavy seas and a taut anchor chain. Was the planking popping? He'd seen that builders had only secured them with two nails, when ten was more common. He'd known the risk; he'd considered it worthy at the time. Now? Now, he wished he'd insisted on better craftsmanship.

Beneath him, waves gnawed at the interior clamp that held the anchor to the ship. It took only one more massive, watery monster to yank the teeth from their sockets. The captain felt it at once.

"We're moving again!" Alvarez screamed, glancing frantically to the swiftly approaching reef, white waves spraying upward. "Abandon ship!"

Seeing that they were drifting, his man on the upper deck swiftly threw a second anchor, unaware that the interior clamp was gone, and that there was nothing below to keep the anchors from merely sinking beyond the wounded ship. He threw a third. A fourth. Holding the last one, he gazed hopelessly from the quickly approaching rocks to the chain in his hand, knowing that all was lost.

—◊—

The Gulf Coast of Texas
Five Years Ago

In this region, Mitch had rarely scuba-dived with visibility as great as this: eighty feet in any direction. He looked left to his friend Hans, provoking a moray eel with a stick, then right to Chet, meticulously studying the coral reef and its inhabitants. He smiled around the regulator in his mouth. As far as he was concerned, this was heaven.

Catching sight of a lavender-and-gold striped Spanish grunt fish, Mitch stroked through the water with legs well used to such exercise, following the beauty with ease. Over the rise of coral he discovered a huge pile of rocks and moved to investigate. Such exploration had lately become the focus of Mitch's dreams. On each dive he imagined finding vases, ballast piles, anchors: the beginning clues of valuable and ancient wreck sites. Ever since his introduction to Nautical Archaeology 101, he'd had nothing else on his mind, much to his mom's chagrin. Mitch knew that she was just biding her time before bringing up law school again.

He tried to dismiss the thought of actually finding a wreck on a casual dive off Galveston, but as much as he tried to banish the idea, he found himself returning to it again and again. It would only take one treasure salvaged to convince his mom that it wasn't just a pipe-dream. Or maybe she'd have to have an emerald necklace that once belonged to a Spanish queen or a Celtic cross that once hung from a devout monk's neck... *Yeah, that might convince her.*

He smiled. *Then.* Then she would not keep hounding him about the cost of a "perfectly good education squandered away on a schoolboy's dreams." Just one. *Come on, God. Cut me a break?* He laughed at himself, recognizing that God had more important things to do than hand him a treasure map. Yet he couldn't stop himself from hoping that he just might.

Mitch fully realized that chasing the siren call of one ship after another might leave him perpetually poor. Yet it was not just wealth that enticed him. It was the anticipated thrill of a find. That was the spark that lit each successful treasure hunter's eyes when telling of their discoveries. *Just one, God.*

The Spanish grunt darted away, and Mitch turned his attention to several multicolored queen angels, their heavenly wings waving to him as they ate from the pile of ballast stones on the ocean floor.

Ballast stones.

Mitch caught his breath and held it. He closed his eyes slowly and then opened them, expecting the pile to disappear.

It did not. He rose fifteen feet—to a depth of about forty-five feet—eager to catch the attention of his buddies. Hans spotted his wave first and pointed Chet toward him. Seeing his pals en route, Mitch moved back to the pile, carefully examining each rock—without moving them—as Professor Sanders had advised.

Sometimes the kind of ballast rock—used to weight a ship—could help a diver narrow down the ship's port of origin. *If there really is a ship around here*, he chastised himself silently, willing himself to calm down. He dusted off the rocks but couldn't tell what kind they were. Chet was better at geology; when he got a look at their color and texture, he might identify them. Mitch moved on when Chet arrived and began studying them.

Thirty feet away, in the direct line of the current, he found another large, lichen-covered pile. After investigation, Mitch discovered that the pile was made up of hundreds of earthen jars, such as the kind crews once carried, filled with fresh water or delicacies, like olives. Many were intact, covered with crusty coral and mussels.

Mitch abandoned the vases to see what else he might discover. As he crested the next rise, his breathing became more labored. Could he possibly be seeing this? There, scattered between what was clearly the rotting remains of a ship's timbers, lay thousands of gold coins.

His friends soon joined him, and the trio excitedly filled the mesh bags at their waists with as many coins as possible, then swam to their raft sixty feet above. Clinging to the sides, they hooted and shouted while throwing their bounty on board.

"Well, boys," Mitch said, grinning broadly, "I think I finally know what I want to do when I grow up."

CHAPTER 1

Boston
Present Day

After Bryn's grandmother's funeral, Christina Alvarez agreed to go grab breakfast with Bryn and her cousin, Trevor, before they all flew out to their respective homes. As college friends, they'd spent tons of time together. But this was the first chance they'd had to catch up in years, and Christina was eager to help remind Bryn of some good things in life, perhaps easing some of her pain she suffered from losing her grandmother. It didn't prove to be too arduous a task. In short order, she and Trevor had pried it out of Bryn—she was falling in love with Eli Pierce, up in Alaska.

Back in love, Christina corrected herself. Bryn had always had a thing for that man. She hoped that they'd finally be able to make that summer romance something that lasted through the year this time. And yet doing so would certainly compromise her friend's dreams. Christina knew she'd long wanted to work for a prestigious hospital here in Boston. She studied her friend; Bryn fairly glowed as she talked about flying with Eli and the beauty of Alaska. Was she seriously contemplating risking her dreams for some guy?

Christina took a deep breath and let it out slowly. She wouldn't challenge Bryn about it now. She had enough to deal with. And they weren't as close as they once had been; did she really have the right to ask her? *All I know is that I'd never let a guy get in the way of my dreams...*

"So what's up next for you, Christina?" Trevor asked, turning toward her and taking a sip of his coffee.

"Well, I've completed my degree with my graduate thesis on the Spanish sea traders and the importance of the port of Veracruz—"

"Ah, the long awaited Ph.D. has finally been attained," Trevor teased, stabbing a piece of sausage. "Took you long enough. Now what?"

She ignored his friendly jibe. "I could teach, in time. But this summer...well, I've still got those doubloons and family folklore on my mind. I want to know, once and for all, if *La Canción* existed as anything other than a figment of my ancestor's imagination. So I'm going to spend the summer investigating."

"You've always thought it was more than family legend," Bryn said gently. "But you must've learned something new to commit the whole summer to the task. I can see the spark of intrigue in your eyes—what'd you find?"

Christina grinned and nodded. "Last Spring I went to Seville and spent weeks in the Archives of the Indies."

"The Archives?" Trevor asked.

"Yes. *El Archivo de las Indias*. It's the best resource that treasure-ship hunters have today. Unfortunately, it's also in the worst shape. There used to be records kept of every Sevillian ship that came back from the New World loaded with gold. The records themselves are highly detailed, but poorly kept. You should see the place," she said, taking a sip from her mug. "The basement of the building is filled with old documents in stacks five feet high. It's a total disaster. But I have a grad school friend living in Seville—a historian named Meredith Champlain. She's an expert in translating Spanish documents dated from the fourteenth century on. So she helped."

"And you found another clue?" Trevor prodded.

"I did," Christina said, feeling a thrill of excitement roll down her neck. "I got a lead on where my ancestor's ship might have gone down." She kept the location to herself, even though she knew it was silly; these two were old friends. But in the field of treasure hunting, one only shared what they had to; it was a cardinal rule.

"Well if you ever give up on your ancestor's ship, maybe you could find our great-great-grandfather Shane Donnovan's final resting place," Bryn said after a long moment, glancing at her cousin. "I don't know if he carried anything of great value at the time, but he was last seen leaving Rio. They think he was caught in a storm. All hands went down with the ship."

"I actually wanted to talk to you guys about that. Before I finished school, I learned more about another Donnovan," Christina said.

"You did?" Bryn asked, blinking in surprise. Trevor leaned in too.

"Yes. Part of our graduate work was to dive and record a wreck captained by a man named Donnovan off the coast of Maine."

"Not our great-great-grandfather's last—"

"Oh, no. If I thought it was him, I would've given you two a call. But the location wouldn't make sense for him. I did find reference to another wreck off the coast of California, and the records show it was captained by a Shane Donnovan. Your ancestor was a part of the Gold Rush, right?"

"Yes. It's really what made him a success," Trevor said excitedly. "So...you think he went down with that ship in California? Not off of Rio?"

"I think it's possible."

"Would you like to see his logs? I think our grandfather still has them. Maybe his ship went down with some of that California gold. Could be worth your while."

She nodded in agreement. "Maybe. Someday. Right now, I just..." She looked to her scone, carefully breaking off a piece. "I think I'd better chase *La Canción* while I have the chance. As soon as I take a job at a university, I'll likely be chasing other people's dreams. *Donor's* dreams and the like."

"I know a treasure hunter," Trevor said. "He was a classmate of mine at Texas A&M. Found a gold ship right there in the Gulf. He made a mint and outfitted his own operation. Been at it for five or six years now." He sat back in his seat, scowled and took another sip of coffee. "Ah, never mind. Last I'd heard, he'd turned into kind of a jerk. You probably don't want to work with someone like that."

"Treasure hunters aren't known for their stellar personalities," Christina said. "Nautical archeologists team up with them for their equipment and permissions to excavate in certain waters, not to date. What's his name?"

—⁓—

Mitchell Crawford lay awake in his bed, roiling in unhappy thoughts. He had failed to find sleep's peace the night before, consumed as he was by thoughts of his only sister's death. Each time he dropped off for a moment, he had been awakened by his niece's incessant crying. As the little girl let out another wail, he glanced at the clock—5:05 A.M.

Mitch threw a pillow over his head and willed the child to go back to sleep. He had his own grief. How could he deal with the sorrow of two small children? *Heck, I don't know the first thing about kids.*

Ten minutes later, he heard the kid quiet. Talle, his Cuban housekeeper of five years, opened his door without knocking and went straight to the long vertical blinds. She drew them back from one dramatic window, then went to the next to do the same.

"Talle!" he moaned. "I'm trying to sleep!"

The middle-aged woman dolefully glanced back at him and pulled the third window's blinds open too. Then she paused, took a deep breath, and gazed out at the ocean. "It is a beautiful day, sir. It would do the children good to go out with you." Her English was nearly perfect, each syllable carefully enunciated.

Mitch sat up, rubbing his face in irritation, trying to focus. "They said they want me to?"

"No. But you see, sir, I cannot take care of them all the time and clean this huge villa and cook." She busied herself with picking up his clothes from the night before, gathering them in a wicker basket.

"It's not forever, Talle—"

"It's been two weeks. The girl cries all night. The boy is sullen, angry. He sneaks food like a little thief and yesterday, he threw mud into the pool!"

"They're just kids—"

"Kids who need a full-time nanny. I cannot do all that you've asked of me. You must hire a woman. For now, I can arrange for my niece Anya to come. She can stay through the summer."

"Fine," Mitch said wearily. "Just get her here within a couple of days, okay? If I don't get some sleep, I'm gonna scream." She cast him a cold look, reminding him that she'd been missing as much sleep as he had. "I've taken the liberty of calling her already. She'll be here tomorrow." That said, she left the room.

Mitch flopped back against his pillow and shook his head. Even though she pretended as if he were the boss, Mitch knew Talle kept him in order as tidily as she ran the house.

After a moment, he made himself rise and walked to his window. Kenna had stopped crying at last. He looked out over the blue-green Caribbean sea, in the direction of the big island, San Esteban. The palm trees lining the beach swayed in the trade winds, sending the salty, musty smell of the water to his nostrils. He loved his tiny island, Robert's Foe. But was it really the best place to raise his sister's children?

"Oh, Rachel," he said sadly. "What were you thinking in sending them to me? I don't know how to raise kids!" His fingers raked through his hair. How could she have given him this burden? Couldn't she have made her friends their guardians, people who knew the children? Someone who knew anything at all about children?

Kenna and Josh had stayed with the Johnsons, Rachel's friends, for the two months that Mitch needed to finish work on his current dive site. In reality, he'd stretched out the work, still trying to decide if he could take them. But from the start, the Johnsons—with five kids of their own—had said they could only help through the transition. And the children's father, a deadbeat who'd abandoned Rachel when she was pregnant with Kenna, was not to be found. With no other family members, either Mitch had to take them or put them up for adoption.

That thought had been intolerable. His own flesh and

blood out in the world with strangers? He knew his own mother—a woman who had died while he and Rachel were in college—would turn over in her grave if he sent them off to live with another family.

But as soon as the children arrived, Mitch feared he'd made a mistake. Within twenty-four hours, he knew it. The kids needed a mother. And a father with more patience than he had. Who was he to even try? He'd envisioned a life as a bachelor sailing the islands; not settling down, getting married, having a family.

Mitch left the window and went to take a shower. The hot water did little to alleviate his angst. He stood under the spout, thinking. *Why, God? My sister and mom are gone. Why take them and leave these poor kids no one but me?*

Mitch heard no answer. Glumly, he turned off the water, toweled off, and dressed. There were bigger things to worry about than the kids, he decided resolutely. Like locating another find.

It had been almost six years since Mitch and his friends happened upon the mother lode of treasure ships, *La Bailadora*. Afterward, he and Hans had established Treasure Seekers, Inc., while Chet invested his portion of the profits and went after an academic career as a geologist. Since then, Treasure Seekers had located and salvaged eighteen ancient ships. None had held such wealth as the first, but the excitement of the work and the substantial potential riches to be gained drove them onward. They made a nice living and had chosen for their headquarters the island of Robert's Foe: a tiny spot on the map, amid a chain of islands northeast of Cuba.

On Robert's Foe, their modest wealth went a long way. Mitch's home sat on the crest of a hill that sloped down a hundred feet to meet white sand beaches. The house had been built by a drug baron caught by international agents, and Mitch had purchased it for half of its worth. He loved it, and Robert's Foe became his private paradise.

Paradise, except for the loneliness. Hans had married a loving Cuban girl named Nora some years back, but Mitch never had time to date many women. His work consumed him. Nothing was more important than the next find. When he was bored or lonely, he sought solace in his library, scavenging facts from ancient ship logs, tracking down valuable clues, and studying the nautical maps that lined the room's walls.

But this morning, after another long night, the need for a companion to help him negotiate the challenge of adjusting to life as a parent weighed on him. He sat down at the breakfast table and sullenly helped himself to a freshly baked roll and the fruits that were typical fare on Robert's Foe—papaya, banana, kiwi, and star fruit. He tried to eat quietly, hoping the kids, playing in the next room, wouldn't discover him yet. He needed more coffee flowing through his veins before—

"Good morning!" Hans's booming voice startled him.

Mitch scowled over his shoulder at his friend and partner. "Do you always have to be so cheery, Hans?"

"Sure! There are many reasons to be happy!" The big man slapped Mitch on the back, nearly causing him to choke on the bite of roll he was swallowing. "Think of it! You live in paradise and we have a great business. And now you have a couple of kids to love you."

"I don't love him!" Joshua yelled from the corner, his small four-year-old fists at his side. "I don't want to stay here! I want my mommy!"

Both men turned to the boy and housekeeper, who had quietly slipped into the room.

"Joshua," Mitch said, rising and moving toward the boy, hands outstretched. The child's words eviscerated him, making Rachel feel farther away than ever. But Josh ran around Talle's skirts faster than he could reach him, escaping down the marble hallway. Kenna began to cry, her wail echoing down the hallway and penetrating his ear drums like tiny, piercing needles.

"I'm not cut out for this, Hans," Mitch said, pushing his shoulder-length, blond hair away from his face.

"Talle tells me her niece is coming to rescue you tomorrow," Hans said, grabbing a piece of star fruit off Mitch's plate. "That'll help. Give it some time. You all are still grieving. Probably will for some time, yet."

"Yeah, well, she can't get here fast enough," Mitch said, wincing as Talle carried Kenna into the kitchen, her cry even more piercing in person. Wordlessly, the maid dropped the child in his lap and left the room.

CHAPTER 2

Three days later, Mitch and the household had not fared any better at getting some sleep. Exhausted, crotchety, and roaring with anger at the fact that Talle's niece was two days late, Mitch ripped aside the gauze living room drapes when he heard the boat.

"Finally! She had better have a good excuse!" He hurriedly dressed and strode down to the launch, where he would make it clear to the girl that he was the boss around here. Things on Robert's Foe would run his way, on his time.

As he neared the girl on the dock, he slowed. Not a girl, like he'd expected, but a young woman. She was slim and well proportioned, with long, dark hair pulled back in a ponytail. Drop-dead gorgeous, really. *Well, that's a welcome surprise...*

When she grabbed her big backpack and a duffel from the boat captain and turned to Mitch with a friendly smile, he faltered and took an odd step. Still, she's late, he reminded himself. *Two days late. She's lucky I'm not going to toss her right back on that boat.*

"Hello," she started and held out her hand. "I'm—"

"—*late*," he finished for her, ignoring her outstretched hand and folding his arms. "You agreed to be here three days ago, and because of your lack of respect for me, your new employer, I have lost three solid days' work. Do you know what that means financially?"

Christina was stunned speechless for a moment. "I don't think you understand…"

"Save your breath. You're here now, so we'll just make the best of things. If I had any other option, you'd be outta here so fast it'd make your head spin." Mitch whirled around and began climbing the hill to the house, not offering to help carry her bag.

She let out a stunned laugh. "I don't think you…" she began, but her words were cut off by the engine's roar as the boat reversed and sped away. Christina looked helplessly from the retreating launch to the broad back of the rude, arrogant man who strode away. No doubt about it, the guy was handsome. But his attitude made him ugly. *No wonder Trevor had said he was kind of a jerk.* Swallowing her anger, she swung her backpack up onto one shoulder and followed, resolving to straighten things out at the house.

Upon reaching the mansion, she paused to catch her breath, her inquisitive eyes catching every detail. Huge windows opened to the fresh breeze off the ocean, and glass doors folded up, accordion style, sheer curtains at the edges billowing in the breeze. The effect was one of a luxurious tent, strewn with soft, over-stuffed couches, chairs, and pillows. *Whoever decorated the place has great taste.*

"Don't stand there and gawk. You've got work to do."

Her eyes focused on him, standing by a corner table.

"Listen. I, uh—"

"We'll speak later about how things are going to roll here. Right now I've got to get to work I've had on the back burner for weeks now. Talle will help you get settled and introduce you to the kids. We'll talk after you get to know each other. Until then—" He turned and picked up a piece of paper, clearly dismissing her.

Understanding dawned. He thought she was some sort of babysitter. Nanny. Childcare provider. Whatever they called themselves these days.

Christina set down her bags, seeing that the man had finally calmed down enough to listen. He was arrogant, haughty, and out of line, but she noticed despite herself that his furrowed brow made him appear even more handsome. She shoved that thought away. "Allow me to introduce myself. I am Christina Alvarez. I've come to talk business, not to babysit."

He lifted his chin and could practically feel the color drain from his face. *Of all the idiotic moves...* "Dr. Alvarez." He shook his head and rubbed his neck. "I'm so sorry. I... Look, you shouldn't have come here without contacting me first. Clearly, you've caught me in the middle of a crisis."

Mitch knew very well who she was. He recognized her face now, from the journals. She'd led the team working that Civil War ship off the coast of Virginia. But his priority was figuring out how to care for Josh and Kenna; not networking with pretty nautical archeologists. He couldn't think about anything—or anyone—until that was resolved.

"I'm sorry I've come at such a poor time. But I tried to reach you several times on the phone. I left messages. Emailed."

"I didn't return them because I have no time, Doctor.

And I already have a partner."

"I know. But the least you can do is hear me out."

"No, I don't even owe you that. Talle!" he bellowed. "Try and reach the launch and tell them to come back for Dr. Alvarez!"

"It has to be you who partners with me," she said, taking a seat when he didn't offer.

"Me? Why me?"

"Well, your company. Because Treasure Seekers is the only company that has unlimited access to waters from the Florida Keys to Cuba and beyond. Ask for a permit, and it's yours. Other treasure hunters' permits can take three years. I can't risk waiting."

She rose and began pacing, clearly excited about the prospect of a find. And she really was gorgeous. She spoke quickly, and Mitch felt himself getting sucked into her passion.

"I've been after this for years, Crawford. It's my ancestor's ship, and I've got insider evidence that no one else has. I've been to the Archivo de las Indias and found one document. If I went back, I bet I could find more. I've got a friend there who would help me." She stilled and looked him in the eye. "I think I know where the wreck might be."

She'd gotten his attention. He fell into his chair, leaned back and steepled his fingers. "Which wreck are we talkin' about?" he asked wearily.

"*La Canción.*"

Mitch drew in his breath, dropped his hands and leaned forward. "No way." The ship was a fable; she was on every treasure hunter's dream list, said to have gone down with a hold full of gold. But nobody had any idea where she was. Mitch and Hans had decided years before that she didn't exist.

But there was something in the glint of her eye that told him that Christina just might. "I'll show you what I have," she said, "if you make me your partner, sixty-forty."

He scoffed. "If we ever took you on as a partner, it'd be seventy-thirty, our way. We're the ones who have the equipment, the access to permits—"

"I'm the one who has the information that will lead you there."

"Look," Mitch said, gathering his hair into a pony and securing it at the nape of his neck with a band. "I'd go broke if I chased every beautiful woman's dream. As I said before, I don't need a partner. I have one. And we have plenty of our own dreams to chase."

Christina was stunned into silence, and Mitch instantly regretted being so harsh. But he had too much on his mind— and heart—for this.

"B-but you haven't even h-heard what I have," she stuttered. "Of all the closed-minded—"

"I'll call the launch back," Mitch interrupted, suspecting Talle had ignored his shouted order. "It'll take a couple hours for the launch to get there, gas up, and return. Please make yourself comfortable while you wait."

She took a step toward him, really angry now. "You listen for just a minute. First of all, I am not just some woman chasing a dream; I am a woman who has a doctorate in nautical archaeology with some solid field experience. Second, after such a rude, awkward greeting, I would think twice about working with you, but you're my only option. Somebody else might find her by the time I get through all the red tape."

He looked at her, trying to hide his smile. She was fired up, her brown eyes huge, her cheeks taut. *A Spanish beauty's anger is best avoided,* he remembered reading on an ancient ship's cannon graffiti. Out of the many slogans he had seen carved into ships by sailors long dead, that one had stuck in his mind.

He took a deep breath and let it out. "I need a nanny before I can consider adding a colleague and going after another wreck. I don't think you understand what I'm dealing with."

"I hear you need a wreck," she shot right back, "and quick."

Kenna began wailing again. Mitch ignored her. "What do you know of my business?"

"Our circle's not all that big, Mitch. It's been a while since Treasure Seekers found a super profitable ship to salvage, right?" She winced as the girl's wail turned into an earsplitting shriek.

Mitch looked over his shoulder angrily. "Talle! Could you keep her quiet for just a minute?" He turned back to Christina. "Look, I don't have time for this. Hans and I are actually close—really close—to something big. If I could get a little peace and quiet around here, I could concentrate enough to peg it. But between the kids crying and people like you barging in on me, I can't do squat."

"Well, I'd heard of your reputation for arrogance, but had hoped that it was purely rumor. Call that launch." She angrily slung her backpack strap over her shoulder. "I look forward to the day when you read about me finding *La Canción* without you."

"Sorry you came all the way out here," Mitch said. His head hurt already from their confrontation. *Women. Total distractions.* He grabbed his cell, found the launch company's number and dialed. It rang and rang. "He's probably not back yet," he grumbled after a moment. "Look. Make yourself comfortable, Dr. Alvarez, and I'll try again in a few minutes."

With that, he stormed out of the room, bent on giving Talle a piece of his mind for not taking better care of the children…nor making sure her niece arrived on time. Was Anya still coming at all?

—ᗢ—

Christina paced the room for twenty minutes, feeling helpless and angry. *How could he not even hear me out? Who does he think he is?* The child's incessant crying only made her more anxious. *Whose kid is that anyway?* Trevor Kenbridge had never mentioned Mitch having children, and she had not heard anything about it in the industry gossip stream. The guy acted like the kids were strangers to him…only a nuisance that some nanny might magically make disappear.

The girl's sobbing continued. *Is no one watching her? Comforting her?* She couldn't ignore the frantic wailing. She made her way down the marble-floored halls, following the sound.

The ceilings were high, lending a palatial feel to the building. As she peeked into the individual rooms, Christina noticed ocean breezes blowing through gauzy, fluttering curtains and well-crafted floors of wood and stone. *So he's ridiculously rich, but can't be bothered with his own children,* Christina thought resentfully. *Just another guy who wants to pawn his kids off to a nanny and take no responsibility.* Where was their mother?

The cries grew louder. Christina turned a corner and watched as a Cuban maid walked stiffly down the hallway in the opposite direction. Christina peeked into the room from which the woman had apparently come. There, on a small bed covered in white eyelet, a little girl lay on her side, sobbing. A little boy sat beside her, patting her hand, repeating over and over, "It's okay, Kenna. It's okay."

"Hello," Christina said gently. The boy's face shot around to search hers.

"Are you our nanny?" he asked.

"No. I'm a…friend of your father's."

The boy looked puzzled. The little girl momentarily stopped her crying.

"You know where my dad is?" the boy asked suspiciously.

"Well, of course. He's right down at the other end of the house."

The boy turned away to look at his sister, his expression unusually grave for a child of such a young age. "That's not my dad. That's my uncle."

"Oh," she said, faltering for a moment. "Well, I'm Christina. What are your names?"

"I'm Josh, but my whole name is Joshua. That's my sister, Kenna."

"Joshua, it's good to meet you. And hello, Kenna."

Joshua nodded his head solemnly. Kenna sniffled and took a deep, shaky breath, rising on one small arm. Christina reached for a tissue and wiped her snotty face.

"Why are you guys cooped up in here?"

"'Cause Talle doesn't want us unnerfoot, and Uncle Mitch doesn't want us outside, gettin' into trouble," Joshua replied.

"Is that why Kenna's been crying?"

"No. She's sad 'cause Mommy died."

Christina took that in, fighting not to let her eyebrows rise in surprise. "That is sad," she said, sitting down on the corner of the bed. "And you don't know where your dad is?"

Joshua shook his head gravely.

"I see." And she rapidly was beginning to see. So Crawford was the reluctant guardian uncle, clearly out of his depth with these two kids. "Well, it looks like I'm stuck here for a bit while I wait for the launch to come back. Why don't we go ask Talle if you can show me a little of your island? I think we'll all feel better if we get some fresh air."

—∿—

Mitch and Hans were arguing vehemently when the noise ceased. Hans noticed it first. "Sh, sh, sh. Listen! The girl's stopped crying. It's a *sign*."

Mitch snorted. "A sign? Let me guess…That Christina Alvarez is a God-sent messenger waiting to take us to the treasure marked with a big red X?"

"That she'll be good for you, maybe in more ways than one… She's that hot, young nautical archeologist, right? Led the university team on the Civil War ship off of Virginia?"

"*Hans*. I need a nanny. And you're my partner. Why would you want somebody else—especially some Ph.D.-twit—to step in between us?"

"She wouldn't be between us. Our company of two would just temporarily take on a partner. If it doesn't work out, we can just say good-bye to Dr. Alvarez. But if it does work…"

"Threes are never good. Particularly when a woman's in the mix."

Hans leaned back in his chair. "I think it would be good for Treasure Seekers to add a 'brain' to the team, even for a bit. C'mon, Mitch. At least hear the woman out. If she's on the trail of *La Canción*…"

"No. I've got enough to worry about without a Spanish hot-head on my team."

"Because you're the only hot-head we can manage?"

Mitch ignored his jibe and hit the speed dial to the boat launch on the big island again.

"Mitch, I—"

"I said no way." He let out a sound of disgust as the phone rang and rang. "Where is Rodrigo? He should've been back at San Esteban an hour ago!"

CHAPTER 3

Christina led the children—holding each other's hands—out of the mansion and down to the water. She didn't know a whole lot about kids, but she knew one thing: Water was a magic elixir for every one of them. After all, she reasoned, you never saw a sad kid on the sand or among the tide pools. In short order, she was lifting and identifying different seashells, placing them in Kenna's tiny, chubby hands, and helping Josh dig for sand crabs.

The scurrying crustaceans dug madly to avoid the boy that sought them, to the delight and intrigue of both children. Kenna caught her breath and squealed as the waves slowly crept forward, tickling her feet. Christina thought both kids were adorable with their white-blond hair and deep blue eyes. Their uncle had probably looked the same when he was their age. Had their mother?

"How old is Kenna, Josh?"

"She turned one just before Mommy died."

"How long ago was that?"

"I dunno. A couple months ago, I guess. We came to Uncle Mitch's island a couple of weeks ago."

"I see," Christina said, managing to keep her tone even. So these two had lost their mother—clearly their only real caretaker—just a few months ago. And Mitch had lost his sister. *A crisis*, he'd said. She'd never had a sister herself. But she knew well the pain of losing loved ones.

The trio walked along the beach for an hour, then back toward the house. That's when they spotted Mitch, striding toward them angrily, a large man trailing uncertainly behind. "Where have you been?" Mitch asked, when they were in earshot. He seemed infuriated, immediately putting Christina on the defensive again.

"We went for a walk," she said.

"Without telling me?"

"*You* were unavailable. I told Talle." Feeling suddenly protective, she scooped up Kenna. "Obviously it's been days since these kids have had any attention to speak of."

"I told you," he said, roughly taking the child from her. The girl began to sniffle. "I'm trying to get a nanny for them. She was supposed to be you!"

"Well, I'm not a nanny, am I? But anyone with any feeling would reach out to these two sweet kids." As if to emphasize her point, Josh clung to Christina's leg and Kenna pulled away from him.

Their easy bonding seemed to agitate him all the more. Mitch ran his fingers through his hair and gestured toward Hans. "You see how she is?"

The big man behind him looked amused, apparently enjoying the spectacle. He stepped forward and offered his hand. "Hi. I'm Hans Carlson."

Mitch looked between them, clearly exasperated. "You

can't just up and take my kids without telling anyone."

Christina drew in a deep breath, unwilling to mention Talle again. Clearly, the man was stressed out. "Look, I'm sorry if I worried you. All I wanted was to distract them. I figured since I was just waiting around for the launch, I could help."

"See that?" Hans said. "She doesn't sit around and dawdle, like some lame partners would."

"Hans!" he barked. Kenna started sniffling in earnest, big tears welling in her eyes. Joshua hugged her leg tighter.

"Oh, for crying out loud," Mitch said, rolling his eyes and at last handing her back to Christina.

The child looked back at her uncle in clear distrust. Josh was beginning to cry too. "Don't you have any sense?" Christina said in exasperation. "You have to keep your cool around kids. They absorb negative stuff. Look…Why don't you two just go back to the house and I'll bring them up in a few minutes?"

Mitch's mouth worked, as if he was considering another angry retort. At last he sputtered a simple, "Fine!" and strode off angrily. Christina trembled with frustration and concern, patting Kenna's back and sitting down to hug Josh. The man was impossible! Who could've handed over their children to someone so unfeeling?

Hans stared after him too. He let out a big sigh and sank to the sand beside her. "Don't mind him," he said, reaching over to take Kenna. "Come here, you," he said, placing her on his shoulders. The child wound her fingers in his ash-blond hair. "Mitch hasn't been himself since…" He paused and his lips twisted. "Well, you know," he said, gesturing to Josh and Kenna. Josh straddled her lap, a leg at either hip, as she stroked his back.

"But don't let his bark scare you off just yet. I hear you

might want to link up with Treasure Seekers."

Christina huffed a laugh. "I'd had thoughts of it, yes. But your partner is an"— she looked up at Kenna, her dripping nose holding a trace of sand against her skin, and stopped herself. "A *challenge*. I came here hoping Treasure Seekers was going to be my partner on the biggest find in a decade, but now I wouldn't don a tank with you-know-who for a thousand bucks."

"Ah. But I hear you know where *La Canción* lies. Isn't she worth far more than a thousand bucks?" He tickled Kenna's feet and the girl sniffled and then covered a smile with a fist. Josh rose and moved back to the water, letting it tickle his toes, as he stared at it with wide, unseeing eyes. Thinking about his mother? Missing her? Kenna squirmed off Hans's shoulders and toddled down to stand beside her brother in the inch-deep water.

Far more than a thousand, he'd said. *And he was right. Thousands upon thousands. Millions, maybe.*

"Why don't we go sit in the shade and you can tell this Treasure Seekers partner about it, at least. Mitch still hasn't been able to reach the boat launch, so I think you might be stuck here a while." The man gestured to a set of three net hammocks gently swaying in the wind. "Maybe we can get the girl to sleep," Hans said, walking over to Kenna. The child rubbed her eyes wearily. "I don't think she's gotten any more shut-eye than her uncle has. And to his credit," he said, giving Christina a meaningful look, "it's been a really tough few weeks."

Christina took a deep breath. This man seemed reasonable. Maybe he'd be a good sounding board. She nodded and headed toward the palm trees and the waiting hammocks, calling to Josh to join them.

—ᴍ—

Mitch pounded his fist on the windowsill as he watched his partner set Joshua into a hammock, then settled into another beside Christina. How dare Hans befriend her! He knew how angry it would make Mitch. "I can see right through your plan, old buddy," Mitch said quietly. "You'll listen to her and then plead her cause. Leave it alone! No partnership that starts off like *this* works out."

He pulled out his cell and dialed the launch number again. A woman's voice greeted him.

"Buenos días, Señora Rodrigo," he said with some relief. *"Dónde está su esposo?" Where is your husband?* Rodrigo always answered his own phone.

"His boat not work," she responded in broken English. "He in shop."

The launch, broken down? Of all the rotten luck…

"When is it going to be up and running again?" he asked tightly in Spanish, trying to relax.

"Yo no sé." I don't know.

"Okay," he said, stifling a groan. "Please have him call the Crawford house when he returns." Mitch slammed his cell to the desk. He closed his eyes in prayer. *I don't need these complications now, Lord. I've got enough to take care of, can't you see?*

"Sir?"

"Yes, Talle," he said, his voice barely controlled.

"Anya called when you were down at the beach. My sister is ill. Anya cannot come until she is well."

"Of course. Of course!" he said, lifting his hands to the ceiling. "The perfect end to a perfect week."

—ᴍ—

Hans set Joshua's hammock to swinging. The boy laid back, smiling for the first time, watching the palm fronds sway back and forth above him. Next, Hans grabbed his own net bed and indicated that Christina should take the third. "You okay with her?" he asked, gesturing to the babe.

"I think so." Christina pried Kenna's hands from around her neck and held the toddler in front of her. Carefully she sat on the hammock's edge and swung her legs upward. She leaned back and pulled the girl around to rest on her chest. Kenna was asleep in less than a minute, apparently lulled by the swing and the steady beat of Christina's heart.

Hans looked from the drowsy boy to Christina and the little girl on top of her. "So," he whispered. "Tell me about *La Canción.*"

La Canción. The Song. To Christina the whole story was a sweet, lyrical vision. Exposing what she knew might put her dream at risk. Men had been known to kill for such information. For even less. But something about the big man's wide, friendly face, and clear, blue eyes stilled her fears.

"I first heard about *La Canción* from my great-grandmother," she began. "I was just a little girl, but I clearly remember her pressing a gold doubloon into my hand and telling me that it came from my 'grandfather's ship,' which sank near land called Point of Murder, or Punta de los Asesinos. I did some research at the Archive of the Indies and found out some things that helped me narrow it down to two or three potential locations."

"That sounds promising. What'd you find?"

"By a stroke of luck, I found one document that verifies *La Canción*'s destination and known cargo when she left Veracruz. But it was a map I discovered, with a notation of 'Asesinos' by a land mass that I'd never seen before that might prove to be my best tip."

Hans's eyes widened in surprise, obviously realizing Christina had gotten further than anyone else. "And what land mass did you decide it might be?"

"Ah, no," she said, giving him a slow shake of her head, lifting one brow. "I'm not going to get into details like that until we have an agreement. In writing."

"Wise woman," Hans said with an appreciative nod. "Can't fault a treasure hunter for trying. Listen, give me a chance to talk to Mitch. I have a plan," he said, grinning and gazing from the sleeping child to Christina, "to help him see it my way."

"How?"

"Are you willing to care for the children while I convince him? We're wrapping up a small salvage operation off of San Esteban. Let him get that done, and he might be much more reasonable."

Christina considered it. The kids had clearly taken to her, seemingly only requiring a little attention and love. Her heart went out to them. And Treasure Seekers—for as much as she disliked one partner—was still her best bet, with their immediate access. No one else could get her so far, so fast. And if she was to find *La Canción* this summer, she needed fast access.

"I think I could spend a bit more time with the kids," she said, smiling back at the man.

—⁂—

Mitch heard Hans's footsteps as he approached down the long, marble corridor. "Don't even start," Mitch warned as he entered, lifting a hand.

"You're gonna listen to me," Hans said flatly, plopping into a chair on the opposite side of the desk. "I am part owner of this operation, and if you weren't such a pigheaded fool, you would've discovered for yourself that she has some legitimate reasons to think she's on *La Canción*'s trail."

"Hans—"

"No. For once, I'm calling the shots. And you will do this because I ask you to. I am your friend and your partner. I'm looking out for you on both fronts, brother."

Mitch stifled a sigh. "How so?"

"Talle told me Anya cannot come for a while. The children clearly like Christina. She has agreed to look after them for a few days while we wrap up the San Esteban operation, if you'll hear her out come evening."

Mitch rubbed his forehead, trying to push back the throbbing ache there. Then he rose from his leather chair, walked to the window, and leaned on the sill, gazing down at Christina and the sleeping children in the hammocks. "That's the first time I've seen those two nap since they arrived," he quietly admitted.

"So I'll tell her you'd appreciate her help. And you'll look forward to hearing her out." Hans sounded like he could barely contain his glee.

"I'm only doing it for the kids—"

"Yeah, *right*. For the kids. Not for the millions of dollars that ship might hold. Or the chance to work with the hottest archeologist around."

"Hans…"

"Right. I'm going, I'm going," he said, lifting his hands in mock surrender as he exited.

CHAPTER 4

While the men of Treasure Seekers moved out each morn on their search and salvage vessel, Christina spent hours observing Joshua's pent-up rage—evidenced by him ripping leaves to bits as they walked, as well as Kenna's sorrow, keeping the child hovering on the edge of tears, day and night. They were grieving deeply, and Christina felt sorry that their uncle—apparently lost in his own grief—seemed incapable of reaching out to them. She agreed that they needed a nanny; Mitch had to be free to do his work. But if the children were to ever heal, they'd have to find their way to their last living relative, and he to them.

And yet Mitch proved to be as unapproachable for Christina as he was for the children. Hans's request that he hear her out was met each day with a "tomorrow, after we get back." But each time he returned to the dock, it was either too late, or he was too tired to "think straight."

By the third day, Christina suspected he'd just settled into using her as a temporary nanny and never really intended to hear her out. *Well, so be it*, she thought. *I'll just have to find someone else.* He had avoided her quite successfully, taking a late dinner in his study when he dragged in. Hans had been away too, apparently going directly to his home on San Esteban each night.

She'd find another partner. She had to. Of greater concern to her were the children. To her surprise, she felt a growing responsibility for them. Her! Someone who didn't intend to find The One and settle down for a number of years yet. But that morning, Josh had awakened Christina by bounding onto her bed and as they played, she heard Joshua laugh for the first time. It was this that drove her to Mitch's study that third night, even more than her burning desire to discuss *La Canción*.

She paused at the study door, hand raised to knock. Hans was there. She could hear them engaged in a heated discussion. "We can't go on like this, Mitch. It's fruitless. We're as far away from *El Cielo* as we've ever been. I think Hobard managed to feed us bad information and is going after the old girl himself."

Tate Hobard. Christina had heard of the man and the unspeakable lengths he would go to salvage a wreck. There had even been rumors of murder in the nautical archaeology circles, but nothing was ever proven. The guy was as slick as Teflon.

"How would he have done that?" Mitch asked.

"Think about it. We found that one lead that took us off course. And it was that email from Chandler that sealed it— we moved into Cuban waters after you got that. How do we know he was who he said he was? We were sure it was in the Keys before that. It changed our whole strategy."

Mitch threw down what sounded like a large book. Outside the door, Christina started.

"I'd like to get Hobard in a room by himself and make him pay for the ways he's screwed us over. Why, Hans? Why does God let somebody like that guy beat the two of us, over and over?"

"It has nothing to do with God. We make our own choices. And Tate's a bit off his rocker. We're better off just steering clear of him from here on out. And verifying every source doesn't have ties to him."

"I'd give him all the room in the world if he'd allow it."

"You know as well as I that he's never gotten over the fact that we beat him to *La Bailadora*. Three college kids from Texas A&M. He'd been after *The Dancer* for four years. And we just stumbled upon it!"

"Fine. I get that. But that's just part of the biz. Luck favors one, and then the next. Why doesn't Hobard?"

"Hobard thought *La Bailadora* was going to be our one and only find. And he was busy enough with his own discoveries. But now that finds have gotten more scarce, he's apparently decided it's easier to leech off of us. Figures we owe it to him, somehow. Least, that's what I've heard."

"Well, now his leeching is driving us into the poorhouse. What's our financial situation? How much longer can we make it?"

"We have the cash to float two more months of active search and salvage—that covers the crew and the equipment. Then, we'll have to resort to liquidating assets."

"Two months?"

"Two months."

Mitch paused. "Maybe I should finally talk to our resident archeologist tomorrow," he allowed. "I guess we don't have anything to lose." He let out a sound of disgust. "Wipe that smile off your face, Carlson! I'm just going to talk to her!"

Christina tiptoed away, smiling as well. She knew if he discovered her hovering outside the door, he might just explode and it'd all be over.

She'd waited this long. She could wait one more day.

—⁂—

The next day, when Christina brought the children down to breakfast, she was disappointed to find that Mitch was not there. After what she'd heard the previous night, she was confident that they'd finally meet. But when? Or had he had second thoughts? She shook her head. Clearly, it was ridiculous to think Crawford would give her a shot. He'd used her. And she was done. She deserved more respect than this.

"Talle, did Mitch and Hans already go out this morning?" she asked tightly.

"Yes. At five," Talle said, placing some dishes in the sink. "My niece called. She should arrive this afternoon."

"Oh…good." Christina watched as Joshua and Kenna ate hungrily, looking worlds happier than they had a few days before. It surprised her, thinking that it'd be hard to leave them. But she couldn't stay forever. She had bigger things to do than become the world's most educated nanny. But she could prepare them for the woman who was coming to care for them next.

"Hey, Josh, let's go explore the lagoon today," Christina said.

"Yeah!" he said around a mouthful of croissant. Then he frowned. "Are there any monsters in there?"

"No monsters. Just some neat things."

"Yeah!" he repeated and smiled.

Kenna uttered something unintelligible in happy agreement.

Christina hoped Anya would be right for the job. As much as she had traded care for the kids in order to connect with Mitch, she didn't want to hand them over to just anybody.

It was a glorious day. Sunny, but not too hot, with the constant trade winds that had been present since she arrived. Christina stood, with Kenna on one hip and Josh firmly in hand. Kenna was undressed to her diaper, and Joshua wore only shorts.

The little girl squirmed to be released, and Joshua strained at Christina's hand. "Come on! Come on!"

The lagoon, not more than a hundred feet from the mansion, was a beautiful green-blue and very calm. A wall of rock at the mouth protected it from the soft waves that lapped at the rest of the island's shore. The maximum depth of the pool was three feet, which Christina had discovered the day before while the children slept.

"Want to learn how to swim, Josh?"

The boy stood with his feet barely in the water, coyly toying with the idea. "No!" he frowned, kicking up a splash.

"Are you sure? I think you could be as good a swimmer as a dolphin!"

His blue eyes shifted to meet hers. "You think so?"

"I know so." All the boy needed was some love and attention. He was starved for it. "Come on, Josh!" she said, waving toward the water. "It's the greatest! When you're older, your uncle Mitch can teach you how to scuba-dive. Then you get to swim with the fish *under* water. You don't even have to hold your breath!"

"For *reals*?" He moved to the side, observing how his feet made perfect prints in the damp sand.

"For reals. It's the coolest. To be way down deep, watching your air bubbles rise to the surface...I love it. But *first*, you have to learn how to swim." Christina moved in and picked up Kenna, who was busy patting the black-and-white sand around her. "Come on, little sister. Let's show your brother how much fun swimming is."

She dropped the towel that was wrapped around her swimming suit and waded into the water. Standing thigh-deep, she held the toddler and dipped the child's chubby feet in the water. Kenna picked them up right away, curling her tiny toes and holding her legs straight out from her body. Christina laughed, and soon Joshua laughed with her. He was in up to his waist before she saw him.

"Oh, bud, wait for me. Don't come any farther out."

He looked down, a little unsure after seeing the slight alarm on Christina's face. "Okay."

"Doesn't the water feel good?" She dipped Kenna again, who giggled at the game.

"I think it does."

Christina laughed at the adult conviction in his voice. "You think you want to swim now?"

"Maybe," he looked away shyly, all child again.

—◆◆◆—

Mitch came across the crest of the hill and spied them at last in the lagoon. It was a perfect children's pool, he admitted, now that he saw them in it.

Regardless of how he'd begun his day, at least some things would be resolved. Anya would arrive shortly. He would hear Christina out, then send her back home on the launch he'd scheduled to arrive at five o'clock, if her evidence wasn't as good as she promised. Meanwhile, Hans would get the huge water fans, or "mailboxes" as they called them, on his main boat up and running. They needed those for the next site. If it was truly a site of note at all...

The sight of Christina interrupted Mitch's thoughts. Every time he saw her, he found himself doing a double take, which unnerved him. It had been a long time since he'd been so attracted to a woman, which wasn't exactly what he wanted to feel for a business partner. Wasn't his life complicated enough at the moment?

But he stood there, admiring her olive skin set off by the white one-piece, her toned arms and legs... She was drawing Joshua out deeper and deeper, getting him to trust her as he became more comfortable in the water. She bent to teach the boy how to hold his breath and blow bubbles. Kenna giggled in her arms as she observed. After a few minutes, Mitch decided he had to make himself known. If she saw him spying on her, she'd think he was a total creeper.

He walked down the sandy dune toward them, as if he'd just arrived. "Hello there! So you decided to give them some swimming lessons, huh?"

Christina warmed to the first friendly tone she'd heard from the man. And he was home early, not staying out until he could again claim weariness. "Seems it must be in their blood. They love it."

"Looks like they have a good teacher."

"Guess it's in my blood too. I've always loved the water."

He waded in. "Look, I'm sorry I haven't had time to talk in the last few days. I know you've been fulfilling your end of the bargain. I appreciate it. I have good news though. You don't have to take care of them anymore. Anya arrives today. You can tell me what you've got. If it's enough, we'll talk some more. If not, we can call the launch."

Joshua stood abruptly from where he had been squatting in water up to his chest. He looked up at Christina anxiously.

"You're goin' away?"

Christina scowled at Mitch. She had wanted to choose her timing with the kids, introduce Anya, spend less and less time with them over a couple of days…It didn't take a genius to know that these kids didn't need any further sense of abandonment. She walked to shore, holding Josh's hand. "Would you please be a little more careful before you say things?" she asked Mitch.

"I was only…"

But she walked away, talking in hushed tones with both children. He started to go after them, then paused and threw up his hands. "You see what happens when I try to be nice?" he asked no one in particular. Frustrated, he trailed them.

"You goin' away?" Josh asked Christina again, looking back at his uncle.

"Maybe. I have to get to my job. But there is a really nice woman who is going to come and stay with you all the time."

"Our nanny."

"Yes, your nanny. I hope she'll take you exploring and play games with you. And maybe she or your uncle will keep teaching you how to swim."

"For reals?"

"For reals." She paused and knelt in front of Joshua. "I hope you'll love her, Josh. I'd like to stay, but I might need to go. I have a dream I need to chase."

"You're not leavin' before I go to bed, are you?"

"No. I'll stay for a couple of days while you get to know Anya, if it's okay with your uncle."

Mitch folded his arms. "Fine."

"But just as soon as I get these two down for a nap, you're going to hear me out," she said.

Joshua nodded gravely at his uncle, as if he totally backed her up.

"Come on," she urged, wrapping each of the kids in a towel. "Kenna's so sleepy, she can barely keep her eyes open. I'll read you a story and then you two can get a little rest."

Christina helped the kids change and then settled them in their cool, dark room—more hotel-chic than nursery—reading them a book before easing out. Then she strode to Mitch's office, determined to tell him all that was on her mind, even beyond *La Canción*.

When she arrived, he was studying nautical maps, measuring. "Listen, Mitch, so far you've been rather thoughtless every time we've spoken. You've avoided me for days, not following through on what you promised. I, myself, can handle it. But after these last few days with those kids, I will not tolerate your insensitivity around them. They need love and support, not you blurting out things that upset them. Have you thought about the fact that I'm the first person who's bonded with them since their mother's death? And there you are, basically telling me that you're going to hear me out and then send me packing. Here I am, the only person who seems to have reached out to them, and you're telling me to go home! How does that look to a four-year-old?"

Mitch rose and rubbed the beard stubble on one side of his square jaw, looking contrite. He perched a hand on either side of him on the desk and leaned wearily forward. "I see your point. But you can't stay on Robert's Foe forever. With your education, you'd be too expensive to hire as a nanny." A hint of a smile twitched at his lips.

"You better believe you couldn't afford me. And while I didn't come here to baby-sit, you just happen to have two adorable children I can't ignore. You shouldn't either."

"So," he said, straightening and folding his arms in front of him. What was it with him and his arms, all the time? Did he feel defensive around her? "How do we make this transition work for the kids? I'm the first to admit that I don't know what to do with them. I never thought I'd have kids. Then suddenly..." He lifted a hand and then turned toward the window. "Clearly, my sister Rachel didn't know what she was doing, leaving them to me."

"Or maybe she knew exactly what she was doing," Christina dared. "In time, maybe you three will be inseparable."

He snorted. "Inseparable? You've seen them with me. They hate me."

"They don't hate you. They just don't know you. You have to get down to their level. Engage them. Smile more. Play."

He rubbed his face, casting her a doubtful look.

"You woo children. Romance them. Prove yourself trustworthy. Much like you might with a woman. You've romanced women before, haven't you, Crawford?"

The twitch of his smile tugged at his lips a bit more forcefully. "One or two."

"Over the next day or two, as we discuss how we pursue *La Canción*, I'll help you and Anya get to know the kids. Rest easier, in one another's presence. Then, when we go after my treasure ship, they'll be ready to welcome you home when you return."

"So that's how it will go, eh?" He opened a small fridge, fished out two cold Cokes, and handed her one.

"You can bet on it," she said, opening the can and then clinking it against his.

CHAPTER 5

Two days later, Christina was glad she hadn't placed any money on that bet. Despite every argument that she or Hans could come up with, Mitch decided that he would need more evidence if he was to pursue *La Canción* beside her. "Do you know how many places this could be?" he said, waving her laminated copy of the map. "A point called 'Murder'? Every sailor who ever wrecked on a shore might call that stretch of sand the same."

It mattered not that she had leads to several viable locations. Neither she nor Hans could get him to budge. Bitterly disappointed, Christina hid her tears, said farewell to the children—who thankfully seemed content with Anya—and got off the island, fast.

Rodrigo's boat launch sped her to San Esteban. Once there, Christina rented a room at a World War II–era hotel from an islander with no teeth. *I'll show that pigheaded, arrogant man where La Canción lies.*

After a sleepless night on a cot with springs that had sprung, Christina pulled on khaki shorts, tucked in a white sleeveless cotton blouse, laced a Guatemalan multicolored belt through the loops, and slipped her feet into Keds. Then she placed her Nikon around her neck. After shrugging at her touristy image in the mirror, she stopped in the hotel's run-down kitchen and inhaled a huge breakfast of *huevos rancheros*. With a full stomach, she felt ready to face the day.

It was hot and incredibly humid, typical for the islands in the heat of summer. A fellow guest had told her about a rental dock for floatplanes, and she was determined to go search, by herself if she had to, for *La Canción*. She would begin with the tiny islands off the coast of Cuba, searching for a peninsula that resembled the one on her ancient map.

She reached the docks, where three older-model sea planes were moored. With the owner at her heels, she approached the newest, a Cessna 180—a plane almost as old as her parents—checked the floats to make sure they held no water, and verified that the rudder and flaps were in good working order. She checked to make sure that the gas tanks were full and the fuel lines clear. As she ran her hand along the struts, she frowned at the owner.

"It is completely airworthy?" she asked gruffly, in Spanish.

The fat, older man crossed his arms over his chest and settled in for the bartering process. "You can see for yourself that she is in fine shape. No better plane on the island."

"*Humph*. Perhaps I'll take the time to check out that claim," she said, letting disbelief settle clearly on her face.

His arms fell. "There is no better deal on the island," he said.

"That may be so," she said, nodding once and turning back to the struts. The cross braces were in good shape. "A hundred-fifty American," she offered idly.

"A hundred-seventy-five and fuel," he countered.

"A hundred-fifty and fuel," she said, dying to get up in the plane, but knowing that her wallet grew slimmer by the day.

"A hundred sixty-five and fuel. She is worth a hundred-and-eighty."

Christina turned back to him, knowing the deal would close. "A hundred-sixty and fuel."

He bit his lip, watching Christina. She could see it in his eyes; he was giving in. A slow smile spread across his own lips as he pulled the key from his pocket and tossed it to her.

Christina climbed into the Cessna, finished her cockpit checks, and ran the engine up to 1700 rpm. Everything looked good. The owner released the plane from its moorings and Christina made a 360-degree turn, signaling to planes ahead that she intended to take off and checking to make sure nothing would be in the way. She'd learned how to fly in grad school, when she was crushing hard on a professor who offered to teach her. Bryn Bailey's stories of her own handsome Alaskan bush plane pilot had probably primed the pump, she admitted to herself. But for times like this... knowing how to fly came in handy. *Moments like when I'm about to prove Mitch Crawford wrong. So wrong.*

She raised the water rudders and applied the power, piloting the plane out of the bay. Her heart pounded in exhilaration as the aircraft climbed into the sky and the island became a tiny lush green button on a patch of Caribbean blue below her.

She headed west. After thirty minutes of listening to the steady hum of the engine, Christina came across a series of minute, uninhabitable islands, thirty miles from San Esteban. She had pegged them on a map while doing research in Maine; one had a long, conspicuous peninsula. *Perhaps that is Punta de los Asesinos.*

Drawing upon family legend, Christina had focused on finding a point where a tribe of headhunters had once lived, since family lore said that although Captain Alvarez survived the wreck of *La Canción*, he soon had to deal with a new kind of nightmare on land. Her research had revealed several good locations that had both a peninsula and possible history with headhunters, but she didn't know how many of them she could afford to search, alone.

But now she had reached the first, quickly finding the small peninsula she sought. Perhaps Mitch was right; maybe it was called The Point of Murder because of its wicked curve of ship-ripping coral. Or maybe the headhunter scenario had been an invention of an ancestor's imagination, an addition to the story to make it even more riveting.

But maybe, just maybe, this was it. Perhaps *La Canción* lay beneath the sands she was flying over. It certainly looked a bit like the coastline of that ancient map. But Christina knew coastlines shifted over centuries, giving in to the relentless powers of earthquake and erosion.

She circled lower and lower, searching for any sign that might point to the remains of a ship.

There. Clear as day. Something was beneath those aqua waters, and it wasn't a whale. *La Canción?* Her breath caught.

Christina set the plane on auto-pilot and took shot after shot with her Nikon, flying as low as she dared, then turned around and set her coordinates for Robert's Foe instead of San Esteban, triumphant. She was armed with additional proof now. This would make that jerk see the reality of her dream!

The kids came running from the house, with Anya following behind, as Christina ran the plane up onto the gravelly beach. The girl was clearly doing a good job with the kids. Christina shut down the engine and clambered out of the plane, eager to hug the children. Someday she wanted a family. She wanted a love like her friend Bryn had found in Alaska. *Why are all the bush pilots I meet down here in the Caribbean old men or drunks?* It didn't matter, really. Before love, she would find *La Canción*.

Christina walked along one float to the sand and hopped off. She pulled a long rope to the nearest palm tree, tied it, and stretched out her arms for the kids.

"See?" she said to Josh, pulling them both into her arms. "I told you I'd come and visit!"

"Yeah!" he said. "Come see the sandcastle we built with Anya!"

The foursome walked up the beach, and Christina oohed and aahed over the extensive castle, smiling at Anya. She was so glad the girl was getting the kids out, playing with them.

Christina spotted Mitch standing on the balcony in front of his office. When he saw her look up, he turned and walked inside, closing the French doors behind him. She chewed her lip in frustration. He couldn't even bother to come down to see why she'd returned? In a float plane, no less? "I'm going to go have a talk with your uncle, kids. I'll see you later."

Hans greeted her in the kitchen entry with a warm handshake. "You're back."

"I have evidence," she said, holding up her camera and smiling broadly.

He cocked his head and gestured toward the staircase. "Sometimes he needs some time to adopt other people's ideas. Let's hope what you have there will help."

Christina walked up the main staircase and directly to Mitch's office, Hans trailing behind. "Thanks for the warm greeting," she said to the back of Mitch's leather chair. He was typing on his computer.

"We didn't part the best of friends," he said, not looking

at her.

"You're going to want to be my best friend when you see these pictures."

Mitch swung around, steeling himself to not be moved by the sight of her in his office again. She was so confident, strong…so dang *indefatigable*, that he found her irresistible. But it just wouldn't work to go into business with this woman. She was too headstrong. He was used to being the boss. And to go into business with a woman that sexy was definitely a mistake. Even Hans agreed with that. Lord almighty, when he saw it was her, coming out of that plane? He'd thought his heart must've skipped about ten beats. Gorgeous, smart and a pilot to boot?

No, this will not work.

"You want to see them?" she asked, moving around his desk and handing him the camera. "It's pretty intriguing." She clicked on the button so he could see the photos in the review pane of the camera. "I present what might be *La Canción*. Exactly where I told you we might find her."

She edged behind his chair, watching over his shoulder as he streamed through them. Hans came to his side, leaning in to see.

"See that?" she said, leaning close in her excitement. Her long, brown hair smelled like lemon, her skin like coconut sunscreen. He fought to keep his eyes off the tender, lighter skin on the inside of her wrist as she pointed. "That's gotta be timbers. *Timbers*, Mitch." After four hundred years underwater, cannons, anchors, ballast, and timbers were usually the only clues to finding lost wrecks.

He had to admit it, in spite of himself. "Could be."

"Could be?" she chided. "And you call yourself a treasure hunter!"

"I've been burned on more than one site that looked like timbers. Or she's already long been salvaged. Where'd you find her?" he asked, turning to pull up a map of recorded wrecks on his computer.

"Thirty miles off of Cuba, among these tiny islands here," she said, pointing to a string of uninhabited, rocky isles.

Mitch clicked two buttons, making that section of the map larger.

"This was it," she said, pointing at the one with a small, hook-shaped peninsula.

Mitch's brows went up and he shared a glance with Hans. There was no history of a wreck—or salvage—on that island.

"Here, check this one out," she said, perching on the edge of his desk, and taking the camera from him. Her bare thigh was right by his hand. *Yeah, this will definitely not work out.* She pressed some buttons, magnifying a portion of one of her shots. "What do you see?"

With a sigh, he took the camera back. Then he held his breath. "It could be an anchor," he admitted. He lifted the camera up to Hans for him to see.

She grinned and jumped away from his desk. "That's right! It's a ship, Mitch!"

Her enthusiasm was contagious. He gave in to a breathy laugh with her. "All right, all right, Dr. Alvarez. I will consider an initial, exploratory dive," he said. "But first, it smells like dinner might be on. Acting on your advice, I've been doing my best to eat with the kids each night. Wooing them, if you will. And trying not to anger Talle by being late. Care to join us?"

—∞—

Christina was so excited, she thought she wouldn't be

able to eat. But she could smell the delectable meal before they got downstairs, realizing she hadn't eaten a thing since breakfast. Talle had made an authentic Mexican meal of *tiritas de pescado*, a delightful dish of marinated fish; *budín de calabacita*, zucchini pudding; and fresh tortillas. Hans's shy young wife, Nora, helped serve, and the big man kept them all laughing throughout the meal. Even Mitch seemed not quite so gloomy. Because he was hopeful about her findings?

The kids ate alongside them, with Anya giggling at Hans's jokes and spoon-feeding Kenna. Josh ate hungrily and even smiled once at his uncle, who let out a scoffing laugh after hearing Hans claim he was the one who really discovered The Dancer years before.

After they had eaten their fill, Christina anxiously looked at Mitch again. He knew he could not put her off any longer. "Okay," he said. "Let's go continue our meeting." Hans said good-bye to Nora and quietly trailed after them as they filed into Mitch's study.

Mitch picked up her camera, retrieved the SD card, then slipped it into his computer. "Let's see what you've really got, shall we?" In short order, he'd downloaded the files, and magnified them up on the big screen of his desktop. Hans and Christina came around to watch over his shoulders.

"Here's what you think are the timbers," he said. He grabbed a capped pen and silently traced the outline.

Christina held her breath. "Aren't they?"

He paused, shifting to the next photograph and then the next. Slowly, almost reluctantly, he looked directly into her eyes. "I think it's a secondary coral reef. Coral that *looks* like a ship."

"What?"

"It's coral, Christina. *La Canción* might be out there still, but she's not in these pictures."

"She is! It's a ship that looks like coral because she's probably *covered* in coral!" She glanced at Hans, hoping he'd support her, but doubt hovered at the edge of his eyes too.

"It's a coral reef that looks like a ship, not the other way around."

"What about the anchor?"

Mitch's green-blue eyes shifted back to the screen. He moved to that series of photos. But magnified, she could plainly see what he did.

It was as likely a manta ray, hovering in the shallow sand, than the curve of an anchor.

"It might still be worth a look, Mitch," Hans tried.

"We don't have the money, time, or equipment for wild-goose chases, and I vote against it." He glanced at her. "I'm sorry. But we don't dive at any site unless we both agree on it. Come back to us when you find something else."

"Fine," she said, her voice tight, fighting tears of disappointment. "Good-bye, Hans." She turned and fled the office.

"Christina," Mitch tried.

She ignored him, struggling to keep herself from breaking into a run as she walked down the hall and to the stairs. He caught her there, grabbing her arm. "Christina, stay the night. It's getting dark. I don't want you flying out now."

She wrenched her arm free. "I'll take my chances. Because I don't want to spend another hour on this island with you."

CHAPTER 6

Her cheeks had burned as she left Robert's Foe that night. She knew she was embarrassed by Mitch seeing what she couldn't. But that he wouldn't even give her a couple of days' worth of his search and salvage vessel to check it out? After all she'd done for him and the kids? She figured he owed her that at least.

At dawn the next morning, Christina raced over the water in her rented speedboat, trying to forget Mitch, the night before, and her dwindling finances. Posing as nothing more than a pleasure diver, she would verify that this was indeed the wreck site of *La Canción* and convince someone else to work with her...even if she had to risk waiting for a few years.

After an hour she came to the chain of small islands, then the larger one with the long peninsula. She anchored in the shallow cove, guessing the depth to be about forty feet. But the distinctive hum of another speedboat drew her attention. She looked up, anxious at the idea of anyone finding her diving right on top of what just might possibly be *La Canción's final* resting place.

The blue boat sped around the corner and slowed as it neared her. Mitch. Seeing it was him did not relieve her anxiety. Why would he show up after slamming the door in her face time and again?

He came to a stop and drifted alongside her own boat. Wordlessly he tied them together.

"Second thoughts?" she asked tightly.

"You should know better than to dive alone," he said gruffly.

"Ahh," she said. "Hans convinced you, huh?"

"No. I decided it might be worth taking a look. Besides, I didn't want to feel responsible if you went down alone and got into some trouble."

"Well, thanks for your incredible gallantry," she said. But she was glad he was there. For safety reasons and for the off-chance that she was right. Witnessing him discover he'd been wrong—after all his objections—would be a sweet victory. "New boat?" she asked.

"Thinking about buying it from a friend. Can't trust that launch from San Esteban anymore." He pulled off his T-shirt, revealing six-pack abs, muscled chest and tanned skin. She looked away as he bent to retrieve his tank and regulator. Christina pulled on her bright gold "farmer john" wet suit, which covered her legs and torso and met in Velcro clasps at the shoulder. Then she grabbed her own inflatable vest, weight belt, and underwater breathing apparatus. The wet suit was more for protection from the coral than for warmth; they could only be down for fifty to sixty minutes.

Mitch looped a long line of hose for his pneumatic hammer and attached it to his weight belt. Together they sat on the edge of Mitch's boat. Mitch gave her the thumbs-up sign;

she put thumb and forefinger together, signaling an "okay." Together, they rolled in backward and descended slowly into the ocean.

The water was clear, with perfect visibility for forty feet. Even from far away, Christina could easily make out the intricacies of the coral reef. It did not unnerve her that she couldn't see anything that overtly pointed to this being a wreck site. In these waters it was possible for marine microorganisms to completely swallow a ship, embedding it in coral in less than a hundred years; *La Canción* had gone down four hundred years prior.

They explored the massive structure bit by bit, side by side for forty minutes before they came to the object that had appeared in Christina's pictures to be an anchor. *Not a manta ray*, she thought triumphantly.

Briefly, their eyes met through their masks.

Taking the hammer from his belt, Mitch chipped away at the object. In five minutes he had exposed its core.

There was nothing but coral.

—⁓—

From a luxury jet boat sitting on the water two miles away, Tate Hobard and his right-hand man, Manuel Rodriguez, watched the boats through cameras with telephoto lenses.

"What are you up to now, my friend?" Tate muttered, waiting for Mitch and the girl to emerge. Someone had reported that a float plane had taken off from Robert's Foe the night before, piloted by a woman. That same woman had rented a boat that morning, which had been easy enough to follow. He simply hadn't expected Mitch to show up in another, narrowly missing their presence behind a group of rocks near a neighboring isle.

They watched as Mitch and the woman rose to the surface amid bursting air bubbles and climbed into the boat. They saw them stand face to face, obviously bickering. "Well, well, well, Mitch. Who is this pretty nymph?" Tate whispered.

He snapped picture after picture of the twosome, then more of just the woman. He focused in on her face, and he sucked in his breath. "She's gorgeous," he grunted, looking over at Manuel. "Find out who she is, what she's up to, and what her association with Crawford is."

"With pleasure," Manuel said, still steadily staring at the woman through his own camera lens, and taking more pictures as she peeled off her wet suit to reveal a white one-piece beneath.

***

Mitch was trying not to gloat, but Christina's pride seemed to get the best of her. She waved her finger in his face. "You think you're so smart, don't you? Well, let me tell you a thing or two, mister. You're the one who decided to come out here on your own and join me. You're the one who wouldn't give my idea half a chance. Maybe if you had actually discussed things with me instead of cutting me off at every pass, we would be on to the actual site of *La Canción* by now."

"Oh no," he said, smiling at her frustration and rage. "You can't pin this on me. I'll admit, I haven't been entirely fair in dealing with you, but you own up to this. You were on a wild-goose chase."

"Today," she said, turning away. "But not forever. I'm going to find her, Mitch."

She looked so determined, so heroic with her nose in the air and her delicate jaw set, that Mitch actually believed her.

"I bet you will."

His unexpected agreement seemed to take her aback. Mitch leaned back against the edge of the boat. "Consider an invitation from me."

"What sort of an invitation?"

"Let's start over, Christina. You coming out here alone convinced me that you're more than a Ph.D. twit with a wild dream to chase. You're dedicated and strong-willed, two characteristics that treasure hunters need. I admire your tenacity and grit. And I think I want to be around when you *do* find *La Canción*."

Her wide, brown eyes blinked in surprise. She bit her lip, studying him, trying to figure out why he'd be giving in now. "To be clear, I don't need a boyfriend, Mitch. I need a partner with connections. Experience. Someone I can trust."

Mitch laughed and put his hands on his hips. "I can accept those terms. Because, believe me, I'm not looking for more than a business associate either."

"Well, fine then. I guess we have a deal."

"I guess we do. Let's discuss it over dinner at Robert's Foe, shall we? Come for a few days. As my guest and potential partner. Not my temporary nanny."

"Deal," she said.

They parted ways at San Esteban, she turning in her rented speedboat and he returning to Robert's Foe. She met up with him again at the island that evening, arriving via chartered launch and carrying her backpack. She wore slim white denim shorts and a dark purple cotton blouse, Tevas on her tanned feet.

Mitch stood on the office balcony, watching her walk toward the house. Even with her bulky backpack, she moved with grace and poise. Can I keep my end of the bargain? *Can I really keep it to just a partnership with this woman?* It troubled him that every time she left Robert's Foe, he had difficulty thinking of anything *but* her. But no, it was more likely her hunt for *La Canción*. That's what truly entranced him. Right?

He waved nonchalantly and went inside to collect himself before she came in. Hearing her in the front entry, he swallowed hard and went to the hall railing. She stood below him, holding Kenna and listening to Joshua sing his ABCs in Spanish, then English.

"That's very good, Josh! You're so smart! Did Anya teach you all that?"

He nodded with big eyes.

She turned and winked at their nanny. "You're doing a great job with them, Anya. Mitch is lucky to have found you."

"I enjoy it," she said in untainted English. "The children are a pleasure."

"They *are* a pleasure," Christina said in agreement, looking straight up at Mitch. He ignored the jibe. He'd witnessed a couple of occasions where he had to admit, the kids could be somewhat charming.

He came down the steps and gestured toward the living room. "Welcome back." Anya disappeared with the kids into another wing of the house. "Please, sit down," Mitch said, motioning toward a rattan couch. He went to one of the window walls and pulled at its edge, sliding it along giant tracks. It settled at one end, letting ocean breezes waft through the room.

Talle brought drinks—a lovely, icy, fruity concoction—and announced that dinner would be ready in twenty minutes.

"Wow, suddenly I really do feel like the full-fledged dinner guest," Christina said, taking a sip.

"We started off on the wrong foot," Mitch said as he pushed another wall to the side, letting in even more air. "I'd like to change that. Especially if we're going to work together." Finally, he sat down. "You were making a point out in the entry about the kids," he said simply.

"Yes."

"And it was?"

"You gotta spend more time with them Mitch. They're delightful, and they need you. You're all the family they have left."

"I know," he said, setting down his drink and rubbing his face. "But every time I look at them it's as if they're wearing big signs that remind me that Rachel is gone. I still can't believe it. And honestly, it rips me up, every time I think about it."

"Were you very close?"

"Yeah," he said, looking to the ocean, as if remembering. "Rachel was all the family I had left. And I don't know anything about raising kids. You've seen how I do."

"Where's their dad?"

"Never around. Rachel hadn't heard from him since Kenna was born. I tracked him down using a P.I., figuring he ought to know about Rachel. About the kids. He's not interested. He told me he's not cut out to be a father. But truth is," he said, rubbing the back of his neck, "I'm not sure I am either."

"You can decide to be an uncle, first. They need you, in whatever capacity you can be present for them."

He sat back, thinking about what she was saying.

Christina's face seemed to soften, his willingness to listen perhaps making her more amenable. "You obviously changed your mind about me, coming out on the dive today. Deciding to investigate the potential a bit more. You could do the same thing with the kids. And while we're on the subject, what did make you change your mind about me?"

"Your determination. Believe me, I've met my share of nautical archaeologist wannabes. More than I can count have come looking for me to be their benefactor."

"So when I came..."

"When you came, I thought you were the nanny. Which would've been a God-send." They shared a smile. "And then my disappointment and frustration that you were *not* her..."

"And instead, just another nautical archeologist coming to knock on your door..." she continued for him.

"Made me a tad...unreasonable. I'm sorry." He tossed her a grin. "I said I wanted to start over. I meant it." He rose and offered his hand. "Mitch Crawford, Lord of the sprawling five acres that is Robert's Foe."

She laughed under her breath, rose, and shook his hand. "Christina Alvarez, grad-school indebted serf."

He smiled at her. *Sense of humor too. This is going to be challenging, Lord. Help me keep it in check.* They sat down together again.

"It's gotta be hard to be the famous, rich treasure hunter everyone wants to get to," she said gently.

"You'd be surprised about how un-rich I am, despite my luxurious surroundings," he said, waving about. "Thanks to *The Dancer*, I'm debt-free, but I've gotta land another gold ship soon if we want to keep food on our table. I meant it when I said we can't afford any more wild goose-chases. And I don't want to bring in any new partners unless I have to."

She pursed her lips and nodded. "Sounds like wise business decisions. So what's keeping you from the next find?"

"Hans and I've made a few painful mistakes. And Tate Hobard seems bent on robbing us of anything new, because he somehow thought he deserved to salvage *The Dancer*."

She cocked her head and lifted her brows. "From what I hear, he's a pretty nasty adversary."

"In more ways than one."

She took another sip of her drink. "So you've been sidelined for a few years. Think God was trying to teach you a lesson?"

"I've wondered." He leveled a gaze at her, measuring her surprise that he was open to responding to God-talk. Did she throw that out idly or is she a believer too?

"And what did you decide?"

"He's been reminding me that for all the fame and fortune he's brought me, it can be as easily taken away. I've been kinda keeping him at arm's length for a while. Nothing like your sister dying to make a man think about what he's making of his life. What's important."

"That's good. I've had trouble with that too." She looked him in the eye. "By mentioning what's important, do you mean Josh and Kenna?"

"Sure. They're important to me," he said defensively.

She bit her lip for a moment, considering him. "But they have no idea they are, Mitch. They need time and attention. Go ahead and grieve for your sister, but let the children grieve *with* you. Humans bond with each other through happy and sad experiences."

Mitch knew that she spoke the truth. He leaned over, sighed heavily and put his head in his hands. "I've been a lousy uncle."

"There's no time like the present to change," Christina said softly.

Talle entered the room. "Dinner will be ready in five minutes. I've fed the kids and Anya is taking them to bed."

"We'll be there, Talle," Christina said. "Go on, Mitch," she said, nudging him. "Why don't you tuck the kids in before we eat."

He looked at her and wondered about the measure of fear her suggestion brought him. He was afraid of his own niece and nephew? "Would you come with me?" he asked.

She blinked several times, her long, dark, mink-like lashes making her hesitation all the more apparent. "Sure."

CHAPTER 7

"Where are you going?" Mitch said, surprised that Christina was up, dressed, and obviously headed somewhere. They had talked into the early hours of the morning about family, friends, and faith. He'd found out she was the youngest of three, but not close to her brothers or parents. She thought herself too different; they did not understand her need to leave their small, upstate New York home to pursue her dreams. Somehow, they never did get around to discussing *La Canción*. Perhaps they had avoided it.

"I woke up this morning and knew, clear as day, that you were right when you sent me away. We need more, Mitch. We can go over all I have on The Song, but before I can risk asking you to invest your time and equipment—and your niece and nephew's future—we need more leads. So I'm off to seek one more piece to the puzzle. More of that map, perhaps. Or more first-hand accounts from survivors."

"And where will you find that?"

"Seville."

"Ahh, yes. El Archivo de las Indias." Mitch fought to keep the hurt out of his voice. She was leaving. This morning. Last night... They'd made strides, but it was the beginning of their partnership, not a romance. And heading to Seville was the right next step for said partnership. So why did he feel so disappointed?

"Yes," she said, looking at him curiously. "Seville. I've called Meredith Champlain. She's going to meet me at the airport and will spend up to a week with me if I need her."

"Sounds like you've got it all planned."

"Hope so." She held out her hand. "Wish me luck, partner. Once we get going, it will be sixty-forty, right?"

He took her hand in both of his. "Take care, Christina. And it will be seventy-thirty, as previously explained."

"Sounds good to me." She pulled her hand away uneasily and went to kiss the children. "Teach your uncle Mitch how to build a sandcastle," she stage-whispered to Joshua. He looked back at Mitch doubtfully. They all followed her down to the beach and pier.

"Better cut 'er loose," she said, climbing into the jet boat with Hans. "I've got a plane to catch."

—∞—

On the cliff of an island thirty miles from Robert's Foe sat a lavishly decorated bungalow, the second home of Tate Hobard. He was sitting in a hammock on the deck, sipping a drink and gazing out to the ocean, when Manuel came outside.

"You've found out who she is," Hobard said.

Manuel sat down on a nearby chair, smiling and twisting the gold stud in his ear. His teeth gleamed as he looked at picture after picture of Mitch and the woman, printed in glossy eight-by-ten black and whites. "Christina Alvarez," he said easily. "Ph.D., summa cum laude grad from Columbia, extensive graduate work under Charles Wilson and Samuel Roarke."

"So she learned from the best." He picked up a picture of her in profile. "I've read of her. She led her team on the Civil War wreck off of Virginia, right?"

"Right."

"What does Crawford want with her?"

"It's more a matter of what she wants with him."

"Don't tell me that this beauty has poor taste in men."

"No. She knows that Crawford has an open permit in Caribbean waters, as well as priority standing around Florida."

Tate paused, considering. "She's on to something."

"You could say that."

"What?"

"From what I can gather...*La Canción.*"

Tate inhaled sharply and swung his legs around to sit up. "How far is she?"

"Apparently she has some good leads and is looking for more."

"Meaning?"

"She has a reservation on Iberia Airlines to Seville today."

"I assume you do, too," Tate said.

"I leave within the hour."

—◊◊◊—

Christina was unable to sleep on the long flight to Spain, so caught up was she in thoughts of her new partnership with Treasure Seekers and the change in Mitch. She didn't fully understand the abrupt turnaround in the man, but she was not about to question it. "Thank you, Lord," she whispered, looking out the window.

She watched as the Atlantic waters gave way to the arid land of southern Spain. She loved Seville and relished the opportunity to be there again. The ancient buildings, the colorful sights and smells and the passionate people had drawn her to return again and again. With her dark Spanish looks and mastery of the language she blended in easily, even though her accent was not Castilian.

After they reached the gate, Christina grabbed her backpack and quickly headed out of the airport, anxious to get away from the throngs of people. It was six-thirty, and she was to meet Meredith at eight for a late dinner...which was actually a bit early, by Spanish standards.

She blissfully took in the sights around her speeding cab. There was the familiar Giralda, the minaret of Seville's great mosque that conquering Christians had later converted to a bell tower. The sight took her back to her first trip to Seville as a college student and to thoughts of Matt, the college boy who had been her first love and fellow traveler. They'd had a passionate relationship and had wanted to see the world together. But when Matt became too demanding and she had trouble finding enough time for her studies, she had broken off the relationship. It had been the same with others.

She frowned, thinking once again of her ex-boyfriends and what went wrong each time. Over and over again it seemed that men wanted more than she could give and distracted her from her dream of becoming a nautical archaeologist. Her family was much the same. Would no one ever share her passion? Understand her for who she was, rather than who she was not?

The sights beyond the cab window blurred as she contemplated another man: Mitchell Crawford. As quickly as the thought emerged of him as a potential love-interest, she just as quickly squashed it. *Like a bug,* she thought. *You don't have time for that, Alvarez. Keep it together.*

Christina checked into her hotel, a hundred-year-old two-story adobe casa. There were three guest suites, and Christina almost always got her favorite room.

She threw her backpack down on the mattress of the pine four-poster and went directly to the shutters. The room was stuffy, and the early evening light peeked through the uneven slats, begging to be let in. She unlatched the hook and opened the doors wide, smiling at the sight and smells of the ancient city.

Massive domes climbed to the sky, testimonies to the solid Catholic faith of the people. The curvy, narrow cobblestone street beside the building disappeared quickly in the direction of the Archives. On the road, vendors wearily returned home with the remainder of their wares, and mothers called their children in for their evening *comida.*

The city smelled hot and dry and dusty, and Christina loved it. She wondered what Seville had looked like in the days when Captain Esteban Ontario Alvarez had arrived with shipment after shipment of South American gold. He must have been a hero, treated like a prince by a grateful, greedy, and constantly poor government. She would give a lot for the chance to go back in time and witness just one such arrival.

She glanced at her watch. If she didn't hurry, she'd leave Meredith waiting at the café. She quickly changed into clean clothes and left via the back door, having no time to stop and gab with the mistress of the house, who loved to talk and would certainly make her late.

In five minutes she arrived at their favorite restaurant: Café Mystique. It was not difficult to spot Meredith, with her long blond hair and Nordic features. She waved as soon as she saw Christina, giving her a happy smile. Christina hugged her for several seconds before releasing her.

"Gosh, it's great to see you, Meredith. It's been too long!"

"Well, sit, and let's catch up! I knew you couldn't stay away from Seville for long. After we found that map, I thought you'd be back in a month or two, not fourteen."

"I had to finish at least a bit more work before I had the guts to tell Charles I wanted to go after *La Canción*," she said, picking up her tiny menu, written expressly for foreigners. The locals knew the specialties of the cook by heart.

"How'd he take it?"

"He was disappointed, but he understood. There are many others waiting to take my place. And the study is going well enough that they'll be funded for another three summers."

"I hear everything you touch goes great," Meredith said, with an arched brow.

"Where'd you hear that?"

"Small world. I ran into Trent Anderson in Madrid. He went on and on about your leadership on the Civil War wrecks."

Christina blushed slightly. "Well, I had a super team." She studied the menu again, pleased–but a bit discomfited by–the second-hand praise. *If only Mitch Crawford had heard such great things about me before I arrived on Robert's Foe.*

"What are you having?" Meredith asked.

"I don't know yet. How about you?"

"I can never get away from their *pollo en pepitoria*."

"That sounds good." Christina's stomach rumbled its approval at the thought of the chicken and almond-sauce dish. "That will make right all that the airline did wrong to my digestive track. Now tell me what you've been up to since I've been gone."

As her friend filled her in, she noticed a man enter the

café and take his seat at the bar, never looking in the direction of Christina or her companion. But he took a seat right by their table and ordered a beer and *gambas al ajillo*, a classic garlic shrimp dinner. Then he took a worn paperback from his pocket and began to read.

He seemed harmless enough, but Christina, trained to notice details, thought something about him was odd. There were only ten other people in the café, but the man had failed to look them all over, a trait Spaniards commonly exhibited upon entering a room. Even more odd was his lack of interest in the blonde who sat beside her. Seville was a city of men who coveted the fair, Nordic looks that Meredith had in abundance. He was also reading, not chatting with the bartender or his neighbor at the bar, as was more typical. And he'd chosen the more crowded part of the bar, right by their table, rather than the empty end where a reader could go about his business undisturbed.

She took a sip of her sangria, telling herself she was imagining things. She needed to concentrate on her dear friend more than any oddlings in the café.

"Well, enough about me," Meredith said. "You sounded charged on the phone. Have you found a partner to search for *La Canción*? "

"I think I have," she said with a grin and sat up straight. "Treasure Seekers."

Meredith gasped. "You're kidding! How'd you manage that?"

"I baby-sat for one of the partners."

"You did *what*?"

After she'd told her the entire tale, Christina observed the man behind Meredith finish his dinner, toss some bills on the counter and ease off his barstool. He nonchalantly left the restaurant, never looking toward the women again. He was out the door before Christina saw that he had left his book behind.

It was a Clive Cussler novel. In English.

She glanced over her shoulder, half-rising to call out to him. But he was gone.

—⁓—

Back at his rented room across from Christina's inn, Manuel waited for Christina to return, watched her light go out for the night, and drifted off to a pleasant slumber himself. He had paid handsomely for the master bedroom of the house. But he decided it was worth every penny as he looked out on the street the next morning, watching Christina open her shutters to the day and move about her room. *Cushy assignment,* he thought, not minding this chore of spying upon a young beautiful archeologist at all. *Nope. Not. At. All.*

Outside, she emerged dressed in Spanish clothing, easily blending into the crowds on the street and avoiding the chastising looks of Castilian matrons who frowned upon scanty American clothes. He struggled to keep up with her long-legged gait, determined not to lose her. He focused on her loose, brightly colored skirt and black blouse as she made her way toward the Archives.

The woman whom Christina had met for dinner, Meredith, was waiting for her on the cracked steps. Manuel paused at the edge of the throng, purchasing an apple from a wrinkled raisin of a woman who sat under an umbrella that had the Madonna painted on its border. He chatted with the vendor idly, watching as Meredith and Christina disappeared between the huge columns that marked the entrance to the Archives, and wondered how he might do the same.

—ᴍ—

The Archives of the Indies held within its belly thousands of ancient documents describing the Spaniards' exploration and activities in the New World. Many papers had been lost in fire and flood, but the Archives held the last remaining bastion of ancient, undiscovered, documented Spanish history from the fourteenth through the seventeenth centuries.

The problem lay in the basement of the monstrous building. When the archives in Madrid had been threatened by a city fire in 1632, King Philip demanded that all the documents be moved at once to the new Seville building, which had supposedly been completed. However, when the documents arrived, only the basement was complete, and the papers were stacked haphazardly there, to be sorted out at a later date. Due to the country's financial ruin, the structure took a hundred years to finish, and after completion, there were few people to staff it. By then the official historians had more than enough contemporary documents to fill the rooms above. The older papers sat where they had been left, neglected and in decay.

Christina winced, as she always did, when she looked upon the stacks of moldy, rat-eaten papers. They lay in over fifty lines, measuring twelve feet long by five feet high. Even more frustrating was the archaic language and thick scroll writing that had been popular in the sixteenth and seventeenth centuries. Christina had done enough graduate work to spot interesting clues, but accurate transcription required someone with Meredith's prowess.

The sight did not intimidate Meredith, who spent several days of every week in the basement and was used to the conditions. She had a passion for her work, wanting to read and transcribe as many of the precious papers as she could before they were gone forever.

She opened her backpack and tossed Christina a head-lamp that matched her own.

"Great idea!" Christina said. "I almost went blind last time I was here."

"Come over here," Meredith directed, switching her lamp on. "A couple of weeks ago I found a stack that seems to be mostly late seventeenth-century documents. Since you called, I've been working on it."

"Same stack where we found that first document on *La Canción*? "

"Three down. There's no rhyme or reason to these things. When you catch a whiff of the least bit of organization, you have to stick to it and hope something turns up."

"Agreed. Let's dive in, shall we?"

—◊—

Manuel had a difficult time getting past the Archive basement door. Based on Meredith's connections and good standing with those who controlled the archives, Christina was allowed entrance without question. Access cost Manuel one hundred American dollars to a dozing back-door security guard.

He crept down the stone stairs, moving as silently as a cat. The walls were discolored with age, and tiny rivulets of water oozed from cracks, disappearing into other cracks in the floor. Manuel wiped his hands on his jeans in distaste. The smell of mold invaded his nostrils and threatened to make him sneeze. He pinched his nose and held his breath, waiting for the urge to pass before creeping forward. He wound his way, deeper among the stacks, following the sound of two feminine voices.

—⚏—

Christina and Meredith worked for hours, reading document after document in silent concentration. Finally Christina paused, got off the hard concrete floor, and stretched. "Man! I forgot how hard this is."

"Blocked the pain out of your mind?" Meredith asked absently, continuing to read.

"I don't know how you can do it, day after day."

Meredith looked up, her blue eyes reminding Christina of Kenna, Josh and...Mitch. The sudden pounding of her heart startled her. Christina frowned in confusion. *Maybe it's just the excitement of having a new partner. But I don't think of Hans that way...*

"Christina?" Meredith said. "You look a thousand miles away."

"I am, I guess. Lots of things on my mind. How 'bout we break for some lunch?"

"Now you're talking." Meredith stood and stretched. She bent over and placed a neon-colored paper between the documents they'd read through and those they hadn't touched.

A faint rustling noise caused Christina to snap her head around and search the dimly lit room. "Did you hear something?" she asked in a low voice.

"No," Meredith said, putting her things into her backpack again. "Probably just a rat."

"Yeah. You're probably right." She shivered. "I don't know if I could handle rats week after week either."

"Better than sharks," Meredith said, clearly remembering her friend's attack years before.

"Just a little better," Christina said, smiling ruefully.

"How's your scar?"

Christina raised her shirt to expose the side of her belly

and the ugly, tearing marks that remained. "Not too bad," she said.

"Better than four years ago," Meredith said, bending over to shine her headlamp on the old wound. "Only two shark attacks in those waters in twenty years, and of course, you had to be one who ended up in a great white's mouth."

"Fortunately, I got out," Christina quipped, shoving away a shudder with a measure of bravado.

"Yes," Meredith put her arm around her friend and edged her toward the door. "Now let's go. Maybe we can get some freshly caught shark for dinner."

"Sounds good," Christina said, her smile returning. They walked to the stone staircase. She paused and lifted her nose. "Do you smell cologne?"

Meredith raised her nose too. "Just a whiff. Probably that scruffy guard upstairs thinking he smells sexy, even though he hasn't bathed in weeks."

"Try and keep your hands off him as we pass," Christina warned with a grin.

CHAPTER 8

Hans leaned back in his chair and smiled knowingly. Mitch ignored him and stood at his office window, watching the kids play with Anya in the shallow end of the pool. He raised a hand to Joshua when the boy looked up, and the boy waved back shyly.

That's some progress, I guess.

From the back, Anya could have been Christina. They had the same slim waist…the same dark hair… But Anya was little more than a girl. Christina was all woman. And he couldn't get her off his mind.

"So, are we going out tomorrow?" Hans asked. They had not made any exploratory missions since Christina left. In fact, now that Mitch was committed to it, Hans could not get him to concentrate on any potential wreck other than *La Canción*. The man was knee-deep into reading about seventeenth-century ships and their routes, as well as all of Christina's notes.

"No. I think we should conserve funds until we launch an all-out seek-and-find mission for *The Song*."

"It's a gamble," Hans said, blowing out his cheeks. This tactic was unlike any they'd used before. Usually they pursued their current mission until they gathered enough information to go after a better find. But *La Canción* was different. "It promises to be even richer than the wreck we found as schoolboys, eh?"

"Far richer. I can't get her off my mind."

"Who? *La Canción* or the lovely Dr. Alvarez?"

Mitch turned to scowl at him. "We've agreed that this shall be a purely professional relationship. Neither of us is looking for more. But speaking of our newest partner, I wonder why she hasn't called."

"I'd just like to point out that I'm not the one worrying about her," Hans said casually, picking a speck of dirt from under his thumbnail.

"I'm not worrying!" Mitch bit out.

Hans smiled.

"I'm not," Mitch said more softly, turning to look out the window again. Was he?

—⁓—

After four days in the stacks, Christina's vision blurred from the constant strain on her eyes and brain. She longed to go for a dive, to explore the multicolored reefs she so loved. She thought of Robert's Foe. *Next time I'm back there, I'm going to check it out with Hans or Mitch.* She had spotted several reefs from the floatplane on the leeward side of the island and guessed they might make excellent diving locations.

She looked back to the document in her lap. The thick, ornate writing swam before her eyes. "I need a break," she said to Meredith, who mumbled her acknowledgment but did not look away from the page in her lap. "I'll be back in a minute."

Christina rolled her head slowly to release the tension in her neck, focusing on the crusty old walls and cracks in the ceiling. She shivered. *I'd hate to be down here in an earthquake.*

As she walked to the stone staircase, she again caught the smell of cologne. What kind was it? She knew she had at one time known someone who wore it. Who had that been? She racked her brain, but could not place the person or scent.

Once outside, Christina took a deep breath of hot afternoon air. She paused at the top of the long, skinny stairway that skirted the front facing of the Renaissance-style building, where many poor gathered to beg from passersby. She wondered where they all went at night, worrying for them. Meredith had told her that they suffered constant beatings from policemen sent to clear the streets of "vermin who hurt tourism."

As they reached out to her, Christina sadly shook her head in refusal and concentrated on breathing through her mouth instead of her nose to avoid the stench of urine and unwashed clothing. She moved directly to a nearby fruit stand and paid for a sack of apples. Then she paid for a cheese sandwich and a fruit drink, which was a little too sweet, but refreshing.

—⟋⟍—

Wearing the white T-shirt and black trousers common to Castilian youths, Manuel studied her from a hundred feet away, hiding in the shadows of a vendor's awning. He had spent part of the morning shopping and had purchased a new gold earring—a tiny shark twisting backward with its jaws open. He pinched it at his earlobe as he bent to light a cigarette and continued to watch her.

He blew out the smoke hard and fast. Christina moved back to the steps as soon as she was done eating. Quietly she moved from one sick and homeless man to an elderly woman, then to a young boy without legs, distributing her apples one by one as she climbed the steps of the Archives and disappeared into its entrance.

Manuel shook his head. *What incredible foolishness.* But something in her loving generosity made him pause and think, just for a moment. It had been a long time since he had seen such an act of compassion.

—⦿—

"Anything?" Christina said wearily when Meredith took out her magnifying glass and bent closer. It was nearly quitting time.

"Maybe," Meredith said, struggling to keep the excitement from her voice. "*La Canción* was traveling with four other ships, right?"

"Right. Two went down in deep waters. The other two ships made it back to Spain, believing there were no survivors."

"Wasn't one of those *El Orgullo?* "

Christina nodded.

"Christina." Her blue eyes lifted to meet hers and she lifted the delicate parchment. "This is her manifest."

"You're kidding."

"No."

"We're getting close!" Christina said excitedly.

Just then the guard called to them in Spanish, telling

them it was past closing time.

Both women groaned.

"Let's smuggle it out," Christina whispered.

"I can't do that! If they ever found out, they'd revoke my pass to the stacks."

"Sorry. But we can't just leave this down here! What if something happens to it? What if someone else gets their hands on it first?"

"No way," Meredith whispered. She turned to the stack on her right and counted fifty sheets down. There she slid in the document naming *El Orgullo, The Pride*. She smiled conspiratorially at Christina. "We'll be back first thing in the morning."

Christina sighed, knowing this was the best they could do. "First thing," she urged her companion.

—✕—

After the twosome left the building, Manuel emerged from the guard's office and slid the man a hundred Euros.

He placed his arm around the older man's shoulders, wincing at the officer's body odor. "Now, my friend, I know you cannot let me any farther than the stone hallway of the Archives." This man was more a stickler for the rules than the back-door guard had been. But the back-door guard had been absent today.

"No, señor. It would mean my job. I have children and grandchildren to feed." He looked at Manuel with a sorrowful expression.

Manuel nodded in understanding. "A burden for any man," he said. "Let me help with your burden. We have become friends." He pulled out another crisp hundred-Euro bill. "You have helped me by letting me look at the Archives, if not to touch them. But you have permission to walk among the stacks at any time, no?"

"Sí, señor."

"I have need of a friend's eyes that can come closer to certain stacks and certain documents."

"And certain women?" the guard asked, risking exposing his knowledge.

Manuel narrowed his eyes, then nodded slowly, smiling. "Yes. Certain women. If you will observe the two who just left and report to me if they find anything, I will pay you several hundred more. I have other business in the morning."

The guard's eyes widened. "Sí, señor, it will be as you wish."

—∞—

Christina finally called on the fifth day. "Christina!" he said. "You finally decided to get in touch, huh?"

"Well, I've been busy, *Dad*," she responded in surprise. "Meredith and I have had four extraordinarily fun-filled and exciting days in the stacks."

"Find anything?" Mitch closed his eyes, listening to her voice. He found himself wishing he had a picture of her.

"Just *El Orgullo's* manifest."

He sat bolt upright in his chair. "What?"

"That's right. And if we hadn't been thrown out, I bet we would've found others, too."

"I take it you're going back tomorrow."

"Righto, partner." Her tone was light and happy; Mitch knew she must be floating on air. If he'd had any idea how to translate seventeenth-century documents, he would have been on the next flight to Seville. As it was, he had seen enough of them to know that he'd be of little help.

"Well, congratulations. Unearth any other clues you can find, and then hightail it home. I want to start this expedition."

"You and me both."

Her signal was bad. He only heard half of what she said next. Mitch's heart tightened as he realized that their conversation was over before it had really begun. "I'm losing you. You're cutting in and out. Keep us posted?"

"I will." She paused. "Is everything okay, Mitch?"

"Fine, fine."

"The kids?"

"They're fine too. I even built a sandcastle with—"

But then he lost her for good.

Feeling every mile of the three thousand between them, Mitch clung to his phone, admitting to himself that he wished her voice, their tentative connection, would return. It took him a minute to press the end button. He looked out on the bright morning on Robert's Foe and imagined the steamy darkness of a summer night in Seville. "Good night, Christina."

CHAPTER 9

Christina bathed the next morning in the deep, yellowed tub of the communal bathroom, then tied her hair back and dressed. She could not wait to return to the Archives and, therefore, could not endure the time breakfast with the hotel matron would take. She sneaked out the back door again, hoping the dear woman would not be angry with her.

Out on the avenue, Christina threw her Nikon around her neck and headed off at a quick clip toward the Archives. She paused and purchased from a street-side vendor a tall cup of rich, black coffee and a basket of *pestiños*, then turned to walk away.

The man she had spotted in Café Mystique a few nights earlier sat beside the street, sipping coffee and reading a newspaper. He did not look up at her. Christina walked by, chewing her honey-coated pastries, but wondered at the coincidence of seeing him twice in one week. *Maybe he's just a fellow traveler.*

She dismissed all thought of him and lengthened her stride toward the Archives. Her heart pounded as she thought of the document. By previous agreement, Meredith would devote her day to transcribing the manifest completely, to see if there were any hidden clues, while Christina would continue to dig, scanning the nearby documents for anything that might be related.

To her delight, Meredith was already waiting for her on the steps. "Well, it's about time," Meredith teased.

"Come on," Christina said, pulling her friend up the steps. "I can't wait to get my hands on that manifest again!"

—∿—

The two disappeared into the building as the guard opened the door to the public for the day. The man looked down the steps toward the vendors, searching.

Manuel lit a cigarette. When the guard spotted him and gave a quick nod, he did the same. As the older man turned to follow the women inside, Manuel pulled out his cell, eager to report to Tate all that he knew.

"Manuel," his boss said. "I trust you have good news for me."

"I do. The girl is on to something. I should have it from her by tomorrow night."

"Very good. The Archives?"

"Yes. She's spent days here. She is working with Meredith Champlain. And they seem very excited. They were here as soon as they unlocked the doors this morning."

"Ahh. Very good, very good. I've read of Champlain. She's an astute partner. If they've found something concrete—be certain it becomes ours, yes? By any means necessary."

"Of course."

Manuel hung up without saying good-bye.

—⁓—

Five hours later, Christina could ignore her rumbling stomach no longer. Working at a collapsible table, Meredith had not moved all morning. Translating was a tedious process, and by nature she was meticulous. It was what made her one of the best in her field.

Christina rose and was about to go in search of food when Meredith looked up at her, a slow smile stealing across her face.

"What?"

"This not only mentions *La Canción*," she said. "It's the cargo manifest for the entire armada! Your ship is the last one to be listed. But it's all here. If you find the site, you'll be able to verify that she is indeed *La Canción*."

Christina squealed and threw her arms around Meredith. "Oh, Meredith! That's wonderful! Mitch is going to be so excited."

Meredith beamed as Christina took a picture of her with the document on her cell, so she could send it to the Treasure Seekers boys. "It is pretty terrific. I haven't found one of these on an active shipwreck expedition for a long time."

"It's an amazing stroke of luck! So where was the gold minted?"

"Well, when you find her, the pieces of eight should be marked with a P."

"Potosí," Christina said in a reverent whisper.

"The finest minter of gold and silver in South America." Meredith looked past Christina. "What about you? Have you earned your keep this morning?"

Christina sighed and glanced back to the stack she'd just set back in order. "I'm afraid not. I thought we'd find a wealth of information right around that manifest, but of course it's never that easy. I think the stack must've been shifted into another at some point. Suddenly I'm two hundred years behind *La Canción.*"

Meredith studied the stack and then the others around it. "Maybe we ought to look for papers of a similar color to this," she said, lifting the manifest. Christina looked around. The stacks of papers were almost all a dark brown, but some were lighter than others, like the manifest. She studied the stack two down from where Christina dug, and then the document in Meredith's hand. "Let's move over to that one," she said, pointing. "*After* lunch."

"Sounds good."

"Are you as hungry as I am?"

"I'm dying."

"Let's go grab something."

The two climbed the stairs to the wrought-iron gate and called for the guard, who came down the tiled hallway to let them out. He shoved an enormous iron key in the ancient lock and as usual, Christina felt as if she were being let out of some sort of scholarly jail. He smiled as they passed him. "Buena suerte?"

"Sí!" Meredith said, not catching Christina's warning look. "Very good luck!"

They climbed the steps to the main floor and exited the building.

"Meredith," Christina said, taking her companion's arm and leaning closer. "You've gotta keep quiet. Do you know what this find might be worth?"

"Of course," she said, hanging her head. "I know better. I'm just so pumped."

"I know," Christina said, squeezing her arm.

—⁂—

Manuel spent the morning carefully searching Meredith's studio. He had easily picked the lock and, once inside, methodically looked around. Meredith made her home in one of the taller buildings in Seville, in which she had converted a portion of an upstairs storage room into a comfortable apartment.

Tall screens walled off "rooms" in the rectangular space. White sheets and a soft, cream-colored down comforter covered her bed. The wood floor set off the sparse furnishings. It was obvious that the woman spent most of her time in her corner "office": a mass of organized paper stacks around a huge desk.

Manuel sat down in her antique leather chair. Slowly he read through each paper on her desk, then went through her files, coolly brewing himself a cup of coffee and drinking from her mug. He smiled at the lipstick on the other side of the cup, took another sip, and picked up the next piece of paper.

Meredith was clearly in the midst of many projects, but notes on *La Canción* dominated the stacks. She even had an eight-by-ten illustration of the original ship, and a copy of a map showing a peninsula marked as "Punta de los Asesinos." Was it this that had led Christina and Crawford to dive that day? He pulled out his cell and took pictures of everything relevant. Tate would be very pleased.

Satisfied that he had covered all the business, he spent several minutes meandering through Meredith's personal belongings, curious about the life of a beautiful blond scholar in Seville. He sat on the side of her bed and picked up a framed picture of Meredith and Christina in front of a brick building. They were both beauties. But if he had his pick, he thought, he would choose Christina. He preferred darker looks in women.

He yawned and looked at the inviting bed. *There might be just enough time for a late-afternoon nap.*

—⚜—

Christina gasped when she saw it. Meredith rose and hurried over to her. "What? What is it?"

"You tell me, Ms. Expert. But if I'm reading it right, I think it's the biggest clue yet." She lifted it to her. "Here! Hurry and tell me what you see. And don't take four hours. I don't care if you have it translated perfectly, I just want the general gist of it."

"Okay, okay," Meredith said. "But give me a minute."

"A minute. No more." Christina paced back and forth, biting her lip and rubbing her hands in anticipation.

Meredith's eyes slowly moved from the cracked, blackened paper to Christina. "It's big, all right," she whispered.

"What? What does it say? I saw *La Canción* written at least five times."

"It's a letter from the Minister of the Treasury to King Philip, telling him that The Song and two other ships were lost in severe weather. He was decapitated for being the bearer of bad news. The letter is a full account of how the ship went down and where she lies, as dictated by Captain Alvarez. The Minister of the Treasury assures his king that it can be salvaged."

"But we know it was never found," Christina breathed, edging closer to look at the document again. "Does it list co-ordinates?"

Meredith scanned the paper again. "It does."

"That's incredible," Christina whispered in awe. "It could lead us right to *La Canción*!"

"Or close to it anyway. The coordinates might well be

wrong. If it was easy, the Spaniards would have found her and salvaged her long ago."

"Maybe by the time they got there, she was covered by sand and the sponge divers couldn't locate her. Storms can wreak havoc on a sea floor, especially close to reefs."

"Maybe," Meredith said, nodding. She looked at her watch. "Better take some pictures of this. The guard will want us out on time."

"Good idea," Christina said, reaching for her camera. She took the delicate paper from Meredith's fingers and laid it flat on the ground. In the dim light, the Nikon was more trustworthy than her cell.

"Here," she said, handing the document back to Meredith. "Will you file this away?"

"You've gotten enough pictures?" Meredith asked with a mischievous smile that matched Christina's. "I'll need an enlargement to fully translate it."

"No problem."

"Well then," she said, "Let me take care of this properly. I think it was in the wrong place, don't you?"

"I do," Christina said, grinning as she watched Meredith walk to a stack of twelfth-century documents and count fifty papers down.

She was just walking back toward Christina when the guard called out to them from the stairs. He was leaning forward, crouching to see them. *"Vamanos!" Let's go.* He gestured up the stairs. It was quitting time, and he was obviously ready to head home.

Both women jumped, worried that he had clearly seen where they'd been working. Or even where Mer had stuck that last report. How had they not heard the creaking gate open?

"Sí, sí!" Meredith called. He nodded and walked up the

stairs, where they knew he'd be waiting for them at the gate. "I'll come and refile the document where we found it," she whispered to Christina, "*after* you've made headlines with Treasure Seekers."

"You've been such a help, Meredith," Christina said gratefully. "I couldn't have done this without you."

"Any time," Meredith cooed, as they picked up their bags and moved toward the steps. "But tonight, I think you owe me a wonderful dinner."

"Agreed."

They passed the guard, merrily wishing him a good evening. "*Buena suerte.*"

"Buena suerte," he said, shutting the old, rusted iron gate with a definitive clang.

—𝕞—

"They've found something big, señor," the guard said quickly in Spanish, greedily eyeing Manuel's pocket. They stood in the alley behind the Archives.

"What?" Manuel said nonchalantly.

The guard shifted uneasily. "Well, I am not certain. They spoke in English, but they mentioned *La Canción* over and over." He nodded eagerly, as if that would be enough.

"Do you have the document they were reading?"

"No, I do not know where they placed it."

"You did not see?"

"No. I could only see their general area."

Manuel knew what a "general area" in the stacks meant. It meant the document would be a veritable needle in the haystack. Disgusted, Manuel peeled a twenty from his wad of bills and threw it on the ground as he walked away.

"But, señor," the guard cried out behind him, "you promised me much more."

He hushed when Manuel whirled back. "You got more than you earned," he growled. "You were supposed to get closer to them!"

"Sí, señor," the man acquiesced, nodding his head anxiously and lifting his hands in apology. *"Lo siento. Lo siento!"*

CHAPTER 10

Manuel knew it would be hopeless to spend time in the stacks himself, even if he paid the guard to sneak him in. He'd seen enough when the back door guard had allowed him closer. Besides, if the document was important, they might have taken it with them, rather than risk leaving it for others to find. He trailed them to the west side of town, daring to draw near enough to hear them discussing various restaurants.

His eyes narrowed as he looked them both over. Christina carried her customary backpack and Meredith a tote bag, along with her collapsible table and chair. Either could have the document with her. He would have to ransack both their rooms while they were out. Or had Christina simply taken pictures of it? Was the Nikon around her neck what he needed most? Or their cell phones?

The two women settled on meeting across town at a renowned restaurant. "After all, we deserve it," Christina said.

"I'll bill it to Treasure Seekers," she added cheekily.

"You should call them," Meredith said.

"I will as soon as we get it completely translated tomorrow."

"Okay. See you in forty-five minutes."

Get it translated. So they had it—or a picture of it. Manuel trailed Meredith by twenty paces, pausing occasionally to look into windows or peruse a newspaper left on a street-side table, in case she looked over her shoulder. But she did not. She moved so fast that Manuel had difficulty keeping up with her.

They reached her studio building, and Manuel sank into the shadows of the *biblioteca* across the street. He lit a cigarette and smiled as the light came on high above him, easily picturing her in the room he had scoured earlier.

—·—

From behind one of the tall screens, Meredith peeled off her clothes, threw them onto her bed carelessly, then tossed on a light summer dress. She looked back at her comforter, frowning.

She took special pride in her bed, it being the one true luxury in the huge, spare room. Each morning she smoothed the covers until it looked like a picture. Now there was a distinct mussed section in the middle and edge, as if someone had sat down or even laid there. She racked her brain, trying to remember if she had sat down to tie her boots that morning.

Absently she looked at her watch and realized she had to catch a cab. Casting aside thoughts of her rumpled bed, she turned out the light and walked through the open door, locking it behind her.

—·—

On the edge of Seville and alongside the Guadalquivir River sat the Chambray restaurant, a popular dining spot owing to its ambiance. The food was intercontinental with various southern European influences. Both women were delighted to be there with something so exciting to celebrate.

They clinked their goblets over the table, grinning widely. "Congratulations, Mer. You're going to get a serious bonus if this proves to be what we think it is."

"You're the one who found it. Do you realize that discoveries like that often take years? And here you come and find it within a matter of days."

"Only because you set me in the right direction." She grinned at her friend in glee. "I looked up those coordinates. It's off the coast of *Mexico*," Christina said in wonder. "All this time I've been concentrating on those islands near Cuba, looking for a hook-shaped peninsula. I've read of La Punta de Muerte in Mexico. But I never made the similar-name connection or believed that *La Canción* could've been thrown so far off course."

"It's not the first time we've seen a name evolve over time. Still, it must've been some storm to carry them all the way to Mexico."

"How long did they battle it?"

"That letter says three days. And that was after he'd been chased for days by pirates."

Christina looked out the window, thinking. "Since Captain Alvarez survived the wreck, she must lie close to shore."

"But only six others survived with him," Meredith said. She shrugged. "Could mean it's deeper."

"Maybe people stayed below, praying they'd survive but, in fact, locked themselves into a chamber of death."

Meredith shivered at the thought. "I wouldn't have wanted to travel by sea in those days." She paused, thinking about the bit she'd been able to translate before they left the Archives. "And it sounds like those who survived ended up getting attacked by headhunters on shore, just like your family legend said."

"How do you think the captain survived?"

"I dunno. Maybe his captain's uniform? Let me see your camera."

Christina handed it over and perused her menu as Meredith looked at the view screen and attempted to enlarge a portion.

Meredith nodded. "If I'm reading it correctly, that's how it worked. The rest were murdered before his eyes. The tribesmen thought that Captain Alvarez was a deity of sorts."

Christina nodded soberly. "The Point of Death," she said, translating *La Punta de Muerte* quietly. She mulled over *Punta de los Asesinos*—the Point of Murder—in her mind. "Maybe at one point it was called murder, and later became death, because of all that transpired. It's too easy. Why didn't I see it before?"

"Well, you were chasing the wrong name. Who knew how they all died? You only knew Alvarez had lived to tell about the wreck and that it was off some hook-shaped peninsula."

"Multiple names always throw me for a loop."

"You and me both. I've found over twenty references to what I think is all the same city on Cuba, but all by slightly different names. Sometimes it was the cartographer's whimsy."

—❦—

This time as he ransacked Meredith's studio, Manuel did not take the time to be cautious. The game was over, and time was of the utmost importance. There was nothing new on her desk, so she probably had hidden the document somewhere.

He threw clothing to the floor as he searched each pocket. He pulled the mattress off the bed and turned it over, searching. He tossed each paper aside as he struggled through file after file on her desk and in the cabinets. When he was through, the documents lay in a huge mound beside the desk.

Nothing. Frustrated, he tore pictures from the wall, looking behind them. Still nothing. He drew a deep breath, choosing to regain control. He had simply miscalculated which woman had the precious information. As he left the studio, he closed the door, carefully peeled off his gloves, and set off for Christina's inn, five blocks away.

—⚬⚬—

Mitch smiled curiously at his partner as Hans paced back and forth, deep in thought. They were outside by the pool with Anya and the children, reading and waiting for news from Christina. Kenna was busy picking up pebbles from the path to the beach and carrying each one to Mitch. Anya was in the pool with Josh, teaching him to blow bubbles as she pulled him through the water.

"What's up?" he finally asked the big, blond man as he paced by again. "Clearly, something's on your mind."

Hans stood still at the question, obviously debating whether he should share his thoughts with Mitch. "How long has it been since we've heard from or seen Hobard?" he asked.

"Thank you," Mitch said, smiling at the tiny girl who placed yet another minute stone in his hand, then busily went back for another. "I don't know," he said absently, "Six, maybe seven months."

Hans turned to look at him. "That doesn't strike you as odd?"

"I've just been thankful to be rid of him for a while. Isn't he on the *Cuban Sky* site?"

"They finished a month ago."

Mitch frowned. He could see what Hans was getting at. Tate Hobard routinely tried to leech off of Treasure Seekers whenever he was ready to take on a new project. As hard as they tried to keep information from him, the man had found out about four out of the last six sites they'd been prepared to excavate, beating them to the claims. He was driving them into financial ruin and enjoying the process.

Mitch looked to the pool where Joshua now played with Anya in the shallow end, forcing his voice to be calm. "You think he might be on to us and *La Canción*?"

"I don't think it's out of the question. It's always far more suspicious when we don't smell him than when we do."

Mitch shook his head, not wanting to believe what Hans might be alluding to. "He can't possibly know about Christina and *La Canción*. Not yet."

Hans turned to face him. "We haven't heard from her for almost two days."

"She's busy. Maybe she's found something new. Besides, how would he even know about her? She's a kid, barely out of college."

"You know better than that, Mitch. She's a Ph.D. hotshot who's been making news in the trades for two years. And she's made no secret of her passion for *The Song*. Nor have her visits here been…*inconspicuous*. You know as well as I do that Hobard stakes us out."

"She's fine," Mitch said irritably, more for his sake than his friend's. "We'll hear from her soon and be on our way to *La Canción* within the month. There's no way Tate will take this one from us. She's ours."

Hans looked back to the water, keeping the rest of his fears to himself. But the seed of doubt had been planted.

Might Tate be in Seville even now, attempting to woo Christina over to his operation? Or worse, was she now in danger as a partner of Treasure Seekers?

He pulled out his phone, checking for a message from her for the hundredth time. He thought about messaging her, warning her. But did he really want to do that? She had enough on her mind without looking over her shoulder every minute. And so far, Hobard had never hurt them or their partners.

He had simply robbed them.

—⁓—

Manuel was not having any better luck in Christina's room than he'd had at Meredith's apartment. The camera was missing, presumably with her at the restaurant. Stealthily he moved about the room, trying not to awaken the building's other occupants, again searching for the document. But the only thing he found of value was her logbook. He smiled as he read her entry about the day he and Tate had spied on them, finding interest in her diatribe against Mitch and her wonder at his change of heart.

He returned his attention to the project at hand. Manuel was sure that one of the women had smuggled the precious document out of the Archives. If it was as important as it sounded to the guard, they would never have left it in the stacks to be found by another.

No one he knew would do so anyway.

Manuel stopped and considered Christina's actions on the stairs the day before with the beggars. Perhaps someone as virtuous as she could not actually steal a document from the Archives. She had likely simply taken multiple shots of the document, and then filed it away where no one else might find it.

Tate would kill him if he missed this opportunity to take the upper hand in the search for *La Canción*.

He checked his watch. If he left now, he might be able to reach the restaurant and take the camera from her as they left, then disappear into the dark maze of streets and alleyways.

CHAPTER 11

Almost every other table was empty, but Christina and Meredith were still talking about the only subject that could distract them from nautical archaeology: men.

"So there's no hot romance brewing in the City of Passion, hmm?" Christina asked.

Meredith smiled. "There is a British professor of antiquities at the university I've seen a few times." Her coy smile gave her away.

"Okay, let's have it. What's his name, what does he look like, is he crazy about you, is he a believer, where does he want to live for the next twenty years—"

Meredith's laughter interrupted Christina's list of questions. "Whoa, whoa! One at a time!"

"Well?"

"He's about my height and blond—"

"I can just see the cute little blond kids you'd have." She paused, thinking of Josh and Kenna, and wondered over the pang of longing for them. How had they wormed their way into her heart in so little time?

"His name is Jake Richardson," Meredith said. "He's very happy here in Seville; and he's open to faith, but hasn't really pursued it much."

"Please tell me he understands you're the catch of Seville."

Meredith looked at her empty plate, smiling shyly and blushing a little. "I get the sense that he thinks I'm kind of special."

Christina squealed. "He'd better! Oh, Meredith, I'm so happy for you! You've been waiting a long time to meet someone right. As long as he continues to treat you like a queen, I'll be happy."

"Well, we've only been dating a few weeks."

"But I can tell from your face—something's different about this one, huh?"

"I think so." She took a sip of hot tea and gazed at her comrade. "What about you?"

"What about me?"

"Come on. You have to have let someone in by now."

Christina shook her head. "No way. I've been on the trail of *La Canción* long enough that she's become my one and only love."

Meredith looked at her ruefully and did not return her smile. "Christina Alvarez, someday you gotta let yourself love someone. You spend too much time on your work. There's more to life."

She paused. Hadn't she said something similar to Mitch? But that had been about the kids... "I'm fine on my own."

"Are you?"

"Yes!" Her voice was higher than she wanted it, making her sound defensive.

"What about this Crawford guy?"

Christina snorted. "The man can barely stomach me. I had to finagle my way into an agreement with Treasure Seekers. Trust me, it's all business." She frowned. She could hear how she sounded, as if she was trying to convince herself.

Meredith smiled from across the table. "Whatever you say, my friend. Just ask yourself once in a while if what you're saying is what you want to hear and not the truth."

Christina looked out to the gently flowing river beside them. It was on those waterways that *La Canción* had made her way to Seville from the Atlantic at the end of several successful voyages. And now they were on track to find her final resting place...if Mitch finally agreed to move forward.

She sighed. "I've never met anyone with a bigger passion for his work. It's even bigger than mine, if that's possible. I have to admit, it intrigues me. It'd be kinda cool to share a passion for your work as a couple, like you and Jake."

"So. You'd be open to a relationship with Mitch."

Christina laughed. "Even if we wanted to do that—which we don't—it's never gonna happen." She thanked the waiter and paid him with cash. "We got off on the wrong foot. A very wrong foot."

"Whatever you say." Meredith lifted a brow, clearly unconvinced. "Come on, my friend, let's get some sleep. We have a big day tomorrow."

"Sounds good," Christina said, her mind three thousand miles away, thinking of Robert's Foe. Sleepily she rose behind her friend and followed her to the dark street outside.

"Oh no. I'm so stupid!" Meredith cried, running her fingers through her hair. "I'm sorry, Christina, I completely forgot. The cabbies are on strike today."

"No big deal," Christina said. "I'd forgotten too. But I walked here, didn't you? And I could use the walk after that huge meal." She rubbed her rounded belly.

"Me too, but it's not a good idea to walk at night in this part of town."

"C'mon. We'll be fine. We'll be together for at least twelve of those blocks." She turned her cell on again. "Maybe I can catch a signal between here and my inn. Is this city full of dead zones, or what?"

"Depends on your carrier. I think there's a conspiracy against American carriers."

"Hmm. Surely they haven't blocked mine everywhere in town." They set off, arm in arm. It was a dark night, with a waxing moon just bright enough to cast deep shadows on the street and just dark enough to allow a sky full of stars to shine. The effect was eerie.

"So," Meredith said. "Tell me what the infamous Mitchell Crawford looks like."

"He's pretty cute," Christina said, glad to think about something other than what might be lurking in the shadows. "A little taller than I, broad and muscular, blond, blue-green eyes. Very strong chin and a killer smile—when he actually allows someone to see it."

"So he's the brooding type, huh?"

"His friend Hans says that he's not always that way. He lost his sister a few months ago and suddenly became insta-dad, since she'd named him guardian of his niece and nephew. It's taking him awhile to adjust."

Meredith nodded. "I hope Hans is right. I can't see you with a moody guy."

"Me neither." She caught herself and laughed under her breath. "I can't believe we're even talking about this! It's never going to happen."

They left Paseo de Colon, the main thoroughfare in Seville, and turned the corner onto Calle de San Pablo, and Christina checked her phone again. "Ooo! A signal, and a decent one." She found Mitch's number and clicked the button to dial. "Go home, Meredith," she whispered as it rang. "We're splitting up here anyway."

"No, I'll stay with you while you're on the phone."

"I'm going to be on awhile. Mitch will want to hear all about what we've found. It's late. Go on."

Meredith looked at her reluctantly, then down the deeply shadowed street. "I don't like leaving you."

"I'll be fine. You have just as far to walk alone, and you're in the most danger. I'm just your average brunette Castilian to most eyes. You're the one the bad guys would target. So keep your pepper spray in your hand! And walk fast."

Meredith looked up the street, to where she would turn to reach home.

"Go," Christina said firmly, widening her eyes in mock anger.

"All right." Meredith kissed her friend's cheek. "Come to my studio tomorrow at nine. We can translate the document together."

"Good. I'll be there."

But as her friend left her, Christina frowned as a shiver of fear ran down her neck. She wished Mer hadn't been so worried; it had planted seeds of doubt in her mind. She looked around furtively. If they had not talked so long about Mitch and *La Canción*, she might have waited until morning to call him. But she was too wound up not to call now. She had to hear his voice when she told him what they had discovered. Or after all Meredith's teasing, was she really just wanting to hear his voice?

She stared at her phone, wondering if the connection was working or if she should re-try it, when suddenly Mitch was on the line. "Christina?"

"Yep. It's me. And I believe you owe me dinner."

He laughed under his breath. "I guess you have news for me." She could hear the relief and smile in his voice.

"How'd you know?" Christina surprised herself with her casually, flirting tone. She rubbed her temples.

"Well, it's after midnight your time, and apparently you only call when something big has happened."

"You've been worried about me, huh?"

"A little. So tell me why I owe you dinner."

She glanced back up the empty street. "Because I know where *La Canción* is."

Mitch sucked in his breath. "Don't tell me where."

"Why not?"

"Because my phone line might be bugged."

"Good idea. I'll be at Robert's Foe within a week."

He paused. "If you've found what you needed, why that long?"

"I want to—" Christina's voice caught as a man turned a corner two blocks back and walked in her direction. She couldn't make out his face, but he was moving casually. *Not like he's after me. Get a grip.*

Christina tried to still her beating heart. Maybe he was just walking home, as she was, stuck without a cab. Still, she turned and began walking toward her inn, deciding a dose of caution was worth risking her precious signal.

"Chris-?" Mitch's voice sounded very far away, and he was cutting out just as soon as she'd taken ten paces.

"I want to spend all the time I can with—" She glanced over her shoulder and with a start, saw that the man was gaining on her. She picked up her pace.

"With what?" Mitch asked.

"With Meredith. We have some work to do, and the thing we found might lead us to researching more while I'm here."

She glanced over her shoulder again. But this time, the

man broke into a run after her. She sucked in her breath and began running too, but she was in high heeled boots, and the man soon overtook her. He grabbed hold of her shoulder and rammed her to the building wall, making her cry out. "Stop! No!"

In the dim light of a nearby street lamp, she knew him. The man from the bar. From outside the Archives too. Had he been following her? "Help!" she cried, desperately holding on to the camera strap. "Help!" Was there no one slumbering in the building behind her?

"No!" Christina screamed, gaining more voice as the struggle went on. "Get away from me!"

"Give me the camera," the man said through gritted teeth as she kicked him in the shin again and again. He took both her shoulders in his hands and rammed her against the stone building. Her head hit, and she saw stars for a moment, but when she saw the opportunity, she kneed him solidly in the groin.

He doubled over in pain but when she tried to pass him, he grabbed hold of her skirt. Bound up and yet still moving, Christina fell. Her cell scattered across the cobblestone walk and over the edge, into the gutter.

—w—

Meredith opened her door and gasped at the sight. In all of her years in Seville, she had never been robbed, a miracle in itself. *After such a great night, Meredith thought sadly, I had to come home to this.*

She made her way through the mess, searching for her valuables. She opened her jewelry box, surprised to find her gold rings still inside. Then, on the floor she spotted her video camera and Hasselblad.

Meredith frowned as understanding dawned on her. She hadn't been robbed; her studio had been searched. *La Canción!* She ran to her desk and looked through the chaos for the pictures and documents she'd been studying. No, they were all still there. But she couldn't shake the feeling that this had to relate to what she and Christina had been uncovering. One look at that manifest had told her it might be the richest find she'd ever researched.

She pulled out her cell and dialed her friend, praying the woman was still in that signal zone. When it rang and rang, she grabbed a butcher knife in one hand and her pepper spray in the other, and took off running down the stairs, thinking of little other than reaching Christina's side.

—◊◊◊—

The man was struggling—clearly incapacitated by her blow to his groin—but he was climbing on top of her.

Christina, remembering a move from her self-defense class, clasped her hands together and brought them down quickly at the back of his neck.

He slumped and rolled partially off her.

Her heart pounding, Christina scrambled up and away, using the building as leverage against her back. She turned to flee when she felt his hand wrap around her ankle, and again went down hard, the Nikon cracking this time as it hit stone instead of her body.

What would it take to get away from this guy? She kicked at his hand with her other foot, frantic to get away. "No!" she screamed. "Let me go!"

He pulled back, cradling his hand to his chest, a grimace of pain making his expression frightening.

—⁓—

"Christina! Christina!" Mitch cried until he was hoarse. He could hear her shout, cry out, but from a distance. Had she dropped her phone?

Hans ran into the office, eyes wide with concern.

"Get your cell. Call the police in Seville," Mitch said grimly, still trying to hear. His heart hammered in his chest when he heard no more shouts from Christina. And then doubled when he heard her cry out again.

Hans was already Googling how to reach them. "What am I going to tell them?" he asked, scanning the information on his screen.

Mitch paused. What could they tell them? That his partner was somewhere on the streets, getting attacked?

"Christina! Where are you?" he shouted, hoping that she might hear his voice, even from a distance, and be able to answer. "Tell me where you are!"

"It's ringing," Hans said grimly. He'd gathered what was going on.

But then all Mitch could hear was the dull, long tone that signaled a disconnected call.

CHAPTER 12

Christina quickly turned a corner, desperately trying to throw off her pursuer. But he trailed her like a hungry coyote after a hare. Knowing she could not outrun him in her heels, Christina took a chance. Ducking under the severe arch of an old church entrance, she hid behind the buttress, frantically attempting to gain control of her breath and remain silent as the man lurched near.

She heard his slapping footsteps on the cobblestone street within seconds. She shut her eyes, praying and listening. *Please, God*, she chanted, unable to think of anything else as the man came perilously close. *Please, God...please, God... please, God.*

Her heart pounded in her ears. How could the man not hear it too? She expected him to appear around the buttress, discover her hiding place, and close in. *Please, God...please, God...please, God.*

The man was close. He stilled and turned one way and

then the other, listening for her. Christina held her breath, ignoring her burning, aching lungs. At last he turned on his heel and rushed down the street again, clearly thinking she had escaped him.

Christina's pounding heart gradually eased as the man's footsteps faded away. She remained in hiding while catching her breath and deciding what to do. If she could get back to Avenida de la Constitución, she could figure out where she was; maybe she could even make it to Meredith's house.

It hit her then. Meredith's house was the wrong place to go. The man had not reached for her backpack, that kept her wallet and passport. He had wanted her camera. He had been following her all week. How could she not have seen it? She chastised herself for not being more discerning. *Please, Father*, she prayed, *be with Meredith. Keep her from harm. And help me get out of here.*

—row—

"Christina?" Mitch asked eagerly, recognizing her number.

"No," a woman said a little awkwardly. "It's Christina's phone. But this is Meredith Champlain. Christina's not here. I'm afraid something's happened to her."

"She was attacked! I was on the phone with her!" Mitch slumped to the couch. There was no time for formal introductions and pleasantries. "You don't know where she went?" he asked.

"No. I found her phone in the gutter. There was no other sign of her."

The woman sounded breathless, as if she was running. "When I got home, I found my place had been ransacked. I think it was someone after information on *La Canción*. We found something big today. So I came back to make sure

Christina was okay."

"One minute we were talking, and the next she was gone."

"There's no sign of her here, Mitch. Did she say who it was?"

"No. Nothing."

"I've called the police." Behind her, could he make out the unique sound of a Euro police siren? "I'll call you back later with any news."

"Please. Send me your number too, Meredith."

"I will. I'll call you with any news," she said. "I gotta go." The siren was growing louder.

"Okay." He hung up, anxious out of his mind. *Christina, where are you?*

Hans gave him a grim look. "Hobard?"

"I don't know. Maybe. Probably."

"Do you think they have her?"

"I don't know. All I heard was her cry out, like she was fighting with someone."

"We need to pray."

"Yes, we do," Mitch said, slowly letting his head fall into his hands. "But I…I can't think. You do it. I'll listen."

—∞—

Christina heard sirens and saw the flashing lights of police cars a few blocks away but did not run toward them. She was putting it all together now. The man had to have been sent by Tate Hobard or another treasure hunter to get the scoop on *La Canción*. And anybody with the tenacity and money to chase her all the way to Seville for information on the ship would have the funds to buy off the police. They were notoriously corrupt, easily bribed.

She had to get out of Seville.

Christina hit Calle de Santiago after four blocks of trotting. Guessing that she was west of the train line, she turned right. She would not allow herself to slow down. A police car rounded the corner, with no sirens, but a steady, bright searchlight swept from one side of the street to the other.

Where to hide? There was no place where she wouldn't be spotted.

Something made her attempt it anyway. She stood at the edge of a deep doorway, hoping they would pass her by. She had read enough espionage books to know that Trust No One was a basic code of survival.

But the policemen spotted her vague outline and shone the light directly at her.

"Who is there?" the officer yelled first in Spanish, then in English, as the car screeched to a halt.

Christina emerged slowly, hoping that these might be honest cops. "It is me, Christina Alvarez. I am an American."

"Miss Alvarez! Your friend called us. We will help you." He exited the vehicle and opened the door. "Come, come," he said reassuringly, gesturing inside. "We will protect you. Come with us."

Seeing no option, Christina clambered in. But as she did so, she saw that the driver was looking down the street, then the other way. For her attacker? Or to see if anyone had noticed them?

The driver took off, driving faster than normal. Christina excused it, hoping they were moving quickly to protect her.

—⁂—

Meredith didn't like it. "How could you not have found either of them? They have to be somewhere!"

"I am sorry, señora. They are not to be found."

Another policeman piped in, "We have heard from an old woman that she saw two people who matched your description. When we got there, they were both gone. But the old woman said that she thinks that your friend got away."

"Great! Then where is she?"

"We are canvassing the city," the first policeman said, irritated at Meredith's impatience. "Go home. We will contact you when we have news."

Meredith sighed. She wasn't sure she was doing any good, but she felt driven to push them. "I'm sorry, I'm just so worried..."

"Go home," the man said again, softening. "Do you need a ride?"

"Yes," Meredith said. It was still dark out, although there was a hint of light on the horizon. She did not feel like walking alone. At all.

The policeman waved another car over to them and opened the door for her. He talked briefly to the driver and his partner, who pulled out to take Meredith home.

"Americans," the driver muttered to his companion in Spanish. "They all think they can run the world and demand treatment as if they were royalty."

"Not all Americans," Meredith said tiredly, in Spanish. "Some of us simply seek help when we are in crisis. You know, like when a friend is abducted."

The two glanced over their shoulders in surprise at her perfect Spanish.

"Now how about you two do your job and come up to document my ransacked apartment?"

—∞—

Christina's heart sank when they pulled up to what

looked like an abandoned warehouse, not the police station. "I am an American!" Christina yelled, as they dragged her inside. "There will be people looking for me!" she cried, as they stripped her of her bag and camera and shoved her inside a small cell.

But the policemen ignored her, walking down the long corridor and shutting an iron door behind them, laughing and saying lewd things in Spanish.

Christina struggled to think through her predicament. The cell was tiny, five by eight feet, and was almost filled by the narrow cot, its mattress stained. A hole in the corner served as a toilet. She was far from the first person to be held here.

Christina shivered. *Oh, Mitch, what have I gotten myself into?* It surprised her that she thought of him first, as if he could save her. What must he be thinking, right now? Surely he'd heard her cries before the phone skittered into the street. But what could he do, from three thousand miles away?

She went to the iron bars and tested each one, desperately hoping one might be loose, trying to think of a means of escape. But the bars held strong. Who else had been held here? Corrupt cops like that could find all sorts of uses for their own private prison.

She shivered. If the Nikon was broken, if they discovered the SD card gone, would they come back to torture her to find out what she knew?

Christina curled up into a ball and tried to ignore the scratching of rats nearby. She needed to think, but her eyes burned. She closed them, just for a minute or two...

The clanging door abruptly awakened her. She sat up quickly, rubbing her eyes and standing, chastising herself for giving in to sleep. Had she been out an hour? Two? She wished sunlight streamed through the tiny windows above. Somehow adversity seemed less threatening by the light of day.

But adversity was definitely coming her way. The two policemen walked toward her. And behind them strode the man who had pursued her, one eye black-and-blue.

Adrenaline exploded through her veins, and she felt the color drain from her face. She shrank backward, unable to combat the stark fear that invaded her heart. *Please, Father,* she prayed, *give me courage.*

—∞—

Meredith's phone rang for the fourth time that night. She picked it up, hoping again that it was the police. But with a glance at her screen, she knew it was not. "Mitch, I still haven't heard anything. I told you, I'll call as soon as I do."

"I think I should get on the next plane."

Meredith sighed. "I don't think that's a good idea. Let's wait until we hear something. At least until morning."

"I could be there, trying to help find her."

"I don't see how you could really help."

"I could lend pressure."

"The police are doing all they can. Give it until morning. Let's see if she turns up. She's a bright, resourceful woman, Mitch."

"If she's tangled with someone who is after information on *La Canción*, she'll need all her resources." His voice was tight.

Meredith closed her eyes, fighting back the fear they shared. If Christina had been captured, what would they do with her? "Come on. You couldn't be here until tomorrow anyway. She's on her own. We just have to wait and pray."

"I've done that! Don't you see? I feel responsible that she

was there alone! I should've realized that Hobard was on to us."

Meredith sucked in her breath at the mention of Hobard's name. "Tate Hobard?" she asked.

"Yes, I think he's behind this," Mitch said, sounding exhausted.

"I had no idea," she said. Hobard was a ruthless, dangerous man.

"*La Canción* is the big leagues. Hobard would want her almost as much as any treasure hunter would. He's stolen smaller finds from us."

Meredith took that in. "Should we call the FBI?"

"I've tried before. The man is wise to the game. They can't pin anything on him, and he has powerful friends."

Meredith did not know what else to say. "I'll call, Mitch," she said softly. She hung up without saying good-bye.

—⁂—

Mitch pounded on his desk, not angry with Meredith, but frustrated. Joshua appeared at the office doorway.

"Uncle Mitch, do you want to hunt sand dollars with me?"

"No!" Mitch yelled. "Can't you see that I'm busy?"

The boy ran from the doorway and out of the house. Hans looked at Mitch and shook his head.

"What?" Mitch searched for a place to pin his anger. "Why don't you leave me alone? I need some time to think!" He pushed his hair back and out of his eyes. "I just need some time to think," he repeated, more quietly this time.

Hans rose and left the room.

—⁂—

"Hello, Dr. Alvarez," the menacing man said. "Finally a

chance to talk with some civility. I am Manuel." He gestured for the policeman to unlock her cell and entered, then closed the door behind him.

She backed up to the far wall, her hands in fists.

Manuel watched her and casually sat down on the edge of the cot. "Leave us," he directed the other two. Wordlessly, they did as he asked. He turned back to her. "Let us quit the games. Why did you fight so hard to hold on to this?" He lifted her Nikon in his hand.

"How do you know my name?" She felt as if she whispered the question.

Manuel threw the Nikon to the ground. Christina shuddered as her precious camera blew into pieces. He rose and came over to her. "I asked, why fight for it?"

"It's an expensive camera!" Or it *had* been when it was whole.

"Where is the SD card, Dr. Alvarez?" His voice was deadly calm, a sharp, eerie contrast to his actions. He hovered inches away from her. "Did you give it to Meredith Champlain?"

"No! I...I hid it," she said. "While you were chasing me." The last thing she wanted was for this man to go after Mer.

"Where?" he asked, his eyes narrowing. "Where did you hide it?"

"Out on the streets. On a brick ledge."

"Where?" he repeated, so close she could feel his hot breath on her face.

"I don't know all the names of the streets. Just the big ones. I would have to see it."

Manuel leaned back then, considering. "I don't believe you," he sneered. "Even now, it could be on you. Turn around and put your hands on the wall."

"I don't have it!"

"*Turn around*," he said, pouncing and bodily forcing her

to lean against the wall. He kicked her feet apart and then slowly, methodically searched her, clearly enjoying it so much that Christina trembled with rage. But somehow he missed the tiny card in her bra, perhaps because he assumed it was part of the underwire, or because he was distracted by the cheap thrills he was getting.

When he stopped, she turned around and spat, "I told you I didn't have it."

"Still," he said, giving her a devilish smile, "I had to be certain. If you did indeed hide the SD card, there's no guarantee it's still where you left it."

"It'll be there," she said. "People don't routinely run their hands over ledges they can't see, do they?"

"Why don't we simply go to the Archives and you can retrieve the original—or originals—for my boss? You'll be free of me then."

"We couldn't get in without my friend." Inwardly, she winced. Had she just blown it? What if they kidnapped Meredith too?

Manuel turned on his heel and went to the cell's gate. "Get us out!" he barked.

The policemen hurried down the hall, keys in hand. "We need to take a drive," Manuel said, looking back at Christina. "She will lead us to it," he said firmly.

"You'll let me go in return?" she asked dully.

"We'll see." He grabbed hold of her arm, so hard, she knew he'd leave bruises. "You know, this doesn't have to be so hard. I know a certain benefactor who would be more than willing to make you his partner. You could benefit, rather than suffer."

Yeah, right. As soon as you get your hands on that SD card, I'll be a dead woman. There was no way he was going to let her live; she could identify him. She forced herself to look as if she took heart in his words. "I think it'd be wise to meet such a benefactor."

Manuel smiled. "Perhaps we can arrange it. Just as soon as I have the card in hand."

The three men ushered her out of the cell and warehouse and into the car outside. Manuel sat beside her in the back-seat, and the two guards rode in front.

"I think it's near Calle de Santiago and Avenida Menéndez Pelayo," she said. An escape there was her only hope. If she could get away, she would be less than a block from the train station.

CHAPTER 13

It was a hot night, and the car had no air conditioning. Against his better judgment, Manuel ordered everyone to roll down their windows, gripping Christina's arm as they did so. When they reached the designated corner where two busy streets met, Christina pointed to a small alcove.

"I hid it there last night. The card is on the ledge inside." She hoped her tone sounded defeated.

"We were two blocks away from here," Manuel said doubtfully.

"I circled around, trying to lose you. Which I did," she said.

With a sigh of doubt, Manuel nodded to one of the policemen. The uniformed man exited the car and waited for two women to pass by on the sidewalk in front of him before he climbed the steps. It was early; the city was beginning to awaken.

Christina eyed the rearview mirror, watching as a wall of

cars came forward after pausing at a light. She had seconds to make this work. The policeman stood in the entryway, casing the ledge above. Manuel watched him intently, casually easing his grip on her.

At the last possible second, Christina threw her elbow upward, connecting soundly with Manuel's nose. He screamed, a feral mix of pain and anger.

She reached for her backpack at his feet, threw open her door, and ran across the three-lane street, narrowly missing the speeding cars. Safely to the other side, she dared a glimpse backward. Her adversaries watched for a break in the traffic to pursue her, but there was none.

Christina had the lead she needed. And she ran directly for the train station.

—⟋⟍—

"Four more hours," Mitch said. "That's all I'll wait."

"And then what?" Hans asked, lifting his hands in exasperation. "You'll fly off to Seville? You don't even know she's there anymore."

"I have to do something! This has Tate's fingerprints all over it, Hans. But this time, I'm going to fight him with everything I've got."

"Maybe we should try and contact him. Maybe we should say he can have *La Canción*."

"No way," Mitch said stubbornly, miserably. "Christina would never forgive us. This one's hers. *And* ours. We can't let him have this one!"

"There are more important things than that treasure, Mitch. Like Christina herself, for instance."

"Of course she is! But you've seen her. How she wants this." He turned to the window and stared out to the waves.

"You can bet that she's more determined than ever to outwit Hobard now."

—◊◊◊—

Christina ran through the train station doors and over to the ticket booth. "I need a ticket on that train!" she said in Spanish, pointing to the one nearby, with a sixty-second countdown to departure.

"Madrid?" the clerk said dryly, clearly unmoved by yet another frantic and harried traveler.

"Si, si, Madrid! A ticket, please." Christina fished through her backpack and found the extra credit card she stored in a secret pocket, watching the glass doors at the grand entry all the while. She shoved the card at the clerk.

It seemed as if the clerk operated in slow motion, casually sliding the card through the slot, stamping a pass, idly pushing it toward her...

In horror she saw Manuel and the guards enter the station. And the train doors were starting to close. Christina reached through the window hole, grabbed her ticket and credit card, whirled and sprinted through the crowd.

Judging from her peripheral vision, she knew she'd been spotted. The men ran toward her, twenty paces away. Finally reaching the train, she jumped sideways through a two-foot span and the train's doors slammed shut behind her. The men crashed up against the doors, yelling at the porter and pounding on the glass. But the train was starting to move.

Manuel glared at her through the window, blood from his broken nose streaming down his lip and chin, as he screamed for assistance. But the train kept moving. Gaining speed now. And leaving her pursuers behind. She trembled and sank to the far wall. Passengers on either side of her gaped at her.

"Telefono, por favor?" she asked a businessman.

"There is no signal," he said in English, lifting his hands to the roof, obviously making her out as an American.

"Of course there isn't," she muttered, then slumped in an exhausted heap to the nearest seat.

—⁓—

God smiled, she thought. Christina had managed to leap aboard a high speed train, transporting her to Madrid in a little over two hours. Judging from the train schedule, she had at least an hour or two before Manuel and his goons might show up. Christina hailed a cab, glad they weren't on strike here, as they had been in Seville. Her passport was miraculously still in her backpack, but not her airline ticket. It mattered not. She'd buy a one-way ticket on the first plane out, as long as it wasn't to another Spanish city.

The cab rushed her to the airport, passing perilously close between other cars and lanes of traffic. Christina was too wound up to comment. If she was driving, she'd probably be handling the car—and their safety—in the same way. She only wanted to get there. With some relief, she spotted the curving, mustache-shaped roof of the airport.

Once inside, she made her way to the gift shop and purchased a sweatshirt, shorts, flip-flops and baseball cap. Then she made her way into the women's restroom to change and tuck her long hair up into the cap. She tossed her blouse and skirt—and after a moment's hesitation, her beloved boots too—into the garbage can, then turned to the sink to wash her face.

Outside, she stopped at a cell phone store, purchased a basic phone and then asked where the Red Carpet Club was. Head tucked, she walked quickly toward it. She hoped she remembered that she had enough points on Iberia Airlines to score a one-day pass.

Manuel knew the high-speed train was heading toward Madrid. Would he suspect she'd go directly to the airport? Or try and disappear among the city streets, throbbing with tourists? As she handed her passport to the club receptionist, asking her to look up her membership, she prayed he'd gamble on the city. But if he didn't, at least she'd be in here as she waited for her flight, rather than out in the main terminal.

—⁓—

"You know you're crazy, right?" Hans asked, watching Mitch throw clothes into a duffel bag, along with his passport.

"I have to do something," Mitch said, repeating his refrain of the last twelve hours.

The phone rang.

Mitch reached across the bed to grab it, trying to steady his hand. He didn't know the number, but by the number prefix, he knew it was Spanish. "Hello?"

"Mitch," she said.

He closed his eyes. "Christina! Thank God. I was so worried, I was about to hop a plane to Seville. Where are you? What happened?"

"Madrid." She lowered her voice. "They're after me, Mitch."

He sank down to the bed. "Are you in a safe place?"

"For the moment. We've got somebody with money on our tails. They want *La Canción*, and they're not afraid of a few obstacles. You know, like kidnapping a foreigner. And buying off a few corrupt policemen to help."

"I know. It's Hobard. It's gotta be. How can I help?"

"I need an airline ticket, but I don't think there's enough

room on my card for it. I just want to be on the first flight out of here, then on to Saint Petersburg."

He paused, catching her reference. "Got it," he said, moving toward his computer. "Let me search for the best way to get you there, then I'll call you back with the confirmation number."

"Good. But hurry, Mitch. Okay?"

"I will."

"Have you heard from Meredith? Is she okay?"

"Yes, just super worried about you. I'll let her know. And I'll be in Saint Petersburg, waiting for you," Mitch said meaningfully. He knew as well as she did that it was too difficult to charter a boat or plane to Robert's Foe from there. Miami or San Juan was the most expedient. Hobard knew that too. But if Mitch's line was tapped, it'd make them wonder, at least.

"I'll wait for your call, Mitch," she said. "Pray for me."

"I haven't stopped for a moment."

She hung up the phone and Mitch began searching for the fastest way of getting her out of Spain.

There were four flights to the USA in the next thirty minutes, but she'd likely need more time than that to get through security. But preferably, not much more time. *There.* A British Airways flight leaving in fifty minutes. He sucked in his breath at the cost. Over three-thousand dollars, the only remaining seat available in business class. But it'd be worth it. It was the least he could do for her.

—⦚—

Christina concentrated on walking casually toward the gate as they called for general boarding, fighting the urge to scan the crowd. *They aren't here,* she told herself. She was safe. About to make her escape.

But once she'd stowed her backpack, her leg bobbed in agitation as she watched the last of the passengers get on. *"Tienes miedo de volar?"* the man asked, with a slightly patronizing tone, as he sat down beside her. He let his eyes linger on her bare thighs. *Are you afraid of flying?*

"Algo como eso," she muttered, turning to look out the window. *Something like that.* She hoped he'd feel the full chill of her cold shoulder.

She didn't dare to take a full breath until she heard the comforting ca-thump of the plane door closing and the engines begin to fire up.

CHAPTER 14

Christina got off the plane in London and an hour later boarded the first flight to Munich. Satisfied that she'd lost her pursuers, she waited five hours to board a plane bound for Miami...and Mitch.

The thought of being near Mitch brought her a sense of security and relief. He had dealt with Tate Hobard in the past and would know how to do so now. Her hand rose to her chest, and she could still feel the SD card that she had stowed in her bra. She still had the documents! They were ahead in the race to *La Canción*.

Although she had barely slept in the last forty-eight hours, Christina was too wound up to nap soundly. This adventure was far more than she had ever bargained for. She'd heard that competition for treasure could be a dangerous game, of course. Known of the rumors about Hobard. But this?

She carelessly paged through the airline magazine—with articles in both English and Spanish—but mostly stared out the window. The businessman next to her tried to make conversation, but she kept her answers to one or two words and looked back to the window, giving him the same cool treatment she'd used to fend off the first. He finally gave up, slipped on noise-cancelling headphones and chose an in-flight movie.

When the meal was offered, she picked at it but could not eat, even though she hadn't eaten in twenty-four hours. Her stomach heaved at the sight of the entrée, and even the bread was hard to swallow. Just a little stressed there, girl.

—⁓—

The sight of Christina flooded Mitch's heart with a mixture of relief and guilt. Relief that he could finally be with her—and do his best to keep her safe—but also guilt for opening the gate between her and Tate Hobard in the first place.

She was looking in the other direction, searching the crowds of people for him.

"Christina," he said in a low voice, finally reaching her.

She turned toward him and there was such relief in her eyes, such vulnerability and weariness, he could not contain himself. Mitch took her in his arms and held her for a full minute, praising God for bringing her safely through.

"Mitch?" she asked quietly, squirming a little.

He released her immediately, embarrassed that he had acted so personally with his new partner. But Mitch couldn't help himself. She was plainly suffering from extreme exhaustion, her eyes ringed and swollen. For an instant, he had a crazy desire to pick her up and carry her out of the airport, daring anyone to get in his way.

He glanced down, worried that with another look into

his eyes, she would detect his feelings. "You have to understand...I was worried you might be dead," he said softly, running a hand through his hair.

"Not yet," she said lightly, taking his elbow. "Come on. Let's get out of here. I need to borrow a bed in your guest room and sleep for a week. Or at least a solid eight hours."

He shouldered her backpack. "I'll get you there ASAP." Mitch fought off the desire to put a reassuring arm around her shoulders. He'd already crossed the line. They'd both made it clear that this was only a professional relationship. And she'd managed to escape their foes and make it home, right?

Christina battled the urge to turn and ask Mitch to take her in his arms again, to hold her while she gave sway to the tears that clogged her throat. But what would he think of her? She had worked hard to make him think of her as a respected business partner, not some weak woman, giving in to a meltdown.

Once she was in the privacy of her room, she would allow herself to cry. *Soon, Christina,* she coached herself. *Keep it together until then.* How long had it taken to convince Mitch to work with her? She didn't want it to all come crashing down now. Especially now, after all she'd been through. Thoughts of her pursuers made her keep glancing behind to scan the crowd.

"They're not here, Christina," Mitch said gently, leading her out to the sidewalk and to the rental car. "You're safe."

"How do you know?"

"I don't for sure," he admitted. "But I've been here for hours. I would've spotted any suspicious characters. And your itinerary hardly allowed them to jump on planes to follow you."

"They could have found me on flight manifests. Or going through security. If they have access to dirty cops, couldn't they gain access to that info? Charter a private plane? Isn't Hobard on that level?" She looked around before dropping into the passenger seat. He shut the door and went to the other side. "Hobard himself could be here," she continued, looking through the rear-view mirror, then her passenger side mirror too. "Even now. Manuel could've alerted him."

"Possibly," he said. "But you could've really flown into Miami, or Saint Petersburg or San Juan. They're probably still piecing together where you went." He patted her hand. "It'll be all right. We'll get back to Robert's Foe and figure out what we do from there. Okay?"

"Okay," she said, swallowing hard. Her eyes stung and she shut them, not wanting him to glimpse her tears of relief.

"You can sleep," he said gently, as they got on a south-bound highway. "I'll wake you if there's anything to be concerned about. Go on. We have about a five hour drive down through the Keys. Hans is waiting for us in Key West."

It didn't take more encouragement than that. Leaning her temple against the side window, she closed her eyes and was out in seconds.

Christina forced her eyes to open as she felt the car slow and focused on the clock on the dashboard. She had slept for most of their journey and felt worse for doing so; it was like a teasing taste of something delicious. Every step, every waking moment, felt like pure agony.

Mitch looked at her with a frown. Clearly, she looked as miserable as she felt. "We're almost to the harbor," he said. "Are you...sick? And I didn't even ask. Christina, were you injured? Do I need to arrange for a doctor?"

"I don't know," she said, slowly realizing that every part

of her ached. In her struggles with Manuel, her falls and wrestling, had she just pulled every muscle? Or was it the emotional trauma of her capture that was manifesting in a physical way now?

—⁓—

She passed out again on the jet boat that Hans had purchased two days prior, after the partners agreed they needed their own transportation, especially if they were going to do battle with Hobard. Mitch stayed with her, belowdecks in the luxurious cabin, keeping watch. Once Hans pulled up beside the dock on Robert's Foe, he gently shook her shoulder. But she was out—almost unconscious. Giving in to what he'd been tempted to do in the airport, Mitch gathered her up and carried her to the house, glad that the kids were somewhere else with Anya, not demanding to say hello. She needed rest—days of it, like she'd said. Maybe he'd need to summon that doctor?

Gently he laid her on the guest bed and covered her with a light blanket. He fought the urge to kiss her brow. *What's wrong with me?* he thought in irritation. What would she think, waking to find him kissing her? *That* would royally mess things up. It was already a little complicated between them. Was it just him who felt the attraction between them? Or did she feel it too…a little?

He opened the window slightly to let in a fresh breeze.

Joshua's small voice from the doorway startled him. "Is she dead, Uncle Mitch?" he asked sadly, looking very tiny and alone. He approached Christina, but didn't get too close.

"Oh! No, Josh," he whispered, squatting down to put a hand on his shoulder. His voice caught and he had to swallow hard, thinking of his nephew seeing Rachel after she died.

"Christina's just very, very tired. She'll be up and about soon. C'mon." He escorted the boy out of the room and out to the patio.

"Mama looked like that when she died," the boy said soberly. "Are you sure Christina isn't dead?"

"I'm sure." Mitch considered his nephew. *What must the child's pain be like?* "Joshua?"

"What?"

"I owe you an apology. Yesterday you asked me to go hunting for sand dollars and I yelled at you. I was not angry at you. I was worried and frustrated, and I was wrong to take it out on you. I'm sorry."

"It's okay." The small boy climbed up on the railing of the patio and patted the wood beside him, directing Mitch to sit, as if Joshua was the adult. Mitch complied, smiling a little.

"I miss Mama," he said.

"I do too." The combined emotions of relief at getting Christina back safe and sound and grief over his sister's death threatened to overwhelm him. He thought of how full of life Christina usually was and remembered the way Rachel had been before cancer had eaten away at her. He missed his sister's easy laughter, her love and gentle companionship. How much more might Josh and Kenna be missing her?

He put his arm around the boy, realizing they had never spoken of Joshua's mother. Mitch had been too wrapped up in his own problems and grief to reach out. In truth, he admitted, he had been too much the coward.

"I wish Mama had come here with us. She would like hunting for sand dollars and building castles and swimming."

"I wish...I wish I hadn't been so busy. That I'd had the chance to get you three all down to visit before she died." Mitch pictured her on the beach, walking with her children. Playing with them. Laughing and splashing... Sorrow continued to flood him and, on top of the stress of the last few days, made him choke up. One more glance at Joshua's quivering lip pushed him over the edge.

Sitting on the rail, looking out to sea, he and the boy cried together. And as they gave way to their shared sorrow, Mitch could feel the boy's defensiveness ease. When Kenna's small hand tugged at Mitch's leg, he turned to see Anya standing in the doorway. He picked Kenna up and held her in his lap for a while, and Anya disappeared into the recesses of the house.

"You know, kids, your mom is in a happy place. She's with Jesus in heaven. And someday we'll all get to see her again."

"I know," Joshua said.

Kenna turned on his lap and peered up at Mitch, patting his cheeks with her tiny hands as if to comfort him.

He laughed under his breath and wiped away his tears. "I'm glad your mom sent you to me. I think she knew I needed to play some more too."

Joshua nodded soberly, rubbing his eyes with his fists.

Together the three got down off the rail and walked hand in hand down to the beach, patiently waiting for Christina to wake up.

CHAPTER 15

Christina awakened that evening. While wolfing down her first real meal in two days, she told Hans and Mitch everything that had transpired in Seville. "Oh! And I almost forgot!" she said. She fished in her blouse unashamedly as Mitch and Hans looked away, a bit shocked.

Mitch looked up when he heard a plastic click on the marble table. An SD card. "You held on to it?" he said in a hushed voice, picking it up.

"Well, of course. I didn't go through all that to hand the bad guys a map to *La Canción*, did I?"

Hans stood and whooped, pulling Christina's chair out from the table and hauling her into an embrace. He picked her up and swung her around while Mitch went to pick up a startled-looking Kenna, hugging the tiny girl to reassure her. Mitch carried her to Christina and Hans and embraced them both, then stood back as Hans set Christina to rights.

"You're something else, Dr. Alvarez," Mitch said.

Christina took in his openly admiring gaze. "Why, thank you. I guess I've earned my keep as a partner of Treasure Seekers...at least for a while, huh?"

"I think you're paid up. What do you think, Hans?"

The man pretended to be dubious at the thought. "I dunno...Let me see what's on the card first."

"You guys check it out. I've got to call Meredith and make sure she's okay—"

"I called her," Mitch interrupted. "She was mostly worried about you. Her apartment was ransacked, but she's had no trouble since. You need some R and R. Trust your partners to pick up the slack for a while."

"I know. I just want to hear her voice and apologize for getting her into this mess." Christina stared at him, hoping her expression told him this was a non-negotiable. She'd just gotten twelve hours of sleep; she was eager to shake out the cobwebs in her head.

Mitch threw up his hands. "Okay. But promise me you'll rest all you can. We'll need your help and sharp mind shortly."

Christina hid her disappointment. *So he just wants a partner who will pull her weight; he's not worried about me as a person.* She chastised herself for such a crazy idea. *What is wrong with me? Do you want to be free to do what you want or a hovering boyfriend? Make up your mind!*

"I promise," she said. "I'll be at a hundred percent by tomorrow at sun-up." She reached for her bowl and winced, feeling her pulled shoulder and straightened to rub away the ache. "Well, *ninety* percent at least." She took Kenna and headed toward the kitchen. "Come on, sweet one, let's put away my dish and call my friend in Spain."

The tiny girl tried to stuff her hand in her mouth and gurgled an unintelligible reply, but seemed happy to be swept up into Christina's arms. She smiled at her and winked at Josh, happy to be with the kids again. There was something…reassuring in it. Familiar. Known, after a whole lot of unknown.

But her heart almost stopped when a masculine, firm voice answered Mer's phone. Christina fought for breath. Was Meredith in danger?

"Hello," she said carefully. "Is Meredith at home?"

"Who is this?" the man asked coolly.

She decided to take a chance. "Christina Alvarez."

Meredith's voice came directly on the line. "Christina! You're safe and sound?"

"Safe and sound. I've been worried about *you*! I'm so sorry, Meredith. I had no idea I was getting you into such trouble."

"It's okay. My boyfriend, Jake, has been sleeping on my couch and answering my phone. I'll be fine. I'm coming to the States for a long overdue visit with my folks until things cool down. I'll work from Dad's office."

"Good. We might need you to consult for us."

Meredith paused. "You mean you still have the camera?"

"Not the camera. But the SD card."

"That's great! I didn't exactly want to go back to the Archives and pull the original. I thought somebody might see me. Or follow me there."

"Good call. Especially if these pictures turn out okay."

"I'll call you with a secure email address as soon as I get to the States. You can send the pictures to my father's office Thursday. I went to your inn to pay your bill and collect your things."

"I appreciate it, Meredith."

"No big deal. This is the most excitement I've ever had in my sedate, studious career."

"And more than a man like Jake wants for his woman, I bet," Christina teased.

"It's good for him," Meredith said in a whisper. "Makes

him realize what I'm worth."

Christina laughed. "I'll look forward to your call Thursday. I'm so glad you're okay," she said again.

"Me too. I'm glad you're all right and made it home with the goods. Mitch told me what happened in Seville. You're a walking miracle."

"Thanks to God opening some doors. Meredith, I would swear he saved me."

"Well, watch yourself. First the shark attack, and now this. You've walked the line between life and death a few too many times for my taste. I need you to stick around. You have to be my maid of honor someday."

"And you, mine."

"Talk to you soon."

Christina hung up the phone, so relieved to have heard Meredith's voice and to know that she was in good hands.

Kenna shook the toy tiger she'd discovered under the couch and smiled at Christina. She had changed so much since Christina had first laid eyes on her! Had Mitch made his peace with the kids? Was he reaching out to them?

"Wagooah!" Kenna suddenly shouted, her whole little body practically vibrating with excitement.

"What?" Christina asked, laughing.

"Wagooah!"

"That's her code word for 'Joshua,'" Mitch said from the doorway. "He's out playing with Anya. I'll take her to him. The SD card was cracked." He bit his lip a bit.

"What?"

"No, we think it's okay. Hans took the boat to San Esteban. He'll take it to a guy we know there and see if he can open the files."

"Oh, Mitch. If we've lost it…"

"No, don't worry," he said, crossing over to her and laying

a hand on her shoulder. "You did all you could to get it here safely. Let us take it from here. Besides…" He lifted his hand and rubbed the back of his neck. "You kinda look like you might want to head back to bed. Here…" Kenna went to him easily when he reached for her, testimony of their progress.

"Well, maybe for just another hour or two," Christina said, taking comfort in his assurance. She had to admit…she liked the looks of such a strong man cradling the sweet little girl in his arms. "Good night," she said, grinning at her use of the word at midday.

"Good night," he answered. "Sleep all you can, partner. Because tomorrow, I'd bet we'll have work to do."

"Sounds good."

Did she imagine his eyes followed her as she left the kitchen?

—✺—

Mitch struggled to maintain his hold on sleep, disturbed by the noise coming from the other end of the house. Groggily he tried to place it. He sat up, tense. *Christina.*

She was calling out. Crying. Screaming?

He set off for her room at a dead run, grabbing the gun from on top of his armoire as he did so.

When he reached her room, her screams were continuing but were no longer as bloodcurdling. She was giving way to wailing, weeping. He peeked around the corner.

The shutters were locked tight. He turned on the light and blinked against the brightness. She was alone in her room.

She thrashed on the bed, crying out. Tears rolled down her face. Satisfied that the room was secure, Mitch hurried to her, tucked the revolver in the back of his waistband and pulled her into his arms.

"Christina!" he said firmly. "Christina! Wake up! Wake up, wake up."

She struggled against his hold. "No! No! Leave me alone!"

Mitch deduced that she was still sleeping. "Christina, it's me. Mitch. You're safe now, my friend. You're okay."

She melted in his arms, realizing at last that she was safe, that she had dreamed it all. Gradually her sobs eased. A minute later, she spoke softly. "I'm okay, Mitch. I'm okay now. Please. Let me go." She sounded upset, embarrassed.

He let her go but remained on the edge of the bed. She turned away, gathering the sheet around her and avoiding his gaze.

"Did he hurt you, Christina?" Mitch asked quietly.

"No. I'm fine."

"If you were *fine*, you wouldn't be waking up at three in the morning from nightmares."

"I'm okay, Mitch," she said. "I'm sorry I woke you."

He came around to her side of the bed, tenderly pulled a blanket up and over her, and wiped a tear from her cheek with one knuckle. "You're just overly tired."

"You're right. That's gotta be it. I'll feel more myself, come morning."

"Absolutely." He turned to go and glanced back at her while she turned to her side, then gently shut her door.

Mitch went back to bed in the guest room next to hers, rather than down the hall in the master. He wanted to be close to her should she have another nightmare. Or should a real intruder actually try and enter.

—∾—

Mitch greeted Christina at breakfast as if nothing had transpired the night before. "Good morning!"

"Good morning!" Joshua echoed his uncle. Anya and Kenna smiled too as Christina entered. Apparently no one but Mitch had heard her cries from the far side of the house. The kids slept in the other wing.

"Good morning," Christina said, smiling at everyone but dropping her eyes when she came to Mitch. How could she face him? He'd had to run to her as if she were a child. All that work to gain respect from the man only to lose it during the course of one night…

She shivered, remembering the nightmare. It had felt so real. She could still feel Manuel's hands gripping her arms.

Mitch's eyes narrowed as he studied her, as if he could see the shadows within. "There is a present for you under your place mat," he said smoothly, pouring her some orange juice and passing it to her by way of Anya.

"Oh?" She forced a smile and looked to the cooking bacon. "Talle off today?"

"Yeah. Every Saturday." He gestured over to the table. "Go on. Look."

Christina moved over to the table and looked under her plate. She sucked in her breath as she grasped the corner and pulled out several eleven-by-seventeen photos, just as Hans walked through the French doors, apparently having heard her voice.

"They are perfect, Christina," Hans said, leaning down to smack her cheek with a surprise kiss.

She glanced up in surprise and then to Mitch. Was that a…*jealous* look on his face? He hurriedly turned his attention back to the frying bacon before she could tell for sure.

"You've done it!" Hans went on. "The pictures are clear—almost all of them."

"Now I just have to get Meredith to help me translate a few more of these sections," she said, staring at one of the pictures. "We only had time to capture the biggest piece—the ship's supposed coordinates—before we had to leave the Archives. And you know how things came down after that."

"Is she quick?"

"Quick as she can, which sometimes feels agonizingly slow to me."

Mitch nodded grimly. "So where is *La Canción*?"

"The document mentions La Punta de Muerte. From some of my undergraduate studies, I think it refers to a peninsula in Mexico."

"Mexico?" Mitch said. "All this time you thought it was in the Eastern Caribbean, right?"

Christina nodded. "The first document referred to it as 'La Punta de los Asesinos,' or 'The Point of Murder.' And number two—this one," she said, lifting the print, "called it 'La Punta de Muerte,' or 'The Point of Death.' I was checking out every possible geographical reference and found several in and around the Keys that could resemble it. Where we dove, Mitch, was my fifth try. I never thought that *La Canción* was blown so far off course—maybe even to the Gulf."

Hans nodded. "It makes sense."

"Accuse me, Uncle Mitch, accuse me," Joshua interrupted, tugging on Mitch's sleeve.

"Yes, Josh?"

"Could I please be accused?"

"Finish up that last bite of egg and then you may be excused to play," he said gently. He looked up to see Christina smiling. "I'm making some headway," he said, a little defensive at her surprised pleasure.

"Mexico," Hans repeated, leaning back in his chair and sipping a cup of coffee. "We won't be able to dive until next month."

Christina's smile faded. "Next month?"

"He's right," Mitch said. "We'll need time for the site permit to go through and, most important, an investor to sponsor the dig."

Christina grew more despondent. "You guys can't generate the cash to sponsor it? That's why I came to Treasure Seekers. How is that possible after all of your discoveries?"

Mitch clearly did not like her tone. "It takes money to make money. And Hobard has robbed us of our last three finds. He's driving us close to bankruptcy."

"How much cash do you have left?" Christina dared.

"Enough to float a month's search work. But if we discovered *La Canción* and then had to break to find an investor, it might tempt pirates—either Hobard or others."

"How could anyone do that? We'd have the permit."

"Mexico's instability these days is a threat in itself. With the drug cartels running things...they might attack if they catch wind of us uncovering a treasure ship. So our budget has to include at least twelve armed guards, on constant rotation."

"Others, like Hobard, are more subtle," Hans said. "A boating accident, equipment sabotage...that's more his kind of thing."

"Up to now," Mitch said.

"Yeah," Hans said. "You and Seville...he took it to a whole new level."

"Or Manuel went rogue," she said. "It seems foolhardy for Hobard to risk his freedom—and reputation—by kidnapping me."

"It's possible," Hans said, stroking his chin as he thought about it.

Mitch sighed and leaned against the kitchen counter. "Even if we're just up against Hobard, we have our hands full. The last few big finds...We point the way, he decapitates our efforts—or sends us on a false trail—and before we can recover, he's bought off the officials and taken over our find. The only way we're going to capture *La Canción* is to plan every move and have resources to back us up to counter-attack. Because in his own way, he will attack."

"This isn't archaeology," Christina said in disgust. "This is guerrilla warfare."

"Welcome to treasure hunting," Mitch said. "Until Hobard's put behind bars, we have to match his modus operandi to survive. As well as watch out for other sharks."

Christina nodded, a chill running down her spine at the mention of *sharks*. She thought about the lengths Tate had gone to already to gain the upper hand in the search for *La Canción*. She clenched her fist and tapped it twice on the table. "You're going to beat him this time, boys. Because I'm your secret weapon."

CHAPTER 16

The next few days passed easily as Christina slept long hours, slowly readapting to island life. The nightmares did not return after that first awful experience. Mitch knew this because he crept to the adjoining guest room each eve to make sure he was near to comfort her, should she wake.

The fourth night, Mitch could not sleep. He admitted to himself that he was sleeping in the nearest room to Christina just to be close to her. Her proximity both comforted and agitated him, and he tossed and turned, unable to find rest. Finally he rose, opened the doors to the veranda, and walked out into the cool night air.

He looked back at Christina's firmly closed shutters, wishing that sleep would elude her, too, and that she would step outside and into his arms. Confess that she was feeling an attraction that might match his own. Mitch shook his head. He had to admit it. He was falling for her.

A woman I can't have.

He looked to the sky, staring at a waning moon and its sparkling light upon the gentle seas below. The last four days had been an awakening for him. Suddenly he could see, clear as day, how important the children and Hans were to him. They had become his family, of sorts. And Christina... Combined, the weight of what he felt for them all overwhelmed him.

"Why, God?" he prayed quietly, looking upward to the stars. "I was fine on my own. Happy. Why hand me all this?"

But his words sounded false, even to himself. He knew that he was glad for his new "burdens." Glad for the small, wiggling bodies and shy smiles of his niece and nephew, waking him up in the morning by climbing into bed with him. Glad for Hans's easy camaraderie. Glad for the electricity that charged his body and mind when Christina was near.

He looked back at the still shutters of her room. Did she have any idea? Could she possibly ever return his feelings? Not knowing left him feeling vulnerable, an uncommon emotion for Mitch. Perhaps it was this that burdened him most of all.

"Please, Father," he prayed. "If I'm off track here, please take away these feelings for Christina. And help me protect her and the children." That was it. The love he felt for all of them made him feel open to attack on all sides. A man like Tate Hobard would not hesitate to use one or all of them to get what he wanted.

He went back to bed and tried to sleep, but it was to no avail. Slumber remained far from him, and he was up at five, working in his office, trying to figure out ways to keep his loved ones safe and finance the expedition to Mexico.

By ten o'clock they had their first transmittal from Meredith, retrieved by Hans from a secure fax on San Esteban, which translated the first part of the document in detail. They dared not email back and forth, fearing their computers might be compromised. Hobard had managed that before.

The three partners sat in Mitch's office, tearing apart each sentence and referring to ancient cartographer's maps, pinned to the walls. They agreed with Meredith's conclusion: It looked as though the coordinates given were consistent with *La Canción* lying in waters north of the Yucatan.

The hours sped by, and repeatedly Mitch looked with surprise to Hans, or Hans to Mitch, as Christina came up with yet another astute, educated idea that aided them in their search. It wasn't her knowledge that surprised Mitch—it was that her involvement didn't feel like the intrusion he'd feared. She was fast becoming a valuable partner. For more reasons than leading them to *La Canción* in the first place.

—∾—

From her angle, Christina marveled at their extensive field experience. They gave her practical insight when something that made sense by the books did not make sense forty feet under water. They had excavated all sorts of sites—from those covered by a hundred feet of sand to those encrusted in four feet of coral. Together the trio made a perfect team.

Christina worried endlessly that Treasure Seekers was counting so heavily on *La Canción*. If they did not find her, Mitch and Hans would be in financial ruin, forced to sell the estate on Robert's Foe along with the search and salvage equipment it had taken them years to acquire.

By the following morning, they had exhausted their reserves of energy and insight. The next portion of the document would take Meredith a few days to decipher. The middle section had been badly damaged by water in the stacks, and the already difficult script was nearly unintelligible. They had to give her time to take it to an archivist at the neighboring university, and use his equipment to learn what she could.

One day seemed to melt into the next, with Mitch watching Christina from afar and Christina admiring the changes she was seeing in the man. Despite her newfound pleasure with Mitch, she felt restless and often found herself pacing.

Hans came upon her in the living room one day to find her wringing her hands and talking to herself as she walked back and forth. He leaned against the side of the doorway and watched until she stopped.

"Bored?" he asked.

"Frantic," she admitted. "Last time I was here, I had to take care of the children constantly. But now I have a ton of time on my hands until we hear again from Meredith."

"You need a swim," he said confidently.

"Diving would be better," she said, looking out the window. "It's too windy and, judging from the undertow, visibility would be nil."

"So you want me to go swimming with an undertow, huh? Trying to get rid of me already?"

"No, no," he laughed. "There is a spring-fed pool that you'll love. Take the dirt trail up the hill, and about a half-mile out, you'll discover paradise." He turned away confidently.

"Hans has spoken," Christina said regally, teasing her new friend at his dictatorial tone.

"Yes," he said, puffing up his chest. "I have declared it. Now go and do as I have said." He gave her a wink, padded into the kitchen and grabbed a banana from a bunch hanging on a hook.

Christina laughed, but had to admit that a freshwater swim sounded great. She hurried to her room to change into her white one-piece and cover-up, then passed Mitch in the hallway on the way out.

"Going for a walk?"

"Hans told me about the freshwater pool. I thought I'd take a swim."

"You'll love it." He smiled wistfully.

"Want to join me?" Her question seemed to fluster him, and she immediately regretted it. Was it obvious? That she was hoping to spend more time with him? Alone?

His eyebrows shot up. "Oh no. No, thanks. I'm going to take care of some paperwork."

Christina swallowed her disappointment, covering it with a quick smile. "Okay. See you later." She hurriedly left the house and climbed the hill in the direction Hans had pointed.

She gasped when she saw it. It was as near to perfection as she could imagine, a deep blue waterway with a wide-mouthed waterfall cascading gently downward from eight feet above.

All around was the evidence of freshwater nourishment. Palms waved in the strong winds, and dense undergrowth grew between them. The lush green foliage protected the pool from the fierce trade wind, making it an idyllic hideaway.

She pulled off her cover-up and dove into the cool, refreshing waters. After enduring days of sweltering heat and humidity, then nonstop wind, the sanctuary of this private garden felt like paradise.

—◊◊◊—

Mitch tentatively approached the pool, captivated by the sight of Christina diving and then somersaulting, obviously loving the water. He held back among the palms, half because he felt shy, worried he was intruding, half because he was mesmerized. As he watched, she visibly relaxed and floated atop the still water, eyes closed. Her hands and feet barely moved as she hovered in the center of the pool.

Mitch picked orange and pink and yellow lilies that grew around the pool in abundance and tossed them into the water as Christina continued to float peacefully, obviously hearing only the pounding of the waterfall. Gentle streams of sunlight filtered through the trees and illuminated the turquoise waters—as well as the beauty resting atop them.

Mitch couldn't help but stare. With long waves of dark brown hair streaming around her and flowers all about, she looked like the famous painting of "Ophelia."

No. Better than that. Was there anything about this woman he did not admire? She was intelligent. Witty. Brave. A believer. And beautiful to boot.

How had she escaped another man's arms up to now? He held his breath as a flower edged nearer her face. How long could he wait until he dared to try and take her in his arms himself?

You need to cool down, brother, he told himself. And with that, he dove deep into the water beside her.

—∞—

Christina heard the distinct sound of his plunge and raised her head, looking about. There was nothing but flowers all about her. *Flowers.*

She searched the border of the pond, curious as to how all the flowers got there. Had it been the wind? Or was someone with her? Hans? Her heart pounded. Mitch?

As if in answer, Mitch emerged beside the waterfall, gasping for breath. He smiled at her. "I'm sorry if I scared you. I decided a swim sounded too good to resist."

She smiled in relief. "Do I have you to thank for the flowers?"

"You looked like 'Ophelia' floating there," he admitted, shrugging. He pushed back his wet hair and dared to give her a small, flirtatious grin. "I thought I'd complete the picture."

She turned away from him, a bit taken aback at his frank admiration, his second-hand compliment, comparing her to a famous painting. But as she ducked under the water and took a few strokes, she understood that it also made her feel vulnerable. Did they really want to be doing this? Flirting? When so much was at stake?

They swam in silence for several minutes, stealing glances at each other, then looking away, enjoying the idle flirtation.

"Come over here, Christina," Mitch said, gesturing toward the waterfall. Tentatively, she swam to his side, wondering what he would do next. "Now dive deeply to avoid a pounding by the falls and swim to the other side. You can come up behind it." He disappeared underwater, leading the way. Curious now, Christina took a deep breath and followed.

When she emerged, he was scrambling up a rock ledge. Once on top, he turned to give her a hand up. They stood, side by side, staring at the waterfall from the inside. Centuries of waterworks had eaten away the granite, forming a damp cave. She looked around in awe.

"It's even more beautiful from this side," Christina said over the roar of the falls. They stared out through the water at the shimmering, watery images of green palm trees.

"It is," Mitch agreed, smiling. "It always reminds me of God. Constant. Strong. Just beyond normal human-vision."

"Life giving, never changing," Christina added.

"Yet always new," he said.

Mitch seemed to reach for her hand and then crossed his arms in front of his broad, finely muscled chest. "I prayed for you, you know," he said, just loud enough to be heard over the crush of water. "When you disappeared, for sure. But before that too. For protection. For provision. For a break through in the Archives."

She turned slightly toward him, and he dared to look her in the eye.

"Apparently, you have his ear, Crawford," she said. "Because he answered on all four fronts."

"Yes, he did." Carefully, he reached up and touched the side of her face. "And I'm so thankful."

She did not pull away. He dared to take a breath and another, but still she did not pull away. Instead, Christina turned toward him. She wanted him to keep touching her face. She wanted him to kiss her.

Passion warmed his gaze and she could feel the struggle in him, echoing her own. The draw between them was powerful, and yet had they not agreed to keep things between them strictly professional?

"I...We'd better get back," he said gruffly. He turned and dove through the wall of water as if she might chase him.

Christina leaned back against the rock wall, allowing herself time to catch the breath that Mitch had seemed to steal with his touch. She'd wanted him to kiss her, she reminded herself. Basically invited him to kiss her, turning toward him like that. *What is wrong with you, woman?* Pulling herself out of her reverie, she, too, dove through the wall of water and emerged on the other side.

Mitch was at the end, toweling dry and smiling ruefully at her. She swam toward him, then climbed out.

He watched her as she pulled on her cover-up, then moved closer. "I wanted to kiss you, you know."

"I wondered," she said, pretending to not care either way, but still fighting the draw toward him. She glanced toward the deep green of the swaying palms and the turquoise sea, then back to him. She ran her fingers through her hair, tousling it into waves. "Why didn't you?"

He stilled. Turned to directly face her. "Do you want me to kiss you?"

"I think…I think I might have wanted you to kiss me ever since I returned to Robert's Foe."

He smiled and his eyebrows met in an adorable arch of concern. "What about our pact to keep things professional?"

She swallowed hard as he took her hand in both of his. "Sometimes, sometimes people have to re-think things. We're not always right from the get-go."

"True," he said huskily, wrapping a hand around her lower back and edging closer. "So…Did I miss my chance? May I kiss you now?"

"Maybe," she said.

He edged even closer. "Maybe?" he whispered.

"Maybe," she said, placing a hand on the back of his neck, feeling the thrill of his hips leaning against hers.

He hovered close, so close she could feel the brush of his broad, muscled chest, the warmth of his breath on her face. "I don't want a maybe from you, Christina," he said. "Because you're not a maybe sort of girl. Tell me. Do you want me to kiss you as much as I want to kiss you?"

She looked into his eyes, knowing this was her final out. Her last chance at escape. Because what was ahead was pure vulnerability, mayhem, potential trouble for their partnership…but she did not have the power to turn away. "Yes," she said firmly.

She'd not quite fully uttered the word when he kissed her deeply, for a long, languid minute—or maybe two? She seemed lost in the moment, in him—then reluctantly drew away. "Ahh, Christina," he whispered with a smile, pulling her into a warm hug. "How I hoped it would be this way."

CHAPTER 17

The next morning, Mitch watched Christina approach Anya in the breakfast room. He stood on the adjacent balcony, appreciating a strong cup of coffee, and studying the sailboat that seemed to have weighed anchor off their leeward shore. "I bet you could use a break," she said to Anya. "Let me take the kids this morning."

"That would be wonderful," the girl said gratefully, casting him a questioning glance.

He nodded, giving her silent permission.

"I need to answer some emails," Anya said. "It seems like if Kenna goes down for a nap, Joshua's ready to play, or the other way around."

"It's tiring for sure," Christina said sympathetically. "When I'm around, please don't hesitate to ask me to watch them if you need help. They kind of wormed their way into my heart when I was caring for them. I missed them when I was in Spain."

As if his heart needed any more stimulus...just seeing her walk into the room after their kiss at the pool set it to pounding. But this? She'd missed the kids?

"Thank you," Anya said. She immediately left for her room, needing no further convincing. Mitch felt a stab of guilt—he'd not really thought about it, with all that had been going on since her arrival. But she hadn't had a day off since she'd arrived two weeks ago. *Fine boss you are, jerk.* Clearly, household management was not his forte.

"Come on, you guys," Christina said to the kids as Mitch joined them in the breakfast room. "Let's go build a sandcastle."

"Yeah!" Joshua yelled, raising his arms in celebration.

"Yawah!" Kenna said, imitating her older brother and raising her tiny arms, too.

Christina laughed and met Mitch's smiling eyes. "Good morning," she said, dropping her gaze and turning to lead the children away.

"Good morning..." he said, wondering what was going through her head. She had not come to dinner the night before but had instead requested that Talle send a half sandwich to her bedroom. "How's your headache?" he asked her retreating back.

"Gone!" she said brightly. "See you later." She settled Kenna on one hip and led Joshua away with her free hand.

"Bye, Uncle Mitch!" Joshua yelled over his shoulder. "Come look at our castle!"

"I will," he said, glad for the excuse to join them. He ate a quick breakfast, then followed their tracks in the sand, staring at Christina's footprints and chastising himself for deeming even them perfect. *You're acting like a love-sick fool, Crawford.*

He found the three perched on the crest of a dune, near damp building materials but on dry sand themselves. Christina concentrated on a tall parapet while Joshua happily dug a moat, his favorite job. Kenna sat beside them, intently tasting fistfuls of sand granules and spitting them out all over her tiny purple swimsuit.

"Should she be doing that?" he asked Christina.

She smiled at him and then Kenna. "It won't hurt her. Part of learning what things are and what they're like is to taste them, if I remember it right." She smiled again at the tanned baby with blond hair. "Besides, she's too happy to stop."

"Agreed," he said, kneeling perilously close beside her to help. When their hands chanced to meet on the castle wall, it felt as if a bolt of electricity shot up his fingers and arm.

When Josh suggested that Mitch help him with the moat, Christina quickly agreed. "Just like a woman," Mitch teased. "Wanting to decorate the house herself."

"This is no house," she corrected him with a chastising frown. "It's a castle."

"With knights and horses and swords!" Josh added ecstatically. He picked up a stick and rose, slashing it about. "I'm a knight, and I'm going to kill the bad guys!" He pranced about the beach with a determined face, slaying imaginary enemies.

Mitch and Christina stifled their laughter. "Who's been telling him Knights of the Round Table stories?" Mitch asked.

"Hopefully Anya. No kid should grow up without hearing about Lady Guinevere and Camelot."

"No, I guess not. That would be a serious void in their education," he said.

They worked on in silence. "Tell me, Mitch," Christina said softly, obviously not wanting the children to hear and without moving her eyes from the sandcastle. "That sailboat, a mile out. Think it's Hobard?"

"Could be," he said smoothly, as if it were an everyday

occurrence. He should have known she'd put two and two together.

She gestured for him to follow and they took a few steps away to speak freely. "I need to know these things, Mitch. I'm not a child."

"I know. I just didn't want you to worry. It may be Hobard. It may not. I don't recognize the ship, but if it comes close enough, we'll run the number to find out."

"Do you think he'd dare come that close?"

Mitch pursed his lips. "He's never gone that far before. But he also hasn't ever kidnapped one of my partners before. He's probably just staking us out. That's more his method."

"If he's staking us out, how do we get past him and on our way to Mexico?"

"I don't know. Hans and I have been thinking about that. Bessie isn't exactly a jet boat," he said, nodding over to the giant, heavy search-and-salvage vessel they'd need to take.

"What if you and I lead them to a fake site while Hans gets a head-start on Bessie?"

Mitch raised a brow. "That's not a bad idea. If we could give him a few days, he could reach the coast of Mexico. On our new jet boat, we could join him a day later. Or better yet, fly there, so Hobard has no idea."

"I like it." She glanced over her shoulder. "But what about the kids?"

"I was thinking about sending them to San Esteban with Anya, Talle, and Nora. Rent a house for a month under one of the women's names, not mine or Hans's, so no one can easily find them."

She nodded and took a deep breath, as if relieved. "They've been through so much. The last thing they need is any more trauma."

"Agreed." He dared to put an arm around her shoulders

as they walked back to the children. "I'm going to do all I can to make sure everyone I care about stays safe," he promised.

Happily, Christina did not pull away. Instead, after a tentative moment and a flash of a smile, she wrapped her arm around his waist. It felt like an assent, an agreement. And Mitch had to wonder if that moment was almost better than their first kiss.

Almost.

—\~—

That night after Anya had taken the children to bed, the three partners sat up talking and drinking tea.

"I want to know all about Tate Hobard," Christina said quietly.

Mitch scowled. "Haven't you had enough nightmares?"

"I need to know," she said steadily. "Exactly who we're up against."

Hans did not bat an eye at her interest. "We burned his tail when we discovered *La Bailadora* as college kids. At the time, we didn't realize how close he was to discovering her himself. Then here we come, and the three of us just happened upon the ship. It gave us the seed money for Treasure Seekers, but put his company in jeopardy, both financially and professionally."

"He ignored us for a long time, figuring we were first-timers and soon gone," Mitch put in, "but when we found and salvaged several more big wrecks over the years, I think he decided that Treasure Seekers owed him something. So far, he's stolen three big wrecks from us, in the last two years. He considers it payback."

"Or he decided leeching off our footwork was easier than doing his own," Hans said.

"I think that's it," Mitch said. "It's like he's addicted to taking what is ours." His eyes narrowed. Taking what is ours. For the second time, he thought of how important Hans, Christina, and the kids had become to him. What could hurt him more than losing one of them? What would Tate delight in more than cutting him at the core?

"Since your abduction, I'm now convinced that he murdered—or Manuel had someone murder—one of our assistant researchers at Texas A&M two years ago," Hans continued. "Scott Haviland was really close to something big. He had just returned from Seville when he was murdered. We thought it was an accident. Now..."

"Murdered? How did he die?" Christina asked.

"Car accident. But he went straight into the side of a building. And there was no alcohol in his system. Cops thought he'd been texting or got distracted somehow."

"Might he have fallen asleep?"

"He might have," Mitch said. "But now we think there's a possibility someone ran him off the road."

"Right after the accident, Tate claimed one of his 'surprise' finds," Hans said. "It made him twice the money we've ever made on any wreck, outside *The Dancer*."

Christina shuddered, remembering Manuel all too well and the lengths he had gone to get ahold of her and what she'd found. Was he the same man sent after Scott? "Did you call the FBI?" she asked.

"We did," Mitch said, with a shake of his head, looking out the window to a sunset sky. The breeze that night was gentle, soothing. "But they didn't have much to go on. And I couldn't believe Hobard would go that far."

"He's done other things," Hans said. "Stolen from us. Bribed officials to keep us from staking claims, that sort of thing. But other than your abduction—and maybe Scott's accident—he's never hurt us or those we loved."

"That said..." Mitch's eyes met Christina's. "Hans and Nora are moving into the east wing tonight. I want us all in one place. And Nora can be with the other women and children, somewhere safe, when we go."

Christina shivered again. The thought of being a prisoner in the house made her feel claustrophobic. She rose. "I need to take a walk. I won't be gone long."

—ൡ—

Mitch watched her closely as she set down her teacup and left the room. She wore a simple purple sarong skirt and scoop-necked, white T-shirt that he found very attractive.

Hans laughed, catching him staring at the empty doorway, deep in thought. "Go after her. You've done nothing but moon over the woman for the last week, and she shouldn't be out on the beach alone. Not with Hobard potentially hovering about."

Mitch needed no convincing. For a time he followed Christina at a distance, admiring her long, lean legs as she walked barefoot in the sand, her flip-flops soon discarded and in her hand. Her hair flowed in the breeze, and days spent on the island had turned her olive skin a dark bronze. She was deep in thought, unaware that he trailed behind her. *What would happen to her if I were Tate?* The thought made his pulse quicken.

He could not wait any longer. He walked faster, making his own strides longer than hers, and soon caught up. She looked up at him, saying nothing, as if she had expected him all along. He took her hand in his own, appreciating the feel of her strong fingers interlocking with his. It felt delightful to simply hold her hand, and they walked silently for a time.

As they passed the stream that originated in the pool high above, Mitch remembered watching Christina swim and float, then her soft kiss…her sweet lips on his. He had to act.

He stopped and turned to her, pulling her to him with a swift, sure movement. Slowly, ever so slowly, she raised thickly lashed eyes to meet his, the warm tones of the sunset behind her giving her skin a golden hue, the shadows enhancing her cheekbones. He stared down at her, thinking she was the most innocently inviting woman he had ever met. Then he bent his head to meet hers.

Christina broke their kiss, pushing him a few inches away, although he still rested his hands at her waist.

He frowned in confusion, but held on loosely.

She looked out at the sailboat that continued to slowly circle the island. "Let go of me, Mitch," she said gently.

He dropped his hands.

"Walk with me, will you?" she asked, already a stride ahead.

They walked on as Christina struggled to gather her thoughts. No one had ever matched her lifestyle and interests as well as Mitch, but she could not quite see them together; there was too much in the way—Mitch adjusting to the children, Tate Hobard pursuing them, the search for *The Song*… She lifted a hand to her forehead, trying to rub away the confusion.

"This is not reality," she said, turning to face him. "We're here on this island, in the middle of a mad, dangerous adventure. Is it possible to begin a real relationship in this situation? Would you even want a relationship?"

Her directness seemed to take him aback. After a second, he cocked a grin. "Hey, I live on a romantic island. And by nature, our work is adventurous. I hope Tate won't be a factor for long, but no matter how much I want to, there isn't much of that I can truly control. We just have to deal with him the best way we can, as it comes. And yes, I think I really do want a relationship," he said, his eyes earnest. "I mean, I wasn't looking for one. As you said, I kind of have my hands full right now. But I also think God brought you my way. And I, for one, don't think we should ignore it."

"I came here wanting a business partner," she said with a sigh, still rubbing her forehead with one hand, her other on her hip. "Nothing more."

He stepped back as if he had been slapped. "Is this because of what we told you about Hobard?" He reached for her hand. "Did it frighten you?"

"No!" she said, pulling her hand away and looking to sea, hugging herself. "Well, maybe. I feel…overwhelmed, I think. By you. By the prospect of us." She turned partially away, looking to the sunset, and in silhouette, the sailboat. "By *all* of this."

He ran his fingers through his hair, trying to get a grip on his swirling emotions. "Why the sudden walls, Christina? Can't we figure things out as we go? Do we really need to plan it all out, right now?"

"Things are just moving too fast," she said softly, taking what seemed to be her first full breath since their kiss. "I need you to give me some room. Professionally, I'm so ready for this partnership. Personally? I, uh…"

She couldn't bear to continue to see the direct hurt in his eyes and turned partially toward the ocean, hugging herself.

He stared at her, then shook his head, sorrow lacing every movement. "You told me you wanted me to kiss you by the pool."

"I did," she whispered.

He paused and turned partially away from her too. "Aren't we both old enough to know what we're looking for, even if it's not the best timing? Why not take the opportunity to see if this is it?"

"What if we decided it wouldn't work, halfway through the dig on The Song? What then?"

He looked at her sharply. "Is that what you're worried about? That somehow this thing between us will interfere in your beloved dig?"

"Maybe," she said, crossing her arms. "Is that so wrong? After pursuing her so long?"

"Yes or no?" he pressed. "As I said before, I doubt you're a *maybe* kind of girl."

"Then no," she said, turning to face him, arms crossed. "No, I'm not worried about our relationship becoming an issue, because I think we should put things on the back burner."

Mitch stared at her. "It's been my experience that God offers us gifts at times. And we either grab hold of it or pass it by and regret it."

"I don't know," she said, digging her toes into the damp, cool sand. "I'm a scholar, Mitch. I like adventure, but I don't enjoy being in danger. I was in a diving accident a few years ago...and the thing in Seville..."

He took her by the shoulders, as if he wanted to shake her. "Life is fleeting, Christina! Look at my sister, Rachel. Ever since she died, I've been thinking I shouldn't put *anything* on the back burner. Why are you resisting this—this thing between you and me?"

Her eyes left his, and she looked out to the sailboat.

Mitch dropped his hands.

"It's just too much, Mitch, and we have too far to go." She clenched her jaw resolutely. "After we find her, maybe then..."

"No, Christina," he said, moving to stand in front of her,

blocking any view of the sailboat. "I won't let Tate rob me of you, too. And I won't let you do this. I won't let you walk away from me. I share your passion to find *La Canción*; you know that. And I've realized a lot about myself in the last weeks. You've awakened a love in me for the children that I didn't think was possible, and I'm falling—"

"No! Don't say it, Mitch! Everything will change!" Her face was stricken with concern as she laid a hand on his chest.

He covered her hand with his own, resolute. "I'm falling in love with you."

"No!" she pulled her hand away and started walking back to the house, frustrated that he fell into stride beside her. "It's never worked for me to have a relationship with someone! I'm too committed to my work, and look at you! You're just as bad as I am."

He grinned in the darkness. The sun was almost gone. "I know. Isn't it perfect? You could be a permanent partner of Treasure Seekers. I've already talked to Hans—"

"You've already *what*?"

Mitch paused at the anger in her voice.

"You've already planned out my life? Are you that sure that I'll do anything you want me to?"

"Christina, I—"

"I can't do this. I'm going away. I'll come back when it's time to go to Mexico. I need space, safety. I need time to *think*."

He grabbed her arm as she turned away. "Christina. Hear me. You're the first woman I've ever said those words to. I tell you I love you, and you tell me you're leaving? You're panicking. Don't run. Please don't run."

He pulled her to him, intending to change her mind with another sweet kiss, but she pushed him away. "No, Mitch! Leave me alone!"

He released her without hesitation and watched, in misery, as she stalked away. For a long time, he stood there, despondent...feeling nothing like what he thought he would feel after confessing love to a woman.

Bleary-eyed, he glanced to the twinkling lights on the sailboat and wondered if the observers had enjoyed their little show. No doubt they had seen all of it. He had been so consumed with Christina that he had given them little thought. Now their presence left him feeling all the more adrift at sea.

CHAPTER 18

Mitch shook her shoulder gently. "Christina. Christina, wake up." She looked up at him drowsily and sat up, wondering why he was in her room. *Half-relieved*, she acknowledged, *half-irritated.*

"Come dive with me," he said. It was obvious that he'd had as little sleep as she. Dark circles ringed his blue-green eyes. "It will help clear our minds. Get us back to the task at hand."

Task at hand. Rather than more talk of what they may—or may not—be feeling.

"All right," she agreed at once, thinking that an early morning dive sounded like the perfect elixir to what ailed her. It had been too long since she'd been underwater. "How 'bout that reef to the leeward side?"

"Four Fathom Reef? Yeah. I haven't spent much time there," he sat back, considering. "Let's do it." He turned to leave, every action seeming forced.

When he was gone, Christina rose, brushed her teeth, gathered her hair into a ponytail, then pulled on her swimsuit and shorts and met Mitch outside. Hans waited with him. "He'll come with us to keep watch above, in case Hobard gets any ideas while we're below," Mitch said.

"The kids?" she asked, falling into step beside them.

"There's a storm moving in. And with that sailboat just hanging out, I asked Anya and Talle to pack for their new rental house on San Esteban. They'll be there in a few hours. We can check in on them tonight," he said. "C'mon. It's so hot already, all I can think of is getting under water."

She nodded, well aware of the still, humid air. At the back of the house, Hans picked up her air tank for her, and she grabbed the rest of her gear, which was in a large, black net bag. They made their way to the docks, and Hans took the helm of the dive boat without discussion. He lifted his nose in the air. "Smells like hurricane."

"You think this tropical storm's going to become a *hurricane*?" Christina asked, gazing toward the horizon. With a start, she realized it had been days since she'd watched the news or looked up a weather report.

"It's gonna run a bit south of us. We shouldn't get more than the wing of it, unless it takes a serious turn," Mitch said.

"But it's another good reason for the kids and women to head to San Esteban," Hans said.

Christina looked again to the horizon. There were a few clouds, but nothing that might raise concern. A hurricane seemed impossible. But she'd seen tropical storms and hurricanes swoop in faster than a sailor could blink, so she took their words to heart. After all, they lived in the Caribbean.

Mitch stood at the bow, ignoring Christina and, apparently, worrying about the storm. Was he angry with her? If so, why did he want her to come with him? Why not just grab

Hans for a dive buddy? Christina felt too confused to think it all through, wishing she'd grabbed a cup of coffee to clear her addled brain.

They were on the other side of the island within minutes. The sailboat remained on the windward side of Robert's Foe, about a mile distant, apparently in a slow rotation around their isle. It was a relief to have them out of sight, she admitted to herself. *I can pretend that they're not even here.*

"I'm going to skip the farmer johns," Christina said. "I can't stand the thought of putting on neoprene in this heat."

"You sure? You might want it on with the coral," Mitch muttered, bending to pull on his own. "It'll protect your skin."

Had he paused for a nano-second before he uttered the word "skin," or was it all in her imagination? Regardless, Christina acquiesced, not wishing for any other reason to argue. They suited up—Christina in her bright gold and Mitch in black—then donning weight belts, inflatable vests, air tanks, regulators, and masks. They waved to Hans and gave a thumbs-up to one another, then went over the side.

As soon as they were under, they both knew that the still, hot day made for terrific clarity below. The coral reef was gigantic, and flora and fauna exploded in bright color all around. They had a hundred feet of clear visibility, making it feel more like an aquarium than the ocean.

Christina concentrated on slowing her breathing. With this kind of diving, she wanted all the time below that her air tank would allow.

And she could not help but cast a smile at Mitch.

—⚉—

With the regulator in her mouth, it was difficult to make out a grin, but he could see the smile in her eyes. *She loves it down here too.* He rarely dove at Four Fathom Reef himself; he spent most of his time on professional dive sites and so usually, he couldn't afford to waste underwater time on pleasure. But it was beautiful. As upset as he was with Christina, he was happy to be sharing this dive with her. Maybe moments like these were what they needed to come together. Whether that meant as business partners. Or something more…

She moved ahead of him, using her long fins to propel her with even, straight-legged strokes. He admired her technique. Even her diving form was good. *If I could just make it past these walls she's erected…*

Christina set out after a huge yellow Coney with transparent fins and a large, yawning mouth. Mitch followed, amused at her childish delight in the various fish. First one caught her fancy, then another. Mitch was content to simply follow her around, watching, thinking.

She paused after a while, turning her attention to the reef below. Swimming through giant red fans of delicate coral, she stopped to examine a different variety below it. In the cauliflower-type reef were tiny fish, making their living off the slow-growing coral and creating their own little multi-colored worlds. Christina maneuvered to the far side, exploring several caves that gave way to entire colonies of marine life.

Mitch brought her a purple starfish and then pointed out an octopus—the size of his hand—expertly camouflaged to blend in with the coral around him. Together, they moved into an ancient cave where he knew they could find a bounty of urchins and eels.

After exploring it for a while, Mitch emerged from the cave and frowned as he felt the surge that had not been there moments before. Calm air and seas with large swells that seemed to come from nowhere were common signs of a nearby hurricane. Maybe the storm intended to visit Robert's Foe far more closely than any of the weather forecasters predicted.

He motioned for Christina to follow him out of the cave, wanting to head back. If the storm was indeed heading their way, they needed to prepare the house and consider evacuating. Mitch waved his hand, emulating the surge for her.

Christina nodded, but then froze, her eyes widening in terror.

Mitch turned to see what had alarmed her. His heart pounded as he saw it. A huge female tiger shark, possibly driven this close to land by the disturbing waves of the storm. If they could just keep still, the shark would move away, not even noticing the divers. She'd be far more interested in finding a tasty turtle or even a smaller shark for her lunch than them.

But the shark suddenly looked toward them. With a powerful twitch of her tail, she turned and darted closer, passing by as if on reconnaissance. Mitch slowly turned his head to see what might be attracting her. A turtle? A sting ray?

But it was Christina. She frantically swam back into the depths of the cave. There was no grace, no control in her movement, and Mitch struggled to understand her evident panic. Moreover, he had to catch up and quell her movements before the shark attacked, thinking they were frolicking, tasty morsels to be eaten.

Mitch eased into the small cave after her, intent on not adding to the commotion that might draw the shark. Christina was backed up to the wall, obviously trying to melt in, disappear. He grabbed her shoulders and shook her, but Christina's eyes refused to focus on him, darting left and right. A stream of bubbles leaving her mouth told him that she was burning through her oxygen. Her eyes grew wider as she looked over his shoulder. He looked back too.

The monster cruised by the cave entrance and Mitch inhaled sharply, silently counting off at least sixteen feet of flesh. The tiger was the biggest he had seen; the larger the sharks grew, the more dangerous they were considered.

Thankfully, Christina seemed paralyzed by fear as the shark passed. As soon as she was out of sight, Christina backed up, bumping her scuba tank against the reef again and again, the coral cutting into her shoulder and arms around the wet suit straps, the crack of her tank audible.

Pieces of coral fell to the sand below. Mitch fought to control her, grabbing her arms and turning her around to face the wall so she could not see the shark cruise by again. He held her arms to her side, willing her to still. The sound of escaping air bubbles in mass quantity seemed deafening in the underwater cavern. The shark would return for another pass, he was sure of it. Christina's movement, their air bubbles, and the echoes of the tank colliding with coral would draw her back.

Mitch never expected such a reaction from an experienced diver. How could she not have learned how to handle a fear of sharks in all her years as a scuba diver? She must've seen hundreds by now! Mitch held on to her, shut his own eyes as the tiger shark passed again, and prayed that it would not decide to delve deeper into the cave.

—⁓—

Christina concentrated on slowing her breathing, realizing she was in the midst of a full-blown panic attack and taking comfort in Mitch's proximity. She prayed, crying out to God to save them both. Mitch turned, wrapping her in his arms and making a comforting sound.

Christina's mask was inches away from the coral cave wall. She fought the urge to wrench out of his arms, knowing he held her in order to try and save them both. What if her panic attack drew the tiger shark closer? What if it bit into Mitch, instead of her?

The thought started her heart pounding faster again. *What if he dies trying to protect me?* She couldn't let that happen! Christina had to get control so they could face the monster together. She took a deep breath in, then released it. Repeated the action. Eventually her eyes focused, and she stared at the space where her metal tank had broken coral away.

She realized that within the six-inch span she could clearly see the curve of a bronze cannon. Gradually, her thoughts clicked into place. *Canon. It's a canon. Right here! A wreck, right under our noses!*

She looked up and around. *This isn't a cave. It's the remains of an ancient hull.*

Before she could turn and show Mitch, he was pulling her around and taking her hand. He gestured to the cave mouth, and then lifted the gauge at his hip, tapping it. Noting his alarm, she checked hers too. The shark had left, but they were nearly out of air.

They rose slowly from the depths, belying their anxiety. Even pressed by their dwindling oxygen, neither was anxious to risk the bends. But once they reached Hans and the raft, Mitch ripped off his mask and frowned at her. "Do you wanna tell me what just happened?" he shouted.

She pulled off her own mask and wiped her face, bobbing in the waves. Looked over her shoulder. The storm was definitely picking up.

"What's going on?" Hans asked, offering her a hand. She took it and the giant easily lifted her aboard, then Mitch.

"What happened?"

She wearily unbuckled her tank and weight belt, setting them to the side. "Look," she said to Mitch. "I'm sorry. I should've told you."

"Heck *yeah*, you should have told me," Mitch said, tossing aside his tank.

"What?" Hans bellowed. "What should she have told you?"

"That I'm afraid of sharks," Christina said quietly.

Hans stared at her. He began to laugh, obviously thinking she was joking, but then sobered when neither laughed with him. "Uhh, did you want to rethink that career path then, doc? Because…" he waved at the sea around them. "That there water is full of big scary things with dorsal fins."

"Look," she said, pushing a wet tendril of hair off her face. "I can usually handle it. It's been years since I…since I…felt that way. Down there." Her eyes met Mitch's.

He took a deep breath and then looked to the sky for a moment, then back to her. "What happened? As your future dive partners, we deserve to know."

She swallowed hard, blew out her cheeks and steadied herself. "Six years ago, I was diving a site off the coast of Florida. And a Great White tried to have me for breakfast."

Both men stared at her, as if they couldn't quite believe it. "It was about the time you guys found *The Dancer*. I was on a university crew, working a Civil War ship. I didn't even see him coming. But then he clamped down on me."

"Where?" Mitch said.

"My back and belly. I owe my life to my professor. He stabbed the shark in the eye, which made him release me." She lifted her hands. "Three surgeries later, I was right as rain."

Both men continued to stare, taking that in. Those three

surgeries—and the recoveries in between—had taken two years of her life.

"Right as rain, you say," Mitch muttered. "But does that happen every time you see a shark?" He waved toward the water.

"Only when I see sharks that might want to eat me," she said, trying to make him smile. But he didn't.

"There are lots of sharks that might want to eat us on a dive site. Only a few consider really trying."

"Right. I usually can keep that straight." She heaved a sigh and looked to the island, the wind setting the jungle and trees into a riotous dance of green. "I think...I think after what happened in Seville... Well, I think I'm just not myself."

It pained her to say it. But it was the truth.

"I'm really sorry, Mitch. I didn't...I never meant to en-danger you. If anything had happened to you, because of me..." She rubbed her forehead in deep circles, trying to press away the ache.

"But it didn't," he said, reaching out to put a hand on her shoulder. "I'm fine. We're both fine, right?"

CHAPTER 19

So absorbed were they in conversation that none of them noticed the men approaching until it was too late. The divers emerged on all four sides of their raft, and when Hans reached for the pistol at his hip, one of them shot him.

"Hans!" Christina screamed, as the man whirled with the impact, nearly falling off the raft. She and Mitch both went to help him, allowing all four men to board the raft.

Once he'd steadied his friend, Mitch turned to strike the first, sending him off the side and into the water.

But Christina felt a man behind her, pulling her back and against his chest. "That's enough, Crawford!" he said, pressing a knife to her throat.

Chills ran down her neck. She knew that voice. Manuel.

Mitch whirled, fists clenched. But he stilled when he saw she was captured. Behind him, Hans's legs seemed to crumple beneath him.

"Sit down, Crawford. Hobard will join us in a minute,"

he said, nodding toward an approaching speedboat, coming around the north side of the island.

In minutes, the boat was beside them and Tate Hobard emerged from the captain's cabin. "Ahh, at last the moment has arrived," he said, lifting his arms. He was dressed in a crisp, white jacket. Dark hair, peppered with some premature silver, was drawn into a ponytail, low at his neck. "Come, come. Join me," he said, gesturing toward the wide deck. "We cannot all fit on your raft."

Reluctantly, they did as they were told. Hans gripped his arm, bright red blood dripping between his fingers. "Now, Manuel, was that entirely necessary?" Hobard asked with some distaste, seeing it as he passed.

"He pulled a gun," Manuel grunted. He held on to Christina until they were on the boat, then pushed her toward Mitch.

Mitch caught her and put a protective arm around her shoulders. She half-turned, wrapped an arm around his waist, and glared back at the men. Christina knew that, like the shark below, they would not hesitate to strike if they sensed her fear.

"The beautiful and confounding Dr. Alvarez! I'm so happy to finally make your acquaintance." Hobard gave her a small bow. He was lean and tanned, about forty years old. Smaller than Mitch, but wiry and strong.

"I wish I could say the same," she said.

He ignored her and moved his gaze to Mitch. "I think we may be in for a little storm. We cannot stay out in our boats, so I think we should take our meeting at your home. It's time we sat down for a proper discussion, isn't it?" He made a gesture in the air and the captain of the ship—invisible behind tinted glass—immediately set them into motion.

Mitch helped her take a seat beside Hans, but remained

LISA T. BERGREN

standing.

When they rounded the island, they all caught sight of Mitch's jet boat, speeding away in the distance. The women and children had gotten safely away, either alerted by the approaching storm, spotting their capture, or both. Christina held her breath as Manuel tossed a questioning look toward Tate. "Boss?"

"We agreed that they would go to San Esteban ahead of the storm!" Mitch said. "They know nothing of your presence here!"

"Oh, let them go," Hobard said, waving a dismissive hand at the small boat in the distance, cresting wave after wave en route to San Esteban. "We have all we need here," he said, gesturing to their three captives. He sat down on the other side of Christina. "Children can be rather distracting anyway, can't they?"

She ignored him.

Mitch set his mouth in a tight line. A man was on either side of him, and two others hovered near Hans, who was clearly losing strength by the moment. Blood dripped down his arm. He needed a doctor, but Hobard only seemed to have an interest in Christina, attempting to draw her into conversation again and again. Resolutely, she ignored him.

When they tied up at the dock, the men immediately tied Mitch's hands behind his back, and they all climbed down to the dock. Manuel held her arm, but didn't tie her up, nor did they tie Hans, who was now sweating profusely and turning a ghastly shade of gray.

With a snap of his fingers, Tate wordlessly sent two of his men to search the house and verify they were alone. They threw open the door without pausing, and Christina prayed the women and children were indeed all aboard that vessel, making its way to San Esteban. And that they would find a safe place to hide once there.

Abruptly, Tate moved into her line of vision. "What are you afraid of, Dr. Alvarez? Is someone you care about still inside?"

She stared into his cold, gray eyes and said nothing.

His eyes left hers slowly, shifted to Mitch, and then returned to her. "I can find a way to make you talk, you know."

Manuel laughed as he felt Christina tense.

Christina looked at the ground, wondering what Mitch was thinking as one of Tate's men came to the door and gave them the all-clear sign. *This is not happening... This is not happening...*

"Come, my dear," Tate said over his shoulder. "We have much to discuss." Manuel dragged her along the path, following Tate, and into the house first. The thought of being there with the two of them alone made her frantic. She looked back. To her relief, Mitch and Hans were brought along too. *Misery loves company*, she thought grimly.

She feared looking up as they went inside, terrified that the children or Anya or Talle were tied up, in the hands of their captors. It heartened her to see no one about. They had all escaped! "Which way to Mitch's office?" Tate asked her.

Christina looked away, determined not to help him in the least. He grabbed a handful of hair and jerked her head back. "Enough of the games. I asked, which way?"

She stared back at him, lips in a clenched line.

"Up the stairs and to the left," Mitch said from behind them, obviously wanting to spare her.

"Why, thank you, Mitch," Tate said, tearing his eyes from Christina.

"Very impressive home," Tate called over his shoulder as they climbed the stairs. No one responded. When they arrived at Mitch's office, Manuel left Christina's side and pulled two chairs up to the desk. Guards pushed Christina into the chairs and Hans was shoved into the corner of a couch ten feet away. Hans cried out as the man intentionally shoved his injured arm.

It was more than Mitch could bear. "Why you..." He lunged at the guard, but another swiftly brought the nose of his gun up under Mitch's chin.

"Mitch!" Christina screeched, jumping up.

"People, people," Tate said, as if he were addressing a crowd of misbehaving junior high students. "Please. Have a seat. And somebody get the lady a robe."

Christina sat down again. Mitch and Hans stopped moving. The heat was unbearable, and the neoprene of her Farmer John wetsuit made her feel as if she were suffocating. A man entered with Mitch's forest green robe. As stifled as she felt, she hated to put it on, but she decided the more fabric that separated her from these men, the better. What if they murdered Mitch and Hans and carted her away, forcing her to show them where *La Canción* was? Christina felt as if she were on a cheap carnival ride, dizzy and unable to see straight.

Tate moved toward her and perched on the corner of the desk, nearest her. This was it. He was going to use her to get to Mitch. Knowing how Mitch felt about her, all was lost. She was the weak link. *La Canción will be in Tate's hands in no time*, she thought numbly.

Tate leaned over and whispered in her ear. "You have no need of them. *We* could be partners. I have more resources. As well as experience. This unpleasantness can all be done for you within minutes."

Christina paused, as if she were considering the thought, wondering if it might help them all if she played along. But then Tate leaned forward again and whispered, "We could be more than partners if you wish."

She looked up at him. "Never."

He raised his eyebrows, looking at her skeptically. "Now that's rather uncivil, Dr. Alvarez."

"Yes, well, if I wanted you as my partner, I would have come to you first. But I didn't, did I?" She was impressed with how strong her voice sounded. Inside, she felt like jelly. The gun, eighteen inches to her right, was pointed at Mitch's head, and everything in her screamed she needed to find a way to get the guy to release him.

"More's the pity," Tate said, returning to the other side of the desk.

The wind outside was gaining strength, pushing at the closed shutters of the office and making them rattle. Hans's body slackened next to Mitch, apparently weakened by loss of blood. His head lulled to the side. "He needs a doctor," Mitch said.

"Business first."

"Well, get on with it then!" Mitch growled.

"Very well." Tate sat down in Mitch's office chair and leaned forward, elbows on the desk. "We know this: Dr. Alvarez has been on the hunt for *La Canción* for some time. And we know a lot about Christina herself. She's made waves throughout our industry with her tenacious methods. I figure she can't be far from *The Song* if she came to you. We have in our possession the original document that she and Meredith Champlain unearthed in Seville, so we know what brought her to Treasure Seekers and why you two were diving off of La Punta de los Asesinos a few weeks ago. It looked curiously similar, yes?"

Christina tried to keep the surprise from her face. How had they found that map? Amongst all those stacks?

Mitch scowled. "Nothing better to do than spy as usual,

Hobard?"

"No," he said unashamedly. "Especially when you're attracting prettier partners these days. Manuel was very close to plucking the rest from Dr. Alvarez's hands when she managed to slip away from him. Fortunately for us," he said, searching the inside pocket of his jacket, "she'd taken a picture of Dr. Champlain, holding what appears to be a manifest for the fleet." He set Christina's cell phone on the desk before him.

Christina blanched. She'd forgotten that she'd taken that picture. She heard Mitch's quick intake of breath. *Rookie move, Alvarez*, she chastised herself.

"Unfortunately, Dr. Champlain's hands cover a critical section. We assume we've given you enough time to obtain a complete translation by now?"

"The translator is still working on it," Christina said, which was partially true. Meredith was not done yet.

"We want what you have so far, then," Tate said, "as well as the third document you discovered your last day in Seville. It was enough to send you out to celebrate. Presumably, you think you have the location of *La Canción*."

Christina and Mitch said nothing. Hans groaned, as if half-asleep.

Tate rose. "I assume the documents are in your safe? Because they are not here on your desk. Smart of you, Crawford, to not let such things simply sit about anymore, where anyone can peruse them."

"I try and not make the same mistake twice," Mitch bit out.

Hobard lifted a brow and nodded in appreciation. "So you've learned. But it shall not keep me from taking this from you now. If *La Canción* proves to be as rich a find as people think, then we shall consider your debt to me over *La Bailadora* paid in full at last. Now you can make it easy, or it can be very difficult." He rose, came around the desk again and stopped in front of Christina. "I'll say it once more, Dr. Alvarez. Join me and I'll make you a wealthy woman."

She looked at him, wanting to spit in his face. "Never. *La Canción's* ours."

"She was yours, my dear. *Was,*" he said. "She's about to become mine."

Manuel chuckled, apparently enjoying the torment unfolding before him.

"Let's begin with the location. The first document seems to point to the coast of Florida or the Keys and that mysterious name, Punta de los Asesinos. I've seen you dive in a location that might've well been our mysterious *Punta,* myself. But clearly, it was the right shape, but not the right place. What did the second document tell you? The manifest? Clearly, it covered the entire fleet. But what, specifically of *La Canción?*"

Tate stared at Mitch, to Hans, growing pale as blood continued to seep from his body and into the couch. Then he stared hard at Christina. "What was the third document? What has Champlain deciphered?"

Christina looked away.

The wind outside whistled, gaining speed as the storm neared Robert's Foe. Tate seemed not to hear it. "Take hold of Crawford," he demanded, and the men jumped to follow his command. Mitch looked at him suspiciously as they lifted him bodily away from Christina. He fought to get away, but the men on either side were too strong to escape.

Hans moaned again from the couch, shifting unconsciously. "Separate them further. Put Carlson down on the ground."

"He needs a doctor!" Christina cried, stricken. "He shouldn't be moved at all!"

"I told you," Tate gritted out, placing a hand on either arm of her chair and leaning in. "This can be easy or hard. Where is *La Canción*?"

Once again, she turned her face from him.

"A girl with a mind of her own," Tate said, rising and straightening his jacket. He turned to Mitch. "You, however, are used to giving in to me. And I'd be willing to bet you won't last long when I threaten this woman." He ran his hand through her damp hair, winding it into a knot in his hand. He pulled and Christina leaned toward him, swallowing a cry.

"Someday, Hobard," Mitch seethed, yanking against the men who held him on either side, "you won't be protected by the wings of the Cuban government, and I'll come after you. I swear it. You'll see justice!"

"Yes. Yes," Tate responded benignly. "How heroic and righteous you are! We are all very impressed."

The men laughed like they were part of a Greek chorus. The wind was growing wilder by the minute. Were the women and children safely to San Esteban by now? Christina shivered at the palpable evil these men had brought into Mitch's home. She shut her eyes, praying that they would all survive.

She was unprepared when Tate pulled her up into his arms. He held her tightly, even as she struggled to free herself. "So tell me, Crawford," Tate said, lifting a knife to her throat. "Shall I steal this treasure from you too?"

—m—

Mitch ignored the guns trained on him and strained to get away from his captors. "Let her go!" he yelled.

"Talk to me, Crawford. I want to see the other documents. I want to hear your conclusions. I want everything on the table. Now."

Christina stared at Mitch. "Don't do it, Mitch," she pleaded. "Don't do it!"

Mitch was frantic, glancing from Tate's knife to Christina's desperate look, to his unconscious friend in the corner. He, too, could feel the evil and wanted it out of his house at almost any price. But giving away *La Canción*… It wasn't even his to give away. How could he give Tate something so precious to Christina? He had to act, but how? *Please, God!* his heart cried out. *Help us!*

Higher ground. Get to higher ground. The words ran through his head like a phone alarm. The shutters rattled nervously as the wind beat at the house.

"What do you say, Mitch?" Hobard asked, not taking his eyes from Christina. "Shall we cut off her hand and throw it to the sharks? I understand she has tangled with one before."

Christina's eyes widened in terror.

CHAPTER 20

It was her look that did Mitch in. "All right! All right! I'll give you what you want. Then I want you out of here for good. This is the find of the decade—more than enough payment to make good on whatever you think we owe you for *The Dancer*. Agreed?"

Tate considered him. "Agreed."

"And you'll agree to leave my niece and nephew alone too."

"I am not so low as to use innocent children," Tate said, leaving Christina with Manuel. "Allow him to move, but stay close," he said, motioning to the two guards behind Mitch.

Mitch went directly to a bronze fisherman statue in the corner, and when he twisted it on its pedestal, a safe rose beneath it.

Tate laughed as it emerged from the floor. "Very nice. *Very* nice."

Silently Mitch spun the dial and opened the safe, conscious of Christina's sad eyes resting on his back. He had no choice. The only way to rid Robert's Foe of the men Tate had brought—and to buy Christina's safety and Hans's recovery—was to give away that which was most precious to her. As he turned with the pictures of the documents and Meredith's notes in hand, his eyes met Christina's, begging her to understand.

Tate laughed as he took them from Mitch and gingerly set them out in front of him. "Okay. Now. All of it. Everything you know."

Christina looked away from Tate, staring at the shaking shutters.

Mitch sighed. He would have to do it. Slowly he told them everything they had discovered to date, leaving out no detail.

"Ah, very good," Tate said. "Anything else?"

Mitch shook his head, feeling beaten.

"Good. Still, I think we'll borrow Dr. Alvarez until we find *La Canción* and hear the rest of Champlain's conclusions. Then, if she so decides at that point, she shall be released. But I would bet that I'll have won her over by that time."

Christina cast Mitch an alarmed look. The veins in his temple pulsed and the muscles in his jaw tightened. "That was not the deal," Mitch growled.

The wind outside howled. The shutters threatened to burst, shaking back and forth, the latches rattling so much one finally gave way. The papers on the desk went flying. Tate shouted at a man to shut it. Mitch seized his chance with their momentary distraction, slugging one guard, then lunging at another.

Apparently feigning his unconsciousness, Hans rose and grabbed the rifle from the man who was lifting it to shoot Mitch. He then turned and rammed it into Manuel's ribs, then swung it around to crack it across the face of a man rushing him.

Tate watched the fight, a shocked look on his face. He turned to chase the papers that blew wildly around the room.

When he bent to grab a photo by her, she clasped her hands together in a fist and rammed them down on the back of his neck. He crumpled to the floor, dazed, but not completely out. She grabbed the papers from his hand, the photo by her foot, and scanned the room.

Mitch caught her eye as he continued to fight off a man. "Go! Go, Christina!"

She ran, but Manuel pounced at her, grabbing her hair and pulling her backward. She gasped as Manuel's strong arm came under her chin, choking her. Desperately, she clung to the photos and papers, unable to think of anything but saving them from Hobard.

Mitch was suddenly in front of them, circling, determined to free her. He charged Manuel and Christina, bringing both of them down to the floor, then rose and brought his fist into the left side of Manuel's face. Christina cringed at the sound of bones breaking, but now free, faltered a few steps away, trying to catch a breath through her bruised, crushed throat.

Mitch roughly hauled her to the door and pushed her out, yelling above the wind: "Higher ground! Get to higher ground!"

She looked at him, confused and still struggling to breathe. Higher ground? *The pool*, she thought. *He means the pool.* The crack of a gun's report sounded inside the office. "Go! I'll come for you!" Mitch cried, then plunged back inside.

Tate's voice reached Christina's ears as she ran down the steps. "After her! I need her!" he yelled, even louder than the scream of the wind. More shutters crashed open throughout the house, the storm now blowing in with full force.

Numbly Christina kept moving, tearing down the cold marble stairs and out the open door, into the wildest tropical storm she had ever experienced. Palms bent nearly in half, as if they might tear off in the ferocious wind. The wind was so strong, that gusts at her back threatened to send her stumbling forward. Rain ripped at her face. Raising her arms so she could see, she ran toward the path that led to the pool.

She turned around at the crest of the hill, desperately wanting to see Mitch or Hans leave the house, but only caught sight of the two men who trailed her. Ignoring her trembling legs, Christina ran, remembering that if they caught her, she would most certainly be carted off to Tate's ship. Slippery mud squished between her bare toes. The robe was soaked, and Christina feared that it was weighing her down, slowing her escape. She looked over her shoulder as she turned a corner in the trail. The two men were gaining on her. They'd capture her shortly.

She looked around madly for a hiding place. The thick, waving fern fronds close to the ground seemed to beckon her. With no time for hesitation, she ran into the waving branches. Twenty feet from the path, she rolled underneath the biggest bush and lay prostrate, praying that the fronds would not split apart in the wind, exposing her.

The dark green robe helped her blend into the foliage, and, seconds later, the men ran by. After catching her breath, Christina made her way through the dense branches, but not on the path, trying to keep the men in sight as long as possible. They would soon realize they had lost her along the way and double back. She had to put distance between herself and the place where her tracks led to her temporary hiding place.

She winced as the sharp elephant grass cut her tender feet, and she limped forward, struggling to discern the men's movements from the crazy blur of the storm. She ignored the pain, hearing the words *higher ground* over and over in her mind. *Mitch.* Was he still alive?

Maybe she should have agreed to go with Tate willingly. Maybe she could have found a way to escape him, without endangering her friends. She fought off the urge to sit and weep. *Higher ground. Higher ground.*

Hearing what sounded like a shout, she paused to look and listen. Thirty feet ahead she spied a man running along the path toward her. With no time to run toward a hiding place, she sank into the knee-deep grasses, chanting her prayer. *God save me. God protect me. God be with me.*

The man stopped not five feet from where Christina lay prostrate, praying that enough of the green robe covered her bright gold Farmer Johns. He was waiting for his partner to reach him. She stared at his black boot through the waving grass, her heart beating wildly. Drops of water ran down the blades of grass near her face and dripped onto her skin. She fought the urge to wipe them away, conscious that her life depended upon remaining absolutely still.

The two men bickered back and forth in Spanish. They could not agree on which direction to head. Both sounded fearful at the thought of facing Tate empty-handed. Christina only prayed that one would win the decision soon, and they would set off in a direction—any direction at all except the three steps toward where she hid.

—◊◊◊—

Mitch danced around Manuel's long, ugly blade. Beyond him, Hans fell to the floor as another man punched him in the face, then his shoulder, using Hans's wound to his advantage. Another kicked him in the stomach, bringing him back down as he tried to rise.

Hobard calmly reentered the office and circumvented the fray. He paused by Manuel and Mitch, still circling each other. "The girl has everything we need, Manuel." He handed him his gun. "Kill them both and leave a bit of cocaine for the FBI to puzzle over. They'll write it off as a drug deal gone bad. Then we'll find Christina and be on our way."

As Hobard left, Manuel reached for the gun beside him. Mitch charged, bringing them both down to the floor, the table and gun falling beyond them. Manuel army-crawled toward it, but Mitch got to his feet and pounced, then rammed his head to the ground. When he grew limp, Mitch took the gun and stood to the side of the door, hoping Hobard would return when he heard no report from the gun. When he did so, Mitch surprised him, aiming the pistol to his temple.

"Everybody! Drop to the floor!" Mitch put Hobard's head in a firm chokehold and motioned for Hans to follow them.

"Do as he says!" Hobard said, one hand to his men. Manuel slowly lowered himself to his belly, fists clenched.

The three backed out of the room with Mitch still holding Hobard, the gun now pressed just behind his jawbone. Hans grabbed the other gun from the ground.

They exited the library and moved toward the stairs.

Once they had made it down the stairs, out the front door and into the frenzied storm, Mitch considered his options. Hans was injured, Christina hiding… Maybe if he let him go, God would see justice served by turning Hobard's boat over on the high seas.

"Go! You and your men get out of here, Hobard! The women and children saw you coming and made it to San Esteban. Help is going to arrive when this storm abates, and you better be on your way to Mexico."

"This was not the deal, Crawford," Hobard said. "You

want me out of your life forever? I want what you have on *La Canción*."

Mitch pulled him closer. "Allowing you to leave with your lives is payment enough!" he growled. "Never threaten me, Hans or those we care about again. Or I will shoot first."

Tate's face was slack, and he lifted his hands. His men poured out of the house. He gestured to the boat. "C'mon!" he shouted. "Everybody out!"

Eyeing their boss—still in Mitch's firm grasp—they passed by and moved to the dock, clambering aboard the bucking boat. The seas and winds were high, but Tate's boat was built to handle them.

Mitch shoved Tate away. "Go on! You have ten seconds until I shoot you!"

The man moved backward, hands up. But his eyes went to the jungle beyond Mitch, as if waiting, hoping for...

Christina.

—⁂—

After what seemed like an eternity, the men headed off to the place they lost Christina's trail, just as she had hoped. She forced herself to count before rising. "One thousand one, one thousand two..."

At ten she raised her head slowly from the grass and winced as another wind-swept blade cut her cheek. Unable to tolerate the grass any longer, Christina rose and ran without stopping toward the waterfall, stripping off Mitch's robe at the edge of the pool and tossing it into the jungle.

She dove in, half waiting for bullets to come ripping into the water and into her back. Holding her breath, she swam the length of the pool. As she came up gasping on the other side of the waterfall, she felt a startling and sudden wave of peace settle deep within her. Gradually, she caught her breath, feeling as if she stood behind God's own protective wall.

Exhausted, she forced herself to climb up onto the ledge and curled into a ball. She leaned against the wall and watched the blurry, dancing images of the swaying palm trees beyond the falls, praying that Mitch and Hans were somehow safe.

—⫘—

Mitch looped Hans's arm over his shoulder and helped him through the jungle, climbing up to the pool on an alternate path, hoping that if Tate returned to the dock and dared to follow, he'd become lost. He prayed that Christina had understood him when he'd told her to go to higher ground… and that she'd made it. He knew two men had left in pursuit of her. But right now, he had to focus on Hans. The big man was clearly weakening, leaning more and more weight on him. Mitch prayed that if they could reach the pool, Hans's wound could be treated. *Because with this storm, we're not going to get off of Robert's Foe for hours…*

Once they reached the edge of the pool, and confident they were still alone, they waded into the water. Mitch kept watch, but their only companions seemed to be the wind and rain.

"Uh, bud, I'm not…" Hans muttered, his body growing more and more slack. He passed out.

Mitch could not hold his dead weight. They both went under.

Mitch dropped the gun to the depths. His only thought was to get his friend up before he drowned.

"Hans!" he grunted. He turned the man over, relieved to see him still breathing. *He's just lost so much blood…* Grimly,

Mitch made his way to the waterfall, pulling his friend along in a lifeguard's hold. Beside the falls, he carefully pinched Hans's nose shut, clamped a hand over his mouth, and dove under.

"Mitch!" Christina said with a gasp when they rose in the pool below her. She reached out with trembling hands to hold Hans in place while Mitch climbed up the ledge. Together, they hauled Hans to the top.

Mitch turned to Christina and pulled her into his arms for a brief embrace. "I'm so glad you made it!"

"Oh, Mitch. And I, you!"

They turned to Hans. Mitch ripped aside the man's sleeve to expose the bullet wound. "It went clean through. If we can stop the bleeding, he should be okay. He's just weak from the blood loss." He quickly pulled off his own shirt and tore strips from it to tightly bind the wound. When he had done all he could, Mitch turned to Christina.

"Are you all right?" He asked, pushing hair away and examining the bleeding cuts on her face.

"Oh, I'm fine. I'm fine," she said, touched by his concern and care. "Are you?"

"Yes." He sat against the wall beside her and opened his arms.

She moved into them without thinking, only craving comfort, assurance. "Are they gone?"

"I hope so. When the storm abates, I will sneak out and make sure. Thank God Talle and Anya and the kids got away. Without the threat of the authorities arriving, I think Hobard would have stayed until he had you in hand."

"I was so afraid. So afraid, Mitch. That something would happen to you and Hans."

"I know. I was scared too." He stroked her hair and kissed

her forehead.

"No," she said, lifting her head to meet his gaze. "I don't think you get it. There's so much I need to tell you." Her eyes closed in exhaustion as she leaned her head back against his chest and pulled him close. "I think...I think I was wrong about us. About what we said. About what I said."

His breath caught and he gave her a small smile. "Rest now. There will be time to talk later." He went back to stroking her hair, and she drew comfort in the steady beat of his heart against her own.

Exhaustion overtook her. She slept in his arms for a while, until Mitch had to move his aching shoulder. "I'm sorry. I woke you."

"No. That's okay," she said, rising on one arm. "Here I am, curled up like a child, practically in your lap, asleep. I'm sorry. You've got to be as beat as I am."

"My body is tired. But my brain's still pumped up from all the adrenaline."

Christina nodded. "I still can't believe Tate let us live."

"I told him to leave the island and never come near us again. Because I'll shoot first and ask questions later."

"No," she said. "You and Hans might be willing to play this treasure-hunting game with him, but I'm not. As soon as this storm abates, I'm making a full report to the FBI."

Mitch lifted a brow, as if recognizing the opportunity for the first time. "That's true. Up to now, he's been far more covert with his tactics. He's messed up this time, sending someone you can identify—and now tie to him—to capture you in Seville."

"I think he hoped to simply steal my findings in Seville and slip away. But Manuel took it to another level."

"No matter. This attack on Robert's Foe was all Hobard. The U.S. government won't tolerate such an action against its citizens."

A slow smile spread across Christina's face, the glimmer of justice in her eyes.

Mitch smiled back. "Once we get your gorgeous face on television screens across the country telling the world how Hobard has treated you, there will be a public outcry. How can a decent scholar make her way in the world with men like Tate on the loose? The FBI will be able to nail him with our testimony. He's kidnapped, trespassed, terrorized, attacked, and threatened murder."

"If they can find him." She took a breath. "After all that, I can't believe he left without the evidence he sought."

"Do you still have it?"

She gave him a rueful smile. "The prints are soggy messes now. But we can print more."

He hesitated and looked to the falls.

"What is it?"

He shook his head and rubbed the back of his neck, then sighed heavily. "Hobard has a photographic memory."

"You think...you think his brief glimpses of everything we have were enough?" Christina asked, incredulous. She couldn't comprehend being able to read the archaic script, peruse the old maps, and be able to remember much of any importance at all.

He gave her a grim look. "I've seen it before."

"Well, we'll just have to beat him to the right spot in Mexico, given we still have the originals at our disposal."

"I like the way you think," he said. He turned sad eyes to her. "I'm sorry I gave what I did to him, Christina. I know how important the ship is to you."

She looked back at him. "I know. She was important to you, too. Is important to us both," she said, correcting herself. "*La Canción* still might save your home and Treasure Seekers. Set me up as a premier nautical archeologist in my own right. But we both know our lives are worth more than any ship. I was just stupid being stubborn with Tate. I didn't want to give in to him.

"But as I sat behind this waterfall, wondering if you or Hans were dead because of my refusal, it all came together. I kept thinking about that verse that talks about not storing up treasures on earth, but rather in heaven. In this business, we kind of obsess about treasures, right?"

"Right…"

"But after a day like today…From my panic attack over the shark—remembering how I was saved years ago—to the panic of seeing Hobard overtake us. To the panic that I might be the lone survivor…Mitch, there is so much more." She reached up a hand to touch his face. "So much more that I want. A different kind of treasure."

Mitch stilled, staring into her eyes. There was such hope there. Such desire. So much intensity and joy, it seemed to quadruple what was unfolding in his own heart.

"Well, it's about time," Hans's faint voice interrupted, barely audible over the thunder of the falls, as he came to. "Are you two going to kiss now? Because bud, you really ought to kiss the girl."

Mitch and Christina laughed and turned to him. "Maybe later," Mitch said. He glanced at her. "Make that definitely later."

"Am I going to die?" Hans asked, grimacing as he ginger-ly touched his arm.

"Nah," Mitch said. "You lost a lot of blood, but it's a clean wound."

"Good. You'll need someone to stand up as your best man."

Mitch smiled and glanced quickly at Christina to see if

Hans's teasing was unnerving her. She simply grinned back at him. "I'm so glad you're okay," she said to Hans.

"Yeah. Not half as glad as you were to see that lug there, I bet."

"I have to admit, I was pretty happy to see him, too." She gave Mitch another shy smile.

"Well, when do we get out of this cave?" Hans asked. "It's freezing."

"I think we should wait until the storm abates. By then, Tate will have given up on finding us and be long gone. He'll fear the women and children will send help and want some distance."

"Okay. Well then, snuggle up, you two. This cave is romantic, but a bit chilly."

"Good idea," Mitch said, nodding. He reached across to Christina. "Will you be warm enough on Hans's other side? With our wet suits still on and between the two of us, we should be able to help him ward off hypothermia."

Christina nodded. She curled up beside Hans as Mitch did so on the other side.

"One big, happy family," Hans muttered, before he passed out again.

CHAPTER 21

Hours later, Mitch left and then returned from his reconnaissance. "I think they're gone. And I think I spotted two boats from San Esteban en route to us."

Hans slipped into the water behind Mitch, strong enough now to make it on his own. Alone for a moment, Christina looked around the cave, thanking God once more for their protection. She felt dazed, groggy—definitely like she'd suffered through a crisis. But she'd survived. They all had.

With another whispered prayer of thanks, she dove out after the men, swimming to the end of the pool. She rose, cautiously looking around, half-afraid Mitch was wrong and Hobard's men might spring from the trees.

Mitch offered his hand and she took it. Together, they moved down the path as the two boats he'd spotted drew near to the dock. He'd been right; it was Talle and Anya and the kids, along with a battered police boat. They hurried down to meet them.

"Uncle Mitch!" Joshua yelled, leaping out of the boat and running down the dock. He ran to the man and jumped into his arms. Mitch hugged him back fiercely. "Ow, Uncle Mitch. Not so hard!"

"Oh, sorry, buddy! I'm just so glad to see you!"

"You know what?" Josh asked, leaning back as Kenna toddled near and stared up at her uncle, fingers in a drooling mouth.

"What?" Mitch knelt to offer his arms to Kenna and she shyly came in for a hug.

"We went on a speedboat real fast," Josh said, "and we swung on hammocks inside a little house until the storm passed by! *Inside* a house!"

"That sounds awesome. I'm glad you're okay."

Joshua nodded with big eyes. "Kenna was scared, but I wasn't."

"Oh, that's good. But it would've been okay for you to be a little scared, Josh." He picked up Kenna and together they moved to the women and two policemen, who each had a hand on their holsters as they looked up at the house.

"It's okay," Mitch said, waving them down. "They're gone."

He handed Kenna back to Anya. "Talle, if you're up to it, could you make some food? I'll give these gentlemen our report and be up. I think we could all use a good meal."

She nodded, then gathered her niece and the children and walked up to the house. Nora stayed with Hans as one of the policemen stitched up his wound and put a fresh bandage on it, using an emergency kit in his boat. A trip to the ER wasn't really in the cards.

It was soon clear to Christina that the policemen were overworked, underpaid, and over their heads with this report. Until she could get to American authorities, not much would come of their complaint. The storm was wreaking havoc to the north of them, so all emergency responders had more urgent requests. All while Hobard might be jet-boating away to Mexico…

Mitch led her upstairs and pushed her in the direction of the bathroom. "Your teeth haven't stopped chattering. Take a long, hot shower. Get into dry clothes."

She nodded gratefully. At the moment, nothing sounded better. But she paused at her empty guest bedroom door, feeling the chasm as some sort of quiet threat, rather than the respite she usually craved.

He read her look and squeezed her hand. "I won't be far. Just down the hall."

She nodded again and closed the door behind her but not before she peeked in the shower and in the closet, making sure no one waited for her.

Smiling sheepishly, Christina peeled off her wet suit, swimsuit and put her head under the hot shower stream.

The water felt incredibly soothing, warming her deeply cold flesh and washing away the evidence of the last, nightmarish hours. Afterward, she joined the others for a meal, forcing herself to eat a few bites of the food Talle had prepared. She could not push from her mind all that had happened. What if Mitch had died? What would have happened to the children, orphaned once again? Or Hans? How would Nora have taken it?

Mitch laughed and looked around the table until he spotted Christina's expression. Lowering his voice, he asked if she was okay. Her hand trembled as she raised her glass of orange juice to drink from it. She nodded, lying, but knowing she must be dreadfully pale for him to be looking at her that way.

"What do you need most?" he asked quietly. "A walk on the beach or a nap?"

"Some air would be good. With just you and the children."

"Fine. There's not much we can do here anyway, and the storm will have brought up lots of things on the beach to catch the kids' interest. Let's go." He held out his hand to her and she rose, picking up Kenna. The girl's happy sounds and solid little body made Christina feel safer somehow. Woman and girl followed Mitch and Josh out the door and to the beach.

Even on the more sheltered half of Robert's Foe, the sandy beach banks were strewn with debris, and Joshua delighted in finding odd things that the angry water and wind had blown ashore. There were brightly colored, dead fish, garbage thrown overboard by thoughtless sailors, coconuts, and seashells and seaweed and sticks. To the boy, each was a treasure.

Watching her brother, Kenna squirmed to get down, and Christina reluctantly bent to let her go. She watched as Kenna toddled off, noticing that the little girl's balance was getting better and better. She sat down on the sand to watch them, and Mitch plopped down beside her.

"Kids are pretty resilient, aren't they?" he asked.

"I keep thinking about what would've happened to them if you had been killed last night," she whispered.

He thought about that, looking at the children and out to sea again. "I guess my number wasn't up yet. God apparently has some use for me yet."

"I hope so," she said, wrapping a hand around his bicep and leaning closer. "Any idea of what you're going to do? If you're right—and Hobard has enough to go on—he could reach *La Canción*'s site by tomorrow. He could stake a claim..." She glanced at him. "Even with all the originals, if he manages to remember the coordinates of where the ship lies, we'd be hard-pressed to beat him at this point."

"Yeah," Mitch said, pushing his toes into the sand and then looking out.

"You're going to lose the house and the company, aren't you?"

"Possibly. I can take a loan against the house and, by selling some of our best equipment, have enough to keep Treasure Seekers afloat for another couple of months, hoping we catch another break." He took her hand. "But it's like we talked about, Christina. I think—through all of this—I've come to see that I need to invest differently." He lifted her hand to his lips and kissed it. "If Treasure Seekers is finished, it's finished. I'll find something else to do. Maybe something more tame that a scholarly girlfriend would like better."

She smiled back into his eyes. "Yeah, right. I can't see you at a desk job. Or me, for that matter. I think you were born for this kind of work. And…what'd you call me? We're suddenly boyfriend-girlfriend?"

"Aren't we?" he grinned.

"Maybe. Maybe not," she said coyly. They sat together, enjoying the view of the children and the golden light of sunset. "I'm glad you've found such a peace about it, Mitch. I think…I think God will honor you, trusting him and everything."

They watched as Kenna bent, fell, then picked up a large object and placed it in her mouth. Christina yelped and jumped up. "Kenna! Spit that out!"

"I thought it was okay for her to do that!" he called, rising to come after her. "Didn't you say it was just her way of exploring her world?"

Christina ignored him and stuck her finger into Kenna's mouth. The girl looked uncomfortable with the large object in her mouth, but reluctant to give it up. "Come on, spit it out, Kenna. You're allowed to taste things. You're just not allowed to eat them." The little girl stubbornly kept her mouth shut, so Christina swept her finger in and was startled to find something large on the tot's tongue.

Christina stared, dumbfounded, as she pulled it out. It was a piece of eight. A silver piece of eight. It all came back to her at once. The cannon. Between the shark and Hobard, she'd had little time to assimilate what she had discovered below.

Slowly, she turned to show it to Mitch.

He searched Christina's face, his eyes and mouth widening. "Is that..." His blue-green eyes moved to meet her. "You think there's a wreck here, right off Robert's Foe?"

She nodded, a bright smile making her feel lighter than she had in hours.

"That's impossible! Hans and I have circled this island, experimenting with new magnetometers and other search and retrieval equipment."

"How far out?"

"Past the break," he said, understanding slowly dawning. "But Four Fathoms is within the break."

"With all that's gone on, I haven't had the chance to tell you—and didn't even remember until this moment—that when we were diving, and the shark drove me back into that cave, and I was panicking and my tank chipped away coral from the wall..." She paused and turned to stare into the waves.

"What? What did you see?"

"I don't think that cave's a cave, Mitch. I think it's the remains of a ship's hold...And I think I saw a bit of a bronze cannon."

Mitch sucked in his breath. "A bronze? Right here?" He gave a triumphant yell, raising his arms to the sky, then turned and picked Christina up, whirling her around, laughing. Bronze cannons were carried only on the early, better-funded ships, and their presence denoted a possible rich find.

She laughed. "Okay, okay! Would you please set me down?"

"Of course." He set her down and then danced a little with her before dipping her in his arms and giving her a long kiss.

"Uncle Mitch?"

Mitch and Christina, belatedly remembered the children, saw Josh now stood right beside them, watching them kiss. They quickly straightened.

But Joshua seemed unfazed. "Look at this!" In his sandy palms were several more pieces of eight and a gold doubloon.

Mitch knelt next to the boy. "You know what this is, don't you…?" he said conspiratorially, lifting one of the coins in the air. "Treasure!" he shouted, picking up the boy and swinging him around.

CHAPTER 22

The next morning, a large helicopter arrived at Robert's Foe. Four men immediately set out to dust for fingerprints in the house and take prints of all those in the household for comparisons. Another man exhaustively photographed each room, making a record of how the house was left by Hobard and his men.

While Mitch was desperate to return to the beach alongside Four Fathoms and begin to plan their operation with Christina and Hans, they remained studiously somber while answering the FBI's questions.

One of the agents—a man Hans and Mitch already knew—listened in as Christina finished her tale, still taking notes, as if adding to those he'd taken down when she first told him. Lieutenant Shriver stared at Christina as she told about being only five feet from the boots of the enemy, when she last saw them. "You're a lucky woman, Dr. Alvarez."

"Protected," she corrected. "By God."

The man looked at her skeptically, but did not deny her passionate reply. "I appreciate your time. Will you be here on Robert's Foe for a while if we have more questions?"

She looked up at Mitch, who smiled at her. "Oh yes. I think I'll be here for a while."

"Very good."

"Lieutenant," Mitch asked, following him out. "Do you have enough to put him away this time? Last time we only had circumstantial evidence to tie Manuel to Scott Haviland's death. This time we all saw him act on Hobard's orders. And you have all our testimonies now against Hobard and his men."

"I think so. This should do it—even if we have to file for extradition. I'm getting some pressure from the top. The media is already on top of your story. We've had a couple calls from Joni Johnson, although I'm not sure how she got wind of it."

"So we should expect company."

"I would assume so." The man rose and shook each of their hands. "We'll do our best to get him, Crawford. In the meantime, you three watch your backs."

"We will," Mitch said. He turned to give Christina a wink as he shut the door. Because he had phoned in the tip to Joni Johnson himself.

The journalist arrived a couple of hours later as the FBI had, via helicopter. A reporter for one of the gossip rags, Joni Johnson had a nose for the type of news that created internet click-bait. It was perfect, since Mitch wanted the story publicized around the world. A public outcry might force the FBI to spend a few more dollars in their search for Hobard, as well as feed him exactly the story they wished him to believe.

Christina did as he requested. Joni's eyes got larger and larger as she traced the story from the chase in Seville to the culmination at Robert's Foe. As the interview progressed, they carefully planted the idea that Treasure Seekers was folding; that Tate's attack had driven Mitch and Hans to the edge of bankruptcy and Mitch was retiring from the field. Christina planned to rejoin the university team on the East Coast cataloguing Civil War wrecks. If Hobard read the story, he'd believe he was free and clear to search for *La Canción*. And he'd stay far from their own covert excavation of Four Fathoms.

When she finished, Joni smiled broadly and shook Christina's hand, then Mitch's and Hans's. This story smelled like it could yield a journalism award, and they all knew it. Mitch had paced behind the camera as Joni interviewed Christina and caught a glimpse of how the footage would feel, once it aired. Christina's captivating presence on film, along with her dramatic tale, would likely fill a week of special segments and draw viewers from around the world.

"Do me a favor, will you?" Joni said at the door.

"What's that?" Christina asked.

"Let me come back in a few months to do a follow-up. People will want to know what happened to that jerk Hobard, and to you guys."

Mitch and Christina swallowed their smiles. "Sure," Christina said. "Come find us."

"Excellent."

Christina breathed a sigh of relief when she was gone. "I need a vacation."

Mitch took her in his arms. "How 'bout Spain?"

She smiled up at him, loving the feel of his arms around her. "Sounds romantic. But if I know you, you're not just thinking about fiestas and dinner on the Guadalquivir. You're thinking about the Archives. And which ship might match her Four-Fathoms resting place?"

"Guilty as charged," he said, bending forward to give her

a quick kiss. "But you and I could have some quality time together too. Give us a chance to get to know each other. You know, without all the fireworks." He waved about them.

"Somehow I think there might be different kinds of fireworks," she quipped, lifting up on her toes to kiss him this time.

"Mmm. I like those kinds of fireworks," he whispered with a smile.

"Me too," she said. "Let's spend a few days here. We can rest, get the house back in order and the kids resituated, and do some preliminary excavation at the site to see what we might uncover."

"Sounds good. But I want to keep things very, very quiet. Just you and me and Hans. This one can't be leaked to Hobard."

"Agreed. Let's break the terrible news to Hans, shall we? He's thinking that he might have to go look for a dishwashing job on San Esteban."

They took the big man, already on the mend, down the beach to let him in on the news. As the sun set, Mitch and Christina told Hans about the discovery. His first reaction was much like Mitch's: disbelief that the wreck had eluded them for so long, then jubilation. After that, he was all business, drawing in the sand with a stick and figuring with Mitch how they might fund an excavation and salvage operation.

After much deliberation, they decided they would sell the two older search and salvage boats they had moored near San Esteban; fully loaded but fairly old, they would bring in at least a hundred thousand dollars. *Bessie* would be all they would need for a site so near at hand, and Treasure Seekers would simply operate as they had begun, with the bare basics. Once they had enough evidence, Mitch would get an investor they knew to fund the rest of the operation. If the site proved to be as rich as they guessed it would, Treasure Seekers would be up and running full-force again, as healthy as it had been several years before.

Christina yawned. "I better go get some dinner, partners. I'm so exhausted I'm going to pass out, and I want to get some food in me before I do."

Hans rubbed his stomach. "I'm hungry too. But I'm too wound up to sleep. Can we talk more about this after dinner, Mitch?"

"Yeah. We can talk. We'll let the brains of our operation get her required REMs."

"Well, don't you two talk about anything too interesting," Christina said. "I don't want to miss anything."

"We won't. It's just our standard operating procedure," Hans explained. "We smell a wreck and we have to talk out all the angles, even before we completely explore her. We talk about possible pitfalls, then talk ourselves into believing she was probably salvaged centuries ago by the Spaniards them-selves, so we're happy if we find anything at all."

Christina nodded. "Sounds wise." She yawned again. "Just fill me in tomorrow morning, will you?"

"Sure."

As they walked, a disturbing thought came to Christina. "You two really believe that the news story—and the hunt for *La Canción*—will keep Tate busy for a while, right?"

"If evading the FBI doesn't," Hans said.

But Mitch wasn't quick to enthusiastically assure her, she noted. "Hobard's smart and well connected. And he has enough men working for him that he seems to be everywhere at once."

Christina nodded. "So maybe we'll really need to sell the charade."

"What do you mean?"

"If Joni's story takes off, I should be spotted in Virginia—making it look like I'm truly re-joining the Civil War crew—before we slip off to Seville."

"Perfect," Mitch nodded approvingly. "See?" he asked Hans. "I told you she'd be the brains of our operation."

Hans snorted. "Yeah. That's exactly what you said when she first arrived on Robert's Foe."

Together, they all laughed.

—⁀⁀—

The trio rose before daybreak to sneak into the waters unseen and begin preliminary work on the Four Fathoms site. Mitch and Christina went under, while Hans—still healing—kept watch above. Spreading white plastic poles in an organized grid, they built the network that Christina would use for her archaeological data. Before touching another piece of coral, she carefully photographed each undisturbed section for reference.

Then, breaking out their pneumatic hammers, Christina and Mitch began chiseling away at the rocklike substance that entombed what they hoped would be a large ship.

They began in the curve of what they had once thought was a cave—but now believed was an encrusted hull—concentrating on the area around the bronze cannon. Oftentimes, cannons bore identification marks that helped to name the find. The problem was that many had been salvaged from sunken ships in the fifteenth and sixteenth centuries, then recycled.

The partners' biggest fear was related to that practice; the Spanish had become very adept at hiring sponge divers to salvage those that had sunk at reasonable depths. Ancient divers had been able to save the treasure from countless wrecks, even at depths of eighty feet.

The ship off Robert's Foe was at four fathoms—approximately twenty-eight feet. It seemed likely that it had been cleaned out long ago; yet the doubloons and pieces of eight washed up by the storm gave them hope that the wreck had somehow escaped detection.

As an archaeologist, Christina enjoyed the process, regardless of what remained inside. Her interest lay more in piecing together the story of the ship and its inhabitants. But she knew the success of this expedition for Treasure Seekers demanded that they find something they could sell to museums or private collectors. Therefore, she too anxiously looked for the bright gold doubloons that would help them fund the excavation themselves.

While they did not find any more gold over the next two days of searching, they did uncover the cannon's sides. With all the sediment the excavation sent into the water, it was difficult to make out at first what the cannon said. Waving the floating particles away, Christina held her breath when she could first get a good read of the script on the cannon's side. *El Espantoso. The Fearsome*, she translated.

Where had she heard that name before? She looked at her dive watch. At thirty feet below, they could only remain in the water for ninety minutes at a time, three times a day; they had only a few more minutes before heading up for the night. Anxiously she pulled Mitch's arm, and his face emerged from the sediment they'd stirred up. She nodded her head to the side, motioning him over to where she had been working, so he could see the name too. Then, noting the time on his watch, he gestured upward, and they began their slow ascent, allowing their bodies and lungs to adjust to each level in order to avoid the bends.

Once aboard *Bessie*, Hans stared at them, dumbfounded when neither of them could place the name on the cannon. "You're telling me that the premier graduate of her nautical archeology class can't remember what *El Espantoso* was?"

"There are so many!" she cried, irritated at his teasing. "Just tell me! Is it a merchant ship? A pirate ship?"

"Bing! Bing! Bing!" Hans said, as if she was the winner of a game show. "Just one of the biggest to ever disappear in the Caribbean. Does Bartholomew Robert's name ring a bell?"

"Bartholomew Robert's!" she choked out.

Mitch shook his head in amazement. "We always knew that Robert's Foe was rumored to be tied to Robert, but after we did that initial search, we thought it false. Robert must've turned and made a stand here, right on his own shore!"

"Could have," Christina said. "We have a lot of research to do before we make that claim."

"Agreed," he said. But he waggled his eyebrows. "But it's possible."

"Wait 'til Meredith gets a load of this one," she said, pulling off her fins and grinning at them both.

CHAPTER 23

Mitch and Christina left Robert's Foe the next day as if they were merely going to the big island for the day, as tourists. They carried one change of clothing each in Christina's large purse, as well as their passports and money to exchange for Euros, not wanting for their credit cards to be tracked.

They sped to the island in Mitch's boat and carefully wound around the crazy streets of San Esteban, losing themselves—and hopefully anyone who tailed them—among the hundreds of peasants selling straw hats, jewelry, and hand-carved statues. Christina bought them each a hat, adding to their inconspicuous, touristy look. They ate and laughed and shopped some more. That evening, Mitch hailed a taxi, and they made their way to the airport.

They sat at the back of the plane, able to see everyone who boarded, and breathed sighs of relief when the plane took off without the appearance of any men known to work for Hobard. Holding hands, they dozed as the sun set, oblivious to the flight attendant who was doling out meals. Six hours later they were posting to social media in Virginia. Two days later, they were doing the same in Maine. Four days after departing, they arrived in Seville on a bright, late summer morning.

Most of the European tourists were gradually heading home from their summer vacations, leaving more room on the native-crowded streets of Seville. Mitch hailed another taxi outside the airport, and they were off to find Meredith, who had just returned from the States herself. Because of their past experiences with Manuel, the couple took extra precautions in approaching her. If they had not succeeded in eluding any followers, Meredith would be an obvious focal point.

When they neared Avenida de la Constitución, Christina leaned forward and said to the cab driver, *"Aquí, por favor."* *Here, please.*

Obligingly the driver pulled to the side, narrowly missing several unconcerned pedestrians. Mitch and Christina walked past the Palacio de Yanduri and the Museo de Arte Contemporáneo before reaching the Archives. They stood back among the vendors' stalls, waiting for Meredith to emerge for lunch.

"It could be hours," Christina warned. "The woman is so focused she can be pretty oblivious to the needs of her stomach."

"We can wait," Mitch encouraged. They stood, side by side, holding hands and studying a large tourist map of Seville and the outlying areas. "What day is it?" he asked.

"August eighteenth, I think."

"Have you ever been to Jerez for the festival?"

"No. Every time I've been in Seville, it's been on business."

"All work and no play..."

"I know. So this festival—I take it you want to go?"

"I want to show it to you. They have fabulous flamenco,

street-side booths with the world's best tapas, and hilarious cardboard bullfights. They finish off the three days by closing off the streets for dancing and masquerades. You should see it."

She grinned. "It sounds like fun. Let's see what Meredith knows about *El Espantoso*, do some digging with her in the stacks if she needs us, and then, if we have *time*, we'll go."

"Okay. But if it's not Jerez de la Frontera," he said, pulling her into his arms, "I'm whisking you off to some other place on this romantic coast for a few days before heading home."

"Sounds good to me." After they kissed, Christina looked over his shoulder and her eyes widened in surprise. "Well, what do you know! There she is! She's emerged earlier than usual. Let's let her walk. She'll probably head down to the plaza for lunch."

They followed the tall blonde for several blocks until she paused at a stall to purchase some fruit. Mitch went on ahead to find someplace reasonably private in which they could talk as Christina approached Meredith. "This time, I'll buy. I owe you."

Meredith let out a squeal and turned to hug her. "Christina! I'm so glad to see you!"

"Shh," Christina warned, smiling, but looking around. "Come on. I want you to meet Mitch."

"Mitch Crawford is here? In Seville? I saw you two on Joni's—"

"Yes, yes," she said, shushing her. They were drawing attention. "We have to discuss something with you."

"Okay. I have an hour before I need to meet a colleague back at the Archives."

"Come on." They walked in the direction Mitch had gone and finally saw him wave at them from a block away. He had found one of Christina's favorite Castilian restaurants, out of the main flow of traffic, which was owned by a third generation in a family of informal restaurateurs. Inside, people sat eating, spitting their olive pits and shrimp heads onto the floor.

Mitch had ordered them a traditional jug of sangría; with it came an array of dishes *para picar*, small quantities of various foods to be nibbled at in the finest Spanish tradition. Mitch stood to shake Meredith's hand. "So you're the distinguished Dr. Champlain. Here I am, a lowly treasure salvager, eating with two of the brightest and most beautiful in the business."

"I hear you don't do bad work yourself, Mitch." She sat down. "I saw a clip of you two on TMZ, as well as the BBC," Meredith went on. "Sounds like you're still up to the same ol', same ol'—which is a tad too rich for my blood. Does having you in town mean I should just topple all my furniture and empty my file cabinets out? You know, just get it over with?"

Christina grimaced at her gentle teasing. "If you've seen the Joni Johnson story, you probably know what happened."

"I assumed that the creep who caught up with you here caught up with you again at Robert's Foe."

"And he saw our documents and map. We had to tell him everything, Meredith."

Meredith reached across the table and took her hand. "I'm sorry. I know how much *The Song* meant to you. Maybe Hobard won't find her. Maybe she'll elude him, too. Or the FBI will nab him before he does."

"Maybe. But while he's distracted with my wreck in Mexican waters, and the FBI is chasing him down, we've found something interesting right under our noses at Robert's Foe."

Meredith perked up. "What?"

"We think there's a chance it's *El Espantoso*."

Meredith let out a long, low whistle. "Boy, you guys play in the big leagues, don't you?"

"That's the hope," Mitch said with a smile.

"If she's there and she hasn't been salvaged, Treasure Seekers will be a wealthy company."

"What do you mean?"

"I assume you've researched where the name 'Robert's Foe' originated."

"Local lore seems to point to the pirate Bartholomew Robert."

"It seems dead-on. Robert's Foe has a natural harbor?"

"A shallow one of sorts, but yes."

"Perfect for the lighter schooners that pirates favored and an excellent device to deter the deeper-water demands of the Royal Navy sloops."

"But not very far out."

Meredith nodded. "I haven't read anything about it, other than to know that Bartholomew Robert was driven out of Caribbean waters around 1720. Could it be that he was caught on Robert's Foe and that his schooner sank where it was moored?"

"No. It isn't in the harbor."

"Maybe they spotted the navy approaching and made a run for it."

"It's possible. Since Robert had commandeered so many Spanish vessels and we found a bronze with *El Espantoso* stamped on it, I assumed Seville was the place to dig up information on what he carried." He glanced at Christina. "But maybe we really belong in London."

"Maybe. Let me dig around a little. Alone. Being spotted with you two could make me a target. There might be some record in the stacks of what you've found. If so, it should be easy to find: Eighteenth-century documents are not in the basement, but upstairs...actually very well catalogued. I'm just not sure how far it will get us. The man was a pirate—we might have to go to alternate resources."

"What's really odd is that she's only four fathoms down," Christina interjected. "She should have been salvaged long ago. But we found some coins after a storm. A number of pieces of eight and a doubloon."

"Could be just a cache that was missed," Meredith said. "Right?"

"Right," Christina agreed with a sigh. "But for obvious reasons we'd prefer to hope there might be an alternate story."

"Maybe one of the men hid a portion of the spoils for himself and they remained hidden until now. You brought the coins with you?"

Christina nodded and, after looking around carefully, slipped them to Meredith.

"Potosí," Meredith said, reading the mark on the pieces of eight. "Perhaps you'll get a share of those particular treasure coins after all, Christina."

"Maybe…" She nervously glanced around the crowded restaurant. "Listen, you're right; it's probably best if you're not spotted with us. Do you mind digging around for a few days on this?"

"No problem. My current project can be put on hold for a bit. And I'll call Paul Tillick in London. He'll probably know all about Robert. Why don't we meet up at the Museum of Contemporary Art in a few days?"

"I knew you'd know who to call," Christina said, reaching out to squeeze her friend's hand. "We'll see you Tuesday. Third floor. One o'clock."

"I'll be there," Meredith stood and leaned toward Mitch. "Keep a close eye on our girl," she demanded sternly. "She seems to draw trouble around here."

"I think I'll take her to Jerez," Mitch said.

"Great. You come here, set me to work, and go off for a

romantic holiday," she tossed over her shoulder.

"We'll be eternally grateful!" Christina said.

Meredith merely smiled and exited the café.

—⟪⟫—

That afternoon they left the whitewashed houses, bright purple bougainvillea, and Baroque facades of Seville, riding in the back of a taxicab and talking of pirates and treasure. The banks of the Guadalquivir soon gave way to fertile pastures, muddy marshlands, and chalky vineyards. Mitch and Christina laughed and talked as they passed rice paddies and fields of cotton, orange groves, stud farms, and bull ranches that boasted the fiercest *toros bravos* in the land.

Ninety minutes later they reached the city of Jerez, already in the full swing of Carnival. The cab driver, unable to enter the choked streets, dropped them off on the outskirts with a note directing them to his aunt's house. "You will not find other lodging tonight," he said simply before driving away.

Taking his advice, they made their way to the simple, sprawling hacienda, where they were shown to two adjoining rooms in the west wing. The rooms each had French doors that opened up to a terra cotta patio, covered with trellises of beautiful flowers Christina had never seen before.

After paying the doña a healthy sum to procure the rooms, Mitch took Christina's hand and led her out to the street. Three blocks down, they stood and watched as a holy procession walked by and penitent people cried out, their faces etched with soul-filled pain. "Have you ever been in Spain during Holy Week?" Mitch asked quietly.

Christina shook her head. "When I lived here, I was away that week."

He nodded. "The people walk bare footed, carrying crucifixes. It was the first time I saw people weeping, as they contemplated what Christ had done for them. Holy Week's never been the same for me, since. It...changed me."

She squeezed his hand. "Sometimes I think that we in the West have lost something critical, making faith such a private matter," she said.

He leaned over and kissed her on the temple. "I've never had a girlfriend that shared my faith before."

She grinned at him. "I've never had a boyfriend that shared mine."

They left the procession crowds and headed toward the western side of the city. Mitch paused to buy three sticks of *pincho moruno*: spiced, skewered pork, and olives. They ate as they walked, enjoying just being together and exploring the sight, smells, and tastes of the Mediterranean country.

"How do you know so much about this area?" Christina asked.

"I spent a summer traveling, learning all I could. I felt like I had to be here to understand those I sought. I had to see a little of what Columbus, Magellan, Drake, Villeneuve, and their contemporaries saw, to figure out how they might have lived, sailed, and died."

"See?" she said, weaving her arm through his. "You're an archaeologist at heart."

"I understand what you do. Figuring out what the sailors were once like is almost more interesting than the treasures they carried."

It was getting late: in typical Spanish tradition, the time when the parties really got started. "The best flamenco is seen between midnight and five," Mitch informed Christina, as they approached a group singing and dancing around a bonfire.

LISA T. BERGREN

What Christina witnessed was not anything like the flamboyant dances put on in the streets of Seville for tourists. There were a few castanets, of course. But the music was more complex, with ever-changing rhythms, and it took about an hour for Christina to begin to follow it. It was rather like jazz, she thought, allowing for improvisation, while obeying strict rules. Most captivating were the sensual dancers and singers, lost in their sad and woeful songs.

One woman sat, singing, with her hands outstretched, as if praying. The very act appeared to be painful. Several men pounded on metal drums. The effect was austere and moving, giving the song's name, "Solitude," meaning.

An hour later the tempo picked up, and the group adopted the more lighthearted, lyrical, and cheerful songs known as *canto flamenco*. The dancing began with it. Women moved around the fire in a fluid manner; old men yelled olé at opportune moments. Christina and Mitch clapped, swept up in the festive spirit.

It surprised her when Mitch put his arm around her and showed her the time on his dive watch. "It's three in the morning. Should we head back?"

She looked up at him, his blond hair glinting in the firelight and his eyes soft with love. "Yes," she said quietly. He took her hand, and under a bright white moon they walked back to Doña Maya's and reluctantly parted ways in the hall.

Christina shut the door, exhausted, but her emotions seemed on high alert. "What is happening to me?" she whispered, leaning against the door and sliding to the floor. "Am I really falling in love with a treasure hunter?"

She got up, went to the bathroom and washed her face, thinking about the question over and over.

"Not *falling* in love, Christina Alvarez," she told her reflection. "*In* love. You're done, woman. Cooked. *Fin.*" And with that, she tugged on the chain to the lone lightbulb in the room and fell into bed.

CHAPTER 24

Mitch, holding a sprig of bougainvillea between his teeth, tapped on Christina's French door late the next morning. Pulling aside the curtains to see who had knocked, Christina smiled and nodded when he motioned for her to join him at a table set on the patio.

After freshening up at the small sink, she joined him. It was a hot morning, but the vines shaded them, and there was a slight breeze that smelled like the salt of the ocean. Christina bent and kissed Mitch briefly before oohing and aahing over the food on the table. In small terra cotta bowls were *huevos a la flamenca*, an egg, chorizo, and an asparagus and pepper concoction as brightly colored as the flamenco dancers' costumes from the night before.

Mitch raised his orange juice glass to hers in a toast. They clinked the pottery together and smiled. "Did you sleep well?" he asked.

"Like the dead. And you?"

"Very well. Although I dreamed of you."

"Oh?" She felt the burn of a blush climbing her cheeks. "And what did you dream?"

"Ah, no. That's only for me to know," he said, raising a devilish brow.

She grinned. "So, what do you have planned today, Master Tour Guide?"

"I thought we'd go down to Cádiz for the day, maybe do some shopping and swimming. Then come back here, if you'd like. Even with the tourists disappearing, I think this is about the best lodging we could find."

"I agree. Our own, private discovery, off the beaten path."

"We need to save enough energy for tonight. The street dances begin, and tomorrow night is the masquerade: The whole town turns out to proceed, masked, down the avenue. Then we have to get back to Seville and find out what the marvelous Meredith has dug up."

"Fine. But let's not talk about that now. I want to enjoy this time away and concentrate only on you."

"I like that concept," he quipped, stuffing a bite of egg into his mouth.

The afternoon was a delight. Holding hands, they explored the whitewashed streets built on the hillsides, looked at masquerade costumes, and admired the shock of blue sea against the spare, stark buildings. Green plants grew everywhere: on windowsills, stairs...even rooftops. After a quick dip at a small, private beach, they hailed a cab and journeyed back to Jerez, looking forward to the dances of the evening.

They stopped at a market, searching for proper attire. In short order, he found something lovely for Christina—a white cotton blouse that was trimmed in lace and meant to be worn down on the shoulders, as well as a bright red skirt made of yards of fabric. He could imagine her twirling in it, her skirt billowing out and revealing her shapely calves. He grinned in spite of himself and turned to wave her over.

"Señor?" the vendor questioned, as he turned. Mitch knew he had been caught in his reverie about a certain pretty señorita. The vendor smiled knowingly. Carnival was a ripe time for love, and gringos, especially, found the novelty of it intoxicating. She held up a pair of loose-fitting black pants and a billowing white "pirate" shirt.

"No, no," he said, laughing at the thought of himself in it.

The woman was too good at her job to let him off the hook. She held up the skirt and blouse. *"Para una señorita."* *For a girl.* Then she held up the pants and shirt, as if it was obvious. *"Para usted. Muy bien."* *For you. Very good.*

"Sounds fair," Christina said, nearing them.

Mitch looked from the clothing to the adamant vendor, then back to his determined girlfriend. *What the heck,* he thought. *It's a festival. I might as well dress the part.*

Back at the hacienda, Christina begged for time to bathe. "I feel disgusting. And I must be a sight to look at."

He pulled her to him suddenly. "You sure are."

She huffed a laugh and shook her head. "See you at eight?"

"Yeah. I'm going to take a brief nap and then probably have a bath after you. Knock on my door when you're out, okay?"

"Will do."

—◊—

Christina got out of the tub and dried off, then helped herself to some of Doña Maya's powder, as she had offered. It smelled of lilacs, and Christina loved feeling clean for the first time in days. Even in the heat of Southern Europe, baths were not a priority, and rooms with their own tubs or showers were difficult to find. She slipped on her new blouse and skirt, pleased to not only be wearing what felt like a light, fresh costume, but clothing that was fresh at all. *Maybe I'll wash my clothes in the sink and hang them to dry while we're out.*

Christina tip-toed down the hall, not wanting Mitch to hear her and come out and see her yet. At the last possible second, she knocked on his door to let him know the bathroom was free, then scurried down to her room and inside. She marveled at the girlish feelings whirling through her; she'd forgotten the sheer giddiness of it. Dressed for the street dance in an ancient city, in clothes Mitch had chosen for her, Christina had the notion that they were courting. In the frenzy of all that had occurred with Hobard, it had not been an option.

Now it felt like they had backed up to let things unfold between them as they should have in the first place. But then, perhaps if all that *hadn't* happened, Christina might still be stuck, reluctant to endanger their professional relationship in order to discover just what might be unfolding between them. *God works through all things. Even the bad things. If we let him.*

He knocked on her door an hour later. When she opened it, he backed up, as if struck by the apparently devastating sight of her. She had braided her long hair into a crown that wound around her head, tucking bougainvillea blossoms into it. Soft tendrils had escaped already.

She laughed at his reaction and pointed at him, dressed in the traditional male costume for fiesta. He looked tanned and handsome, a hint of his strong chest showing through the natural V at the neck of his shirt. Even his hair, which usually fell pell-mell into his face, was carefully combed and tucked behind his ears.

He stepped back to the doorway and pulled out a long, red rose from behind his back. Bowing, he asked, "Señorita, would you kindly accompany me to dinner and to a dance?"

She nodded her head regally. "Gladly, señor." She took the rose from him and placed her hand in his. "Shall we?"

—\\\\—

They spent the evening wandering the streets, observing the riotous festival as people laughed and sang and drank and argued, then danced some more. At midnight, the church bells pealed and the true street dancing began, an amazing cacophony of different bands playing many and various folk tunes.

Mitch whirled her from one dance to another, spending an hour at each. Together they learned many of the traditional dances. The locals, used to foreigners, welcomed them. Christina drew many admiring glances, but Mitch casually moved her down the street when a huge fellow looked her way too often. He wanted this to be a night of pure joy for her. *A fight will ruin the whole thing.*

At four in the morning, the dance was at its peak. Christina and Mitch had stumbled upon a group practicing a wild dance from the mountain regions of Andalusia. Women twirled and twirled, were caught by different partners and set back on their feet, then were sent out into the ring again. Christina was laughing, dizzy from the constant motion.

After five or six revolutions of the dance, Christina was whirled again across the ring of eighty men. About fifty women were swung back and forth inside the large circle like turning tops on a table. Christina twirled, around and around, hoping she would not run into another dancer or crush her next partner when she came to the side. Strong arms caught her, and a familiar-sounding voice said, "Hello, *muchacha*. You look enchanting."

Christina dizzily struggled to clear her vision and see him in the dark, shying away as she thought she recognized his voice.

Manuel?

CHAPTER 25

She pushed away from him, holding her head and letting out a scream. Amid the wild motion of the dance and the ecstatic cries of the dancers, her call went unheard. And the man disappeared among the throngs.

Mitch spotted her desperately waving off men who tried to grab her and twirl her back out into the center of the piazza. He hurried over to her, dodging whirling dancers as he did so. Christina's eyes darted back and forth, frantically scanning the crowds, not seeming to focus in on anything.

"Christina? Are you okay?"

"Mitch!" She fell into his arms, clearly relieved, but turned to keep searching the crowds. "I think it was him! *Manuel*. I think he's here!"

Mitch pulled her behind him and led the way through the throngs, looking for the intruder. A head taller than most of the locals, he scanned the deeply shadowed faces for a glimpse of their enemy, but did not see him.

"Are you sure it was him?" he asked, pausing when they'd gone up a building's front staircase in order to get a good look at the street before them.

"I-I think so. I was dizzy, but I thought it was him. He said it was good to see me, like he knew me. And he spoke in English."

"You know Spaniards, and their macho ways. They think they have the right to approach any woman." He put a comforting arm around her. "Sure it wasn't just some creep trying to cop a feel? Someone who looked like Manuel? You've drawn more than one man's eye…"

She frowned and continued to scan the crowd. "I'm not crazy, Mitch."

"I don't think you are."

She took a deep breath and rubbed her forehead. "Maybe it was someone who just looked like him."

"Could be. And Manuel—and his boss—wouldn't be here, right? They have their own issues now, between searching for our ship and avoiding the FBI. And even if they were after us again, there's no way they could have tracked us here. Not after we took so many precautions."

"You're right," she said, aggravated with herself now. What was wrong with her?

"Look, it's really late." He checked his watch. "It's nearly five in the morning. Maybe you're just as tired as I am?"

"Maybe," she said, feeling paranoid, as she looked around. She took his arm and they made their way down the street. "I'm sorry. I've ruined the evening."

"No, no," he said, turning a corner, which led them to a quieter neighborhood. "Christina, you went through a lot in Seville. Heck, you went through a lot on Robert's Foe. Have your nightmares returned?"

"Not after that first week back."

"Well, it was pretty traumatic, what you went through. And it's obvious why you'd half-expect to find Manuel here. You have to give your mind—and heart—time to process and heal. There will be a day that we'll be in Spain and you won't give Manuel—or Hobard—a second thought."

She smiled and wrapped an arm around his waist as they walked. "So you don't think this will be the last time we come here together?"

"I hope not. I hope this is just one of many adventures we'll share."

His arm around her shoulders felt warm and comforting. "I'm still sorry our night ended on a downer note," she said.

"Hey, stop." He pulled her under a streetlamp, took her face in his hands and kissed her. "I had a blast. Well, you know, up until this last bit. Did you?"

She nodded and looked up into his eyes. "I'll never forget it." They were alone. No one trailed them. *It's just us,* she told herself. *It was all in my imagination.*

He smiled reassuringly. "Then let's just remember the good parts, okay? Not let Manuel or Hobard horn in on what is special and...*ours* now. These memories are *ours*. They don't get to invade this time, these memories. We won't let them."

They continued on in silence for a while.

"Thanks for coming back to Spain with me," he said. "I think...I think we needed this time together."

"Me too." They had reached the house, walked around to the back, and stood in front of the French doors.

"I've really loved it, Mitch. Being here with you has made me glad—so glad—that I decided to give us a chance."

He lifted her chin and stared into her eyes. Using his other hand, he tenderly swept aside an errant lock of hair from her face and gently, sweetly kissed her. "I've thanked God for that every morning since. Good night, Christina."

—꿈—

The next day at noon Mitch paid Doña Maya for her rooms and walked into town to rent a car. They had decided to head back to town early and lose themselves in the sights and sounds of the tourist parts of the city, something neither of them had previously found time to do. A trip to Seville usually meant work. They would use the day for pleasure for once, as they had in Jerez.

"Let's pick three places and spend a couple hours at each," Mitch suggested, once they were on the road.

"Good idea. I would love to see Alcazar again. I haven't been there since my college trip."

"Done. And how about the cathedral?"

"I never get tired of it. Then we can finish our tourist rounds with a hike up the tower."

"Perfect." Mitch smiled over at her, then reached over to rub her neck. "You feeling okay today? Are you still worried about running into Manuel?"

"Oh, it crosses my mind about every ten minutes, and I think we should be on the lookout. But I must have imagined the whole thing. He's in Mexico with Hobard, right? Right," she said, answering her own question. "It was just someone who looked like him, sounded like him. I was so tired and dizzy from that crazy dance…"

"Well, I hope you can relax today."

She took his hand in hers. "It's easier when you're beside me."

"That's exactly where I'm gonna be all day."

Their first stop was at Alcazar, a lavish Moorish castle in Carmona that had been rebuilt by the Christians. As they traipsed among the collection of royal courts, halls, patios, and apartments, Mitch had to drag Christina along.

"Hey, don't rush me, Mitch! Can't you *smell* the history? Wouldn't it be wonderful to travel back in time and see the people in action in this incredible place? I close my eyes, and it all comes alive…"

She did just that, seeming to lose herself in thoughts of centuries past. Mitch smiled as he watched her, feeling his heart swell with the love building inside him. She was so passionate, so interesting, so curious…

Christina opened her eyes and caught him grinning at her. "You're laughing at me."

"Not at all," he said, pulling her into his arms. "I think," he said, putting his forehead against hers, "I'm just falling more deeply in love with you, Christina," he whispered. "I love how smart you are and how you care for those around you. How you invest so thoroughly in whatever you're doing, whether that's babysitting my niece and nephew for a few days or researching a wreck or learning a Spanish dance. I love you and I can't imagine ever letting you go again."

She smiled and they shared a long kiss that went on and on, until a disgruntled tour guide coughed conspicuously, and they turned to see a group of delighted tourists staring at them.

Mitch raised his arm. "Shall we make our way to the cathedral now, my lady?"

"Most assuredly," she said, cheeks burning, taking his arm.

Outside, Mitch rushed her down the stairs and into a shady, cool alcove, away from prying eyes. He took her face in his hands and stared tenderly into her eyes. "Our kiss was interrupted. But moreover, our conversation was."

"It was?"

He nodded slightly, the hint of a smile on his lips, knowing she was feigning ignorance. "I confessed my love."

"You did," she said, unable to hold back her grin.

"Last time I tried to tell you, you pretty much ran away."

"I did," she said, nodding once.

He squeezed her in mock agitation, wide-eyed with frustration. "You're not going to make this easy on me, are you?"

"I don't believe I shall," she said impishly. "Let's call it payback for how hard you made *me* work to let me in to *your* life."

"Okay. I deserve a little of that," he allowed. "But will you keep me in suspense forever?"

"No," she said, acquiescing at last. She stood on her tiptoes and kissed him, pulling him close.

His hands slipped down her neck, to her shoulders to her back, pressing her to him. But then he pulled back abruptly. "Hey, wait. No? As in no, you won't keep me in suspense forever? Or no, you aren't as in love with me as I am with you?"

She laughed. "No, as in, I don't think you could possibly be as in love with me as I am with you, Mitch Crawford. I love your passion, your tenacity, even your hard-headedness. Your dedication to the kids, to your friends, to your work. I love you. And I don't want to leave your side either."

His face spread in a broad smile and then he was kissing her, kissing her so deeply, so hungrily, that Christina hoped he would never stop. But eventually they had to, aware the day was heating up and they had to get to Seville before the cathedral closed for evening mass.

They sped along the highway and reached Seville within fifteen minutes, each casting the other quiet, wide grins. Echoes of their confessions of love clearly still rang in their ears, making Christina feel impossibly light and deliriously happy. Mitch parked and they walked four blocks in, wanting to blend into the crowds since they were so close to the Archives.

As they neared, Christina held her breath, as she always did at the sight. Built on the foundations of a huge mosque, the fifteenth-century cathedral was gigantic. Flying buttresses and rose windows seemed to shout in celebration.

Mitch whistled. "I hear the clergy renounced their incomes for this project. One of them said, 'Let us build a church so huge anyone who sees it will take us for madmen.'"

"Oh yeah. I'd say they were pretty far gone, wouldn't you?"

They climbed the steps and entered the narthex, grabbing a pamphlet written in both Spanish and English. A small man approached them. "You need a guide. I will show you the halls of wonder," he said, lifting his hands in a grand gesture.

Christina smiled back at Mitch and he shrugged his shoulders. "Lead on, good man. But only for fifteen Euros, tops."

"Deal," he said, smiling and shaking their hands. "My name is Juan. I speak good English."

They followed the man into the dimly lit sanctuary and listened as he droned on about the cathedral being the third biggest in the world, one of the biggest gothic buildings ever constructed, and about the various naves as they passed through.

The Capilla Mayor nave caught their attention with its sixty-five-foot-high, forty-five-foot-wide gold-leaf *retalbo*, or paneled altarpiece. Gazing at thirty-six scenes from the life of Christ, featuring over fifteen hundred figures carved in gold, Mitch felt a wave of reverence: first, for the artist whose passion kept him in one place so long; then, even more for the God who had inspired him.

The rest of the interior was vaguely disappointing, the austere, Gothic beauty buried in ornate Baroque decoration that was later added. Their mood lightened as they approached the monument to Christopher Columbus.

"If it hadn't been for this guy, I wouldn't have much of a business," Mitch quipped.

"Nor I. I think it's especially appropriate that we stop here and pay our respects." She looked up at the four regally robed figures, representing the four medieval kingdoms of Spain, standing watch over his tomb. "Think they'll bury me in such a grand fashion for my work?"

"Sorry, my love. I think you're destined for something much more conservative."

"Ah well, lead on, Juan."

Seeing their waning interest, their guide sped them along to the other highlights: the richest crown in Spain, made with eleven thousand precious stones and the world's largest pearl, carved into the body of an angel; supposed holy relics of thorns, chunks of the cross, and splinters from the table at the Last Supper.

Juan looked at Mitch's raised eyebrows and led them to the Giralda tower. "I think you will enjoy the view from there. With the sun about to set, your timing is perfect."

"Thank you, Juan," Christina said. "You did a good job."

Mitch paid the man, and they climbed the hundred yards up the spiraling, ramp-like steps that had been built to accommodate riders on horseback. It was beautiful in its Moorish simplicity and, after an hour in the ornate, incense- and soot-laden rooms of the cathedral, felt like a breath of fresh air.

They reached the top and crossed from side to side, window to window, admiring the bird's-eye view of the city. Christina was looking out toward the Guadalquivir, imagining Columbus and the city of his time, when Mitch came up from behind, wrapping his arms around her. "It makes me very, very happy to be with you, Christina."

"And I with you," she returned dreamily, hoping he could feel the contentedness that seemed to now fill her, center her.

CHAPTER 26

They found Meredith on the third floor, carefully studying the sculptures of Eduardo Chillida. After pulling her toward a less popular exhibit of an Andalusian painter, they stood behind a wall while Meredith briefed them about what she had discovered.

"Paul was a wealth of information," Meredith said excitedly, leading them to a wide, white marble bench. "Listen to this: Apparently Bartholomew Robert was tried before a 'benevolent' judge, and the pirate was sent to Newgate Prison. Robert lived in cramped, rat-infested, open-sewer quarters for twenty years. At the end, when he was dying of typhoid, he supposedly muttered something about 'buried treasure.' His ship—maybe the one you found—had been salvaged. The Royal Navy didn't find the treasure they expected but couldn't get any more information out of him. The guy was just too stubborn to give it up, and then too sick in the end.

"By the time he died and word spread of the treasure, the

obscure little island had already been lost among a sea of obscure little islands. When treasure hunters began seeking it a couple hundred years later, even the sunken ship seemed to have disappeared, probably encased in the first layer of that coral and sand you guys talked about."

"Wow. Right there in back of the house," Mitch muttered. "But where did he bury the treasure? Somewhere on the island?"

"Paul says that any information is highly suspect, but one man—Robert's cellmate—swore that he talked about it being 'under the water.' Most researchers have assumed Robert was talking about the ocean, and they surmised that in his delirium, he was remembering a previous ship he lost."

"Well, that's pretty vague. Was there anything else?" Mitch said.

"There is a record from one priest who took down his story as he died, and he always said the man kept muttering something about 'the falls.'"

Mitch straightened and his blue-green eyes met Christina's.

It took her a moment, but then she gasped.

Mitch nodded, smiling.

"I take it this information means something to you…" Meredith said slowly, her hands on her hips.

"It does, Mer," Christina said, rising, wringing her hands in excitement.

"You've been such a great help," Mitch said, shaking her hand. "That gives us a solid start."

"But I'll still need all the information you've found on *El Espantoso*," Christina said, grabbing Mitch's arm. Could the falls mean *their* waterfall?

"Sure. I'll email you all I've found." She paused, waiting. "You're not going to tell me what you know, are you?"

"I'm sorry, Mer," Christina whispered, eyeing a portly

gentleman rambling by. "You know how it goes. The more you know, the more vulnerable you are."

"But you'll be the first to call if we unearth a treasure," Mitch promised with a grin.

"Okay, fine. Whatever. But do me a favor and stay out of Seville for a while. I don't need any more trouble," she said, pulling Christina into a hug.

"Deal. But when I return, I want to meet Jake," she said.

"We can double-date on the Guadalquivir!" Meredith said.

"Sounds great. We'll call."

"No need. I'll just keep track of you through TMZ."

—⁊⁊—

Back at Robert's Foe, cuddled up with both children on the couch, Christina and Mitch happily filled in Hans about all they had learned. They talked so long, Kenna and Joshua both fell asleep in their arms.

Hans sat back, grinning. "So from what I hear, you could've accomplished all that with a simple phone call from here. You know, rather than spending thousands of Euros on what sounds suspiciously like a romantic getaway on Treasure Seekers' dime."

"Well, maybe," Mitch said. "But you know how Tate has the capability to intercept our calls. We don't want him showing up on our doorstep again."

"Fine. But next time, Nora and I get to be the ones to jet-set off to Spain. Deal?" he said, rising with mock consternation.

"Sounds fair," Mitch said, sliding Christina a sidelong grin.

She gently set Kenna in the corner of the couch and rose

with them, walking to the hallway. "Everything in me wants to go to the pool and start digging with my bare hands. How can you two stand it?"

Mitch crossed his arms. "I want verification that what we think is *El Espantoso* is truly *El Espantoso*. We need another piece of evidence besides the cannon before I'm willing to tear that beautiful pool apart."

Christina thought of the idyllic falls. It *would* be terrible to tear it up, especially if they were on the wrong track. "Well, Hans. How have things progressed at the site since we left you? Were you able to go down?"

"Yep. I scored a waterproof bandage in San Esteban and Nora and I've worked on the site over the last four days, mostly clearing the cannon and seeing what is around it."

"Anything?" Mitch asked.

"We've found what appears to be a conglomerate of cannonballs. Don't ask," he said, holding up a hand. "I'm still racking my brain, trying to figure out how the magnetometer missed them. That is odd in its own right. And they would've been good pickings for a salvager for sure. We found a few more coins, but not from Potosí. Sam is cleaning them now, so we can read their marks better." After centuries underwater, many pieces of eight became black discs. A quick chemical bath often made them as bright as they once had been.

"Coins minted in Mexico won't tell us that it was Robert. The man was a pirate. He should've had everything—from New England shillings to Portuguese crusadoes. We need that kind of evidence," Christina said. "Any chance the coins are anything like that?"

Hans shook his head. "They're the size of pieces of eight and silver. Unless…"

"Daalders," he and Christina said together. The three partners rushed downstairs, anxious to see what Sam had uncovered.

The bearded man, concentrating on his work, barely raised his head when they rushed in. "Hello there," he mumbled.

Mitch introduced them. "Sam, this is Dr. Christina Alvarez. Christina, Sam is one of our most trusted colleagues."

She shot him a look that said *I hope so.*

"Pleased to meet ya, Doc. Heard of your work on the Civil War ships."

"Word seems to get around."

"Sam works freelance and cleans coins for many treasure salvors," Hans explained. "I called him in 'cause he's the best in the business and he's done some good work for us."

"They're not pieces of eight," Sam said.

"Dutch?" Mitch asked.

"Yeah," he said, raising a brow. "How'd you know?"

"Lucky guess," Christina said, elbowing Mitch with a smile.

"They'll be out of the tumbler in a minute or so. You can see 'em for yourself." A buzzer sounded and Sam shut off the shaking machine, reached in, and withdrew a large silver coin. While they all held their breath, he rinsed and dried the disc, then handed it to Christina. A kingly lion was depicted on its face. "A daalder," she said. "Gentlemen, I think we're on to Robert. Have you collected any books in your library about him, by chance?"

"A few," Mitch said. "Nothing too specific."

"We need to find out where Robert's last escapades took him. Meredith's research says he was being driven from the Caribbean by the navy before he was captured. Maybe he was exploring new territory or had come across new traders who dealt with Dutch merchandise."

"That's a good guess. I bet Paul Tillick's friend in Port-au-Prince would have a load of information. Meredith's notes mention that he has an extensive personal library. Maybe we could get Tillick to introduce us?"

"Good plan," she said with a smile. "Duty calls, Hans. I guess Mitch and I are off for another romantic holiday-slash-research trip."

"No way. You saw how happy those kids were to see you two home. Would you trust my study skills?"

Christina thought about it. "I think so. That makes more sense anyway; I'll send you out with a detailed list of things to research, while I spend some time on the site."

"I'll leave tonight."

"Tell Nora she can keep staying here," Mitch said. "After all she's been through, she might be more comfortable with us than alone."

Hans clapped him on the back. "Nah." He waggled his eyebrows. "I think I'll take her with me."

—⚬—

Christina and Mitch gave in to their jet lag and spent the evening and most of the next day reading and playing with the children, then the following two days twenty-eight feet down in water. Hans did not come back for three days; when he did, he was laden with pictures to download.

They sat down at the breakfast table the following morning, sipping coffee, anxious to sort out the information, and pulled up his pictures on Christina's laptop.

"That was a good hunch, Christina," Hans said, smiling at her. "It appears that Robert spent most of his last years venturing into Northern Atlantic waters, alternately plundering and hightailing it home, hiding among the islands along the way. The Royal Navy almost caught him three times, but he escaped."

"So the daalders make sense," she said.

"What doesn't make sense," he returned, "is the lack of treasure the navy found when they finally did catch up with ol' Bart here. Tillick says that even with the treasure divvied up among the crew, Robert should have accumulated well over twelve treasure chests of valuables."

Mitch whistled. "Finding that would definitely fix our financial woes."

"No, man. It would fix us up for life. We could spend the rest of our days chasing down Christina's beloved *La Canción*. Fund it ourselves."

"What do you mean?" Mitch said, his eyes shifting sadly to Christina's and back. "Hobard's probably on top of it right now."

Hans grinned. "I don't think so."

"What?" Christina demanded. "What? What'd you find out?"

"Well, for one, I called our FBI friends, and they're very close to nabbing him. Two, the Mexican government is hassling him about digging in their waters without a proper permit. It seems that last time he salvaged a wreck there, he didn't give them a fair share and they found out about it. And three, I think they're in the wrong place."

"La Punta de Muerte?" Christina asked.

"I was studying the maps at Jack's house. I think there might be a chance that the real location is four hundred miles southeast from where we sent Hobard. Just south of the Yucatan Peninsula, there's a beach and shallow harbor called El Puerto de Muerte. Any chance those two places might be one and the same? What if the map was not depicting a hook-like peninsula, but rather the harbor beside it?"

Christina frowned and shook her head. "No way. The coordinates are more in line with the northern location." The names went through her mind, though, over and over. *The Point of Death. The Port of Death.* As she well knew, names and places had consistently been confused by early cartographers.

She rose and paced back and forth. "Okay, for the sake of argument, let's say that not only did *La Canción* get blown completely off course, but she was also in the entirely wrong area for a voyage home to Spain. How did she get there?"

Hans sat back, enjoying this moment to the utmost. "You said the letter mentioned a pursuit by pirates, before the storm was upon them. It couldn't have been our own Robert, of course, because he was a couple hundred years later. But maybe it was his great-great-grandfather."

Christina's mouth rounded in a silent O.

"Pirates were just finding their place in the Caribbean," Hans said. "Merchants feared their superior armory and speed. If your ancestor saw one on his tail, he would've hauled sail to get away—wherever the wind would take him fastest. The late armada builders skimped on defensive guns, even on the military escort ships, anxious to save weight so they could fill their holds with the much-needed gold. They mistakenly relied on the notion that there was safety in numbers."

"Enter our unknown pirate," Christina put in. "Licensed at first by the English to take any Spanish ship he could get his hands on, for the royal British cause. He could have been legal before he figured out it was more profitable to go freelance. He picked up a handy-dandy fearsome pirate flag—and bang! He was in business. Then he catches wind of *La Canción's* voyage and the other ships in her flotilla…"

"But consider this," Mitch joined in. "Maybe Captain Alvarez came up against two enemies, a pirate *and* a hurricane at the same time. Maybe the pirate is coming at him through the Florida Straits—which is a huge surprise because of the currents and all, but not beyond the pirate's capabilities—and the captain knows that his armed escorts cannot battle their way out. Also on the wind is that storm, so Alvarez heads to open sea, hoping to weather the storm and escape the pirate. He manages to escape the pirate, but the storm finishes off his ship, driving her into the Yucatán Peninsula. Or nearby."

"Sounds plausible to me." Hans sat back, smiling in satisfaction. "So, what do you think, Professor? You're the expert."

Christina paced. "Maybe the family story has changed drastically over the years. Maybe there were headhunters and maybe there weren't, but after being raked across a few sandbars and reefs, the only one who ultimately survived was my ancestor. He could've considered the mass death of his crew and passengers a murder because pirates and a storm drove them to their demise." She looked at Hans and Mitch, excitement written on her face. "There were monks in the Yucatán by that time who corroborated the family story of his appearance, but his shipwreck could've been anywhere along that coast."

Mitch smiled at her obvious pleasure. "So we have a chance at two different finds. What do you think, partners? Which treasure do we seek first?"

Christina stopped pacing. "I think we pursue Robert's ship and treasure first until Hobard is securely behind bars. If Hans is right with his hunch, he might be excavating, but miles away from *The Song*; if he has the right location, there's nothing we can do about it, besides hope that the Mexicans will boot him out."

Mitch nodded.

"We still need assurance that the ship in Four Fathom Reef is really *El Espantoso*," Christina said. "Meredith didn't discover anything further. What about you?"

Hans said, "Robert's last recorded hit was on a ship carrying a tithe meant to go to the Church. He killed many monks aboard the ship when his group overtook her. There should be many pieces of jewelry or gold bars with markings that denote the monks' destination."

Mitch's brow went up and and he let out a long whistle of appreciation. "I'm all for finding a stack of gold bars. They're so much more gratifying than coins," he quipped, rubbing his hands together.

CHAPTER 27

Ten days later they finally found their clue. After they had excavated several timbers they suspected were part of the hull, Nora found a gold object underneath one of the timbers.

Christina came over to see what it was.

She held in her hand a scallop-shaped gold pendant. Emblazoned on top was a cross, one Christina immediately identified as an early seventeenth-century symbol of the knighthood of Saint James. She struggled not to get overly excited; any ship might have carried religious paraphernalia.

Two weeks later they had removed enough coral to expose a conglomerate of broken pottery: olive jars. Noting the time—and her need to get above water—Christina photographed it all and gathered up sacks full of the material. That night, much to Talle's chagrin, Christina bent over pieces spread all about the kitchen table, cleaning the largest ones.

After putting the kids to bed, Mitch sneaked up behind her, wrapped his arms around her and softly pulled aside her hair to kiss her on the neck. "So, why the inordinate interest in the olive jars?" he asked, sitting across from her and picking a chunk out of the huge stack in front of him.

"Have you ever seen any so smashed?"

He frowned, thinking back. "Don't think so. Usually a few of them survive intact, or they're broken into large pieces."

"Right. These seem like they were broken intentionally," she said, not taking her eyes off the pieces as she studied one after another. "Like someone deliberately picked up each one and smashed it on the floor."

"Why would they do that?"

"I don't know. I'm trying to find out."

Mitch yawned. "Well, you've got more stamina than I do. I'm heading to bed." He kissed her again. "Don't stay up all night."

She smiled at him, then turned back to her work. "Mm-hm," she muttered absently.

—◊◊◊—

Christina woke him at two in the morning. "Mitch! Mitch!" she said, shaking his shoulder and wanting to bounce on his bed. She turned on his light.

"What...Christina? It's two in the morning," he groaned, rubbing his eyes.

"I know! I know! But look!" On the bed, she placed twenty fragments of olive jars, carefully putting the jigsaw together. Each was imprinted with a separate piece of an image and overlapped in places. Still, the image was clear.

"They're not all from one jar. But look! The picture makes sense."

Mitch rubbed his eyes and pushed his hair back with one hand. It was tough to make out, since the images had worn away with time and erosion, but gradually he saw what she saw. The image was of a sea captain and a skeleton drinking a toast to death: the same image that Bartholomew Robert had used as his pirate ship flag emblem.

Mitch yelled, ignoring the danger of waking the children, and grabbed Christina for a big hug. He pulled her down into his lap and kissed her, then paused to say briefly, "Tomorrow. We'll figure out how to dig tomorrow."

Belatedly she remembered that she sat on his bed and that he wore only pajamas. Although they worked side by side in their swimsuits all the time, they were usually in work mode, not in the high mood they now shared. Their kisses became longer, more intimate, and Christina finally pulled away. "Gotta go," she said regretfully.

"No, stay," he pleaded, planting kisses along the inside of her wrist and arm.

"Can't," she said, knowing he didn't really mean it. Well, she knew he wanted her to stay, but agreed, deep down, it wouldn't be wise. She kissed him on the forehead and walked to the door. "Tomorrow, Treasure Seeker. Let's *finally* be after it."

—∞—

Mitch got precious little sleep the rest of that night, dozing fitfully as his mind raced from Christina to the pool where Bartholomew's treasure most surely awaited. Maybe it was even directly below the secret ledge behind the waterfall.

Christina and Mitch sadly watched as the pristine pool was drained by a team of twenty men. "I'll rebuild it," he whispered in her ear, his arm around her shoulders. "We'll find the treasure and rebuild it. After all, I suspect Robert did so first."

"Yeah, but it'd take a couple hundred years to be the

same," she moaned.

He had to agree. The pool was now nothing but a muddy pit, fifteen feet deeper than it once was, to allow access for the digging equipment. The team turned their efforts toward the cave, pulling out rock after massive rock, until they all could see the clear lines of a fortified shaft, made of timber and stacked rock.

"It's really here," Christina said, running a hand over the stones. "Bartholomew—or someone else—went to great lengths to hide it."

"And the only reason to do that is because it's worth a lot," Hans said, rubbing his hands together.

"Just creating the pool and waterfall would have been quite the undertaking," Mitch said. He waved his arm, giving the crew the go-ahead to resume their excavations. Christina took pictures every time they hoisted out a shovel full of dirt Hans filmed it too, so they'd have solid documentation.

Three hours later and twenty feet down, the bulldozer paused. "You gotta come see this!" Hans shouted to Mitch. He climbed a series of ladders and joined them on a small ledge to one side.

"The team's hit a bunch of logs," he said.

"Logs? Do you know what that means?" Christina said, pacing excitedly.

Both men stared at her, puzzled. The motor started up again on the bulldozer. "No! Stop!" she cried. She clambered down to the bottom of the excavation, half-sliding through the muck, and the men followed.

Christina ran her hands down the length of one log, and then the other. "This is a barricade. We have to proceed with extreme caution."

Hans and Mitch eyed each other, clearly in no mood to slow down.

"Why?" Hans asked.

Christina glanced back at it. "The wood's not tropical, so it must've been imported. I need the crew to remove it—carefully—and I'll figure out where it originated." She looked up and around the pit. "And if he went this far, you can bet we're likely to uncover more surprises below. Once we remove these, the rest of the digging will have to be by hand."

But the following hours exposed nothing but twenty feet of sand below the logs.

Two long, tedious days of digging later they hit another barricade: a steel plate, measuring ten by thirty feet. Hans whistled. "Robert was pretty thorough. It's gotta be good, right?"

"Or he was losing it," Mitch retorted, "and got a good laugh, thinking about all he'd put people through if they discovered this shaft."

Hans knocked on it and it sounded as if there was open space below it, not more sand. "Bring me a blowtorch and mask!" he shouted up to a man.

"Not so fast," Christina said, rubbing her chin, trying to think.

"What?" Mitch said. "We gotta get past this thing."

"The log barricade, and now this…Think *Oak-Island* level."

Understanding dawned on their faces. A similar shaft had been discovered on the island off of Maine, and treasure hunters had come across nearly identical barricades. When the steel plate had been removed, it triggered an ingenious set of booby traps; the worst being a flood of water from underground caves.

"You think we're in for trouble?" Mitch asked her.

"It's possible."

"Well, if it floods, we'll just put on scuba equipment and

go from there," Hans said.

"Fifteen men have died at Oak Island; ten of them were professional divers and excavators," Mitch said.

"The tide and caves are intricate," Christina said. "And slowly rising water could be the least of your problems."

"What else?" Hans asked Christina.

"I don't know. It might flood instantly, without warning. There might be a load of quicksand. Clearly, these guys were determined to keep looters at bay. Look at us. We're forty feet down!"

"So what do you suggest?" Hans asked impatiently.

She paced, thinking. "Okay. Blowtorch it. But just a hole big enough for a man to get through. I'd be willing to bet the trap is set off when you remove the plate, releasing some sort of mechanism. Removing only part of the center might keep the trapdoor in place."

Mitch nodded. "Then we can see what happens."

Mitch insisted on burning the hole through himself, not wanting to endanger Hans or any of the crew. Every worker, including Hans and Christina, stood around the edge of the pit, anxiously watching his progress. Mitch completed the red-hot circle and, looking upward with a grin at his comrades, rammed the disc and it disappeared below.

"See anything?" Christina called.

"Not yet. It's deep."

Working with an archaeologist's bent mirror, he picked up a flashlight and slowly circumvented the space, examining the area directly under the steel plate, checking for mechanisms that might set off a trap. Tentatively, he poked his hand down through the hole.

There was no flood. No metal swords emerged to stab an invader. No poisonous arrows shot across the chasm. "Seems okay!" He turned his attention to the sandy floor, thirty feet below.

He blinked, and rubbed his eyes, wondering if his lack of sleep over the last week was making him see things. Eyes wide, he looked again. *Gold. Silver. Emeralds.*

Mitch turned on to his back, laid a hand over his forehead and smiled up at his partners. "I see the bottom. You two had better come take a look."

Christina climbed tentatively down the ladder, with Hans following close behind. Peering in, they shouted and hugged each other ecstatically.

"It's here!" Christina yelled to the crew above. "We've found it!"

CHAPTER 28

After further testing for traps—tossing down sacks of sand—even Christina couldn't talk Mitch out of descending into the shaft. Hans and several men lowered him on a rope, and he hung suspended, twenty feet below the metal floor. "I'm having a serious Indiana Jones moment here," he called up to Hans.

"Go on, rub it in," Hans returned, jealousy lining his tone. His healing arm kept him from even arguing with Mitch that he should be the one to go down. Plus he had a good fifty pounds on Mitch; if an emergency occurred, they needed to haul any explorer up as fast as possible.

They lowered him farther, until he was just five feet above the floor. "Hold!" he shouted. Mitch shined his light around the walls, scanning again for warning signs, as Christina had instructed.

But the treasure soon consumed him. His flashlight reflected back the startling wealth. Mounds of coins from every major seventeenth-century nation were represented: French deniers, English crowns, Indian mohurs, as well as the shillings, crusadoes, doubloons, and pieces of eight he expected. "You're gonna love this, Christina," he called up to her. "There's some serious evidence of Robert's travels and exploits."

"We'll set you down!" Hans yelled.

"No!" Christina cried. "Not yet!" Mitch could imagine the two of them arguing, up top. "What do you see, Mitch? Tell me what the room looks like."

Again he absently flashed his light around the walls. "It's similar to what you see up top. But halfway down, it turned into a shaft that appears to have been carved out of the native limestone. This must've taken Robert's crew *years* to build."

Christina frowned, thinking. What dangers might lie below? Her mind raced, but she could not come up with any specific concerns that would dissuade Hans and Mitch from immediate exploration. Hans's hands shifted on the rope.

"Can you see any of the floor? Is any of it exposed?"

Mitch shined his light around below, clearly anxious to relieve her mind and be free of the rope. She could guess what he was feeling. She'd want to feel those gold coins in her hands too. To send some of those large, uncut emeralds up to the workers who had toiled day and night. "There's a little standing water. Maybe some sand. I think it's a natural bottom."

Her heart pounded. "Okay," she agreed warily. "But please don't touch anything that looks even vaguely suspicious. And keep that rope around your waist in case we have to haul you up."

"Roger that." He looked up. "It's fine, babe. Really."

Hans lowered Mitch the rest of the way, and Christina

breathed a sigh of relief when his weight on the floor triggered no response.

He looked up at her again. "See? No big deal."

She rolled her eyes and watched him walk the room, gathering samples of each treasure and placing them in a bucket. The workers above were captivated by the pail of treasure he sent up, but Christina ignored it, wanting only for Mitch to come back up. She tried to tell herself she was worrying too much, but could not escape the uneasiness that hounded her.

He looked up at her. "Come down here, sweetheart. I want you and Hans to see this too. It's safe." He jumped up and down. "See? Nothing's happened."

She felt like an idiot, like she did that day when she'd had a full panic attack over the shark. "Okay," she said, forcing a tone of bravado. Hans brought up the rope, then lowered Christina slowly. She gasped as she got closer to the floor, her own flashlight catching bars of gold, mountains of coins, ingots of silver, and a sextant embedded with rubies.

Mitch helped her out of the rope and hugged her, swinging her around and around and laughing. "Christina," he whispered. "There's millions of dollars' worth of treasure here. *Hundreds* of millions, maybe."

She gave him the first genuine smile he had seen all afternoon, then moved meticulously about, photographing each pile. "You realize that you disturbed the site before I was able to record it properly."

"You didn't say anything," he said defensively.

"No. I was preoccupied with your safety. That's the danger of being on a dig with someone you love. You lose your edge of professionalism."

"Well then, I hope you're even more unprofessional now," he said, and took her in his arms to give her such a solid kiss, it ended up with him dipping her, much to the delight of the crew above.

After studying the walls and ceiling carefully, they were pulled out of the cave, and Mitch ordered the crews above to cut out all but the last eighteen inches of steel on any side of the plate, giving them the natural light needed for excavating the site. By the time they finished, the sun had set and they called it a day, setting up trusted men as armed guards for the night. All crew members had been required to stay on the island in tents; there was no way that Mitch wanted news to get out, or robbers to come in. They would bring up every single gold coin, green emerald and red ruby before word of the find reached the world.

The trio were up the next morning before the sun. With the aid of a rope seat, Hans joined Christina and Mitch below and continued sending buckets of treasure upward as Christina recorded on her pad of graph paper each coin, ingot, bar, and jewel, and where it had been found. Neither she nor Hans noticed Mitch studying a niche in the far wall, which the rising sun had illuminated.

He shined his headlamp into the small alcove, his breath catching at the sight of a solid gold cross, encrusted with emeralds, bearing the same design as the medallion Hans had found underneath the ship's timbers: the Knights of Saint James.

"Mitch, no!" Christina cried.

But he had already lifted the cross from its pedestal.

As soon as he did so, the floor opened up beneath him and he fell downward. He grunted as he hit a sloping wall and continued to fall, much of the treasure going with him.

He landed with a thud far below, sinking chest-deep into what felt like mud. It was very dark. He heard Christina calling to him, high above, over and over. Somehow, she and

Hans hadn't fallen with him. Had only part of the flooring given way to this new level of the shaft?

"I'm here!" he yelled. "I'm okay, but uh…send down a rope! Water's coming in!" The mud had probably saved him when he landed. But now he was getting sucked down into it. He struggled against it, moving in slow motion, searching the walls for a ledge, a crevice…anything to pry himself out of the sludge. *Quicksand*, Christina had mentioned.

The water climbed. Within a minute, it was up to his waist. "Hurry!" he called.

He forced his legs to move through the muck toward the edge, but the walls were smooth in the five-by-seven-foot room. If they didn't get a rope to him soon, he would drown. The knowledge sliced him like a cold knife.

"More rope! We need more rope!" Hans yelled upward.

"Más cuerda!" Christina reiterated in Spanish. Her own voice sounded hysterical to her. "Más cuerda! Rápido! Rápido!" *More rope! Fast!*

Mitch could picture the crew, paralyzed with fear. They'd seen their boss—and part of the treasure—disappear. He prayed one of them would move.

With effort, Mitch freed one arm from the thick, encapsulating substance. He tried not to panic. *Dear God, what have I done?*

As the water rose to his chest, he begged God to spare him. It climbed up his neck and past his chin. He waved his arms around, desperate to find the rope that Hans must surely be dropping his way by now. But found nothing.

—※—

"Mitch! Mitch!" Christina cried. No call answered her. Their headlamps did not illuminate all the way to the bottom, but they could hear the rush of water. "He's in trouble! Oh, Hans, we have to do something!"

Hans finally got the slack he needed from the crew and threw the rope down. They heard the splash. "The rope!" he bellowed down. "Grab the rope, Mitch!"

No answer came. Both knew Christina's worst nightmare was coming true. The trap had sprung, and Mitch was hopelessly caught in its teeth.

"I'm going down!" Hans wound the rope around a fist beneath him and one above, preparing to rappel down the cavern walls. He clenched his flashlight between his teeth.

"Bring him back, Hans," Christina pleaded as he disappeared down the hole. "Please bring him back."

—⁓—

Below, Mitch felt the water crawl up his outstretched arm. He could see the shaft of light filtering to him as if it were from God himself. *I love Christina and the kids, Lord, he prayed silently. Let them know that I loved them more than anyone I ever loved before. I'm sorry. So sorry...*

His oxygen was giving out. Mitch had been under for more than sixty seconds, and he felt dizzy from the effort of holding his breath. His body called out to him to give up. To give in. To give way. His hand slackened.

Dangling above, Hans watched Mitch's hand go limp, a ghostly image in the cave of death. Assuming that Mitch was somehow stuck beneath the water, Hans dropped into the water and swam over to him, careful to not let his legs go down.

"Mitch!" Hans yelled, grabbing his hand. "Mitch!" He could hear Christina's soft, terrified weeping above.

Holding on to Mitch with one hand, and to the rope with

his other, Hans ignored the searing pain in his still-healing arm as he tried to tug Mitch free. He let out a roar, half-determined, half-frustrated. And slowly, reluctantly, Mitch's body moved toward him, the cavern reluctantly giving up its prize.

Mitch's face emerged from the water, ghastly white in the edge of Hans's headlight beam. He gasped for air, his mouth wide in all-consuming need. Then coughed, then gasped again.

He opened his eyes, and Hans laughed in relief. "If you want to dissolve our partnership, just say so, dude."

Mitch was breathing too hard to find a retort, and the water was still rising. Hans gave another mighty heave, and Mitch found himself floating atop, along with his friend.

"I've got him, Christina! He's okay!"

"Oh, thank God! Let's get you both back up here!"

"The chamber's filling up with salt water!" he yelled. "At the rate it's going, it's going to flood the whole shaft in hours."

"Got it! Prepare to evacuate us!" she cried upward.

Hans looked down at Mitch. "He's too weak, Christina. I can just hold on to him and we'll float up to you!"

"No, I don't like it, Hans! One booby trap might set off another! I want you guys out of there!"

Hans grimaced at the thought. "Hold on to the rope, Mitch. With both hands."

Mitch nodded, clearly exhausted.

Floating on his back and working like an otter, Hans hastily wove another seat out of the rope and, ten feet beyond it, another. He helped Mitch into the first one, then clambered into the second. "Okay!" he yelled above. "Bring us up!"

—⁓—

Having gathered enough information to realize that the

wealth below them might disappear at any moment, the crew had panicked, rappelling downward on individual ropes—which now seemed abundantly available—and stuffing their shirts, socks, and shorts with the valuables. Christina screamed at them, trying to get their attention, their help. But no one listened. Giving up, she frantically climbed the ladder and went to the rope and winch. Grimacing at the effort, she began winding the heavy men upward herself.

—◊◊◊—

Hans frowned at their slow pace. Christina's warning about new floodgates haunted him, and he searched the walls for evidence of such a monster. His headlight beam rested on a square stone panel measuring about four by four feet, located three feet above him and nearly blending with the rest of the wall. He shivered. The same image was etched on it that they had found on the olive jars: captain and skeleton, toasting to death. *A panel of death.*

"Christina!" he bellowed. "Hurry!" *I think we're in for another surprise....*

But no one answered.

—◊◊◊—

Christina clenched her teeth and pushed the taut winch crank down, then pulled it up again. The muscles of her arms trembled from the effort. "*Come on,*" she repeated. "Come on," she gritted out.

Inch by inch, the cable rolled around the wheel. *Hurry.* Tears of frustration poured down her face as she toiled on and on, feeling helpless and weak.

Nora ran into the clearing, alerted by Anya and Joshua,

who had been watching and come to the house for help. Her eyes went wide as she saw the crew clambering out of the gaping hole, with pockets bulging with treasure. But there was no sign of either Mitch or her husband. Her eyes found Christina, frantically working, solely concentrating on bringing in the cable that disappeared into the dark cavern. It was obvious at once to her what was transpiring.

"*Padre en el cielo,*" she muttered, running toward Christina. "*Ayúdanos!*" *Father in heaven. Help us!*

Christina looked at Nora with desperate eyes, sweat pouring off her face. Nora joined her at the winch crank, and together they were able to move faster.

"Look out!" Christina thought she heard Hans bellow. "It's going…"

But his words were drowned out by a crack of stone and a tremendous rush of water. With their mouths hanging open, Christina and Nora watched the sides of the excavated pool disintegrate. The crew, each with a rope around their waists tied to trees high above, swung screaming to the sides as the ground dropped beneath them.

—⁓—

Hanging from beneath the winch, still fifty feet down, Mitch and Hans clung to the rope and watched Robert's treasure fall into the dark abyss below, a twinkling, metallic, and bejeweled rain of millions.

Mitch closed his eyes, saying good-bye to the fortune that should have been theirs. But when he opened them, he counted the crew, hanging like baby spiders from a broken web, scrambling to climb back up to safety. He counted, then recounted. The men were all there. And Hans still dangled ten feet below him, bruised but alive.

When Christina and Nora saw them, clinging to the rope below, they let out cries of joy, then began to pull them up the rest of the way.

Thank you, God, Mitch prayed as they rose, *for sparing us all this day. And forgive my greed...*

CHAPTER 29

Mitch sat in the kitchen, covered with mud, head in hands. "I'm sorry, so sorry," he said to them. "If I hadn't lifted that cross..."

"Just thought things were getting a bit dull down there, huh?" Hans teased. He had his arms around Nora, who hadn't let go of him since they finally got the men to safety. Anya rose and took the children outside so the adults could speak freely.

"I thought it was just some sort of altar piece," he said miserably. "A way to honor a saint or something. If I had stopped to think—"

"If you hadn't done it, I might have," Hans said.

"It doesn't matter," Christina said, kneeling beside him and putting a hand on his thigh. "You survived. We all did. When we couldn't get the men to toss another rope...When you went under...Mitch, that was one of the most awful moments of my life. All I wanted—*all* I wanted—was for you to live. And you did."

He looked at her, and briefly caressed her face. "Thank you," he whispered.

"I'm serious," she said. "In that moment, it didn't matter if I ever cashed in any jewels or coins. All I wanted was you."

"Well, I wouldn't go that far," Hans said, making them all laugh. "But I don't have to. Because we still managed to collect a fair fortune."

"All the men turned in what they collected?" Christina asked.

"They did, although we had to turn a few upside-down and shake loose some 'sticky' jewels and coins. I don't think they'll believe we're going to pay them handsomely until we actually cash out and do so."

"But then they will be very happy," Nora said.

"Ten percent of the treasure, divided between them all?" Christina said. "Oh, yes. They have no idea how happy they'll be."

Hans moved over to Mitch and put a hand on his shoulder. "That leaves ninety percent for the three of us. There's still a good ten million in the next room, friend. More than enough to pay off our debts and fund many more excavations."

"But what we lost—"

"What we lost was not ours to begin with," he said. "We hold it all with open hands, right? Hasn't that been our motto for years?"

"Yes, you're right," he said, nodding.

"And we all got to be part of one of the coolest treasure finds ever," Christina said. "That footage we captured? That shaft? The story itself is something we might be able to sell."

"Joni Johnson?" Mitch asked.

"We could call her in a few days," she said. "But for now, I think we all need hot showers and a good night's sleep."

—∿∿—

Awakening late one morning, a week after the disaster at Robert's pool, Christina was surprised to discover a "treasure map" on her pillow that had been drawn with a leaky inkwell pen and burned on the edges to create a weathered, ancient look. She smiled, thinking it was just Mitch's ruse to woo her away from her studies of *The Fearsome* and cataloguing the wealth they had managed to salvage before the cavern collapsed.

She pulled on shorts, a cotton blouse, and—after perusing the map—a pair of hiking boots. In the deserted kitchen, she stole a muffin and swallowed a few sips of juice before setting out, anxious to see what the household was up to.

Christina studied the paper again. At the top was the slogan *"El Mapa a Mi Corazón." The Map to My Heart.* She grinned. Mitch had certainly gone to great lengths to do this. When had he found the time? He had been as busy as she in the week since they discovered—and largely lost—Robert's treasure.

Taking a deep breath, she walked through the French doors, following the path mapped for her. "Ready or not, here I come!" she gaily called.

Her first stop was just shy of Four Fathom Reef, on a palm that bent "under the weight of my love for you." She knew the one: The elastic trunk of a palm had curved toward the ground years before but continued to grow. She and Mitch had sat on it during one of their walks.

There she found Joshua and Kenna, patiently waiting and dressed in the garb of pirates. Christina covered her mouth to keep from laughing. Kenna came toddling toward her, but

Joshua remained serious.

"Treasure hunter!" he shouted sternly, his small brow furrowed.

"Yes?" she asked, picking Kenna up and kissing the child's belly.

"You must answer the first question before I let you pass."

Christina smiled. He must have been practicing his lines for a week. "What is that question, O mighty gatekeeper?"

"If you answer right, you can pass," he said to her in a stage whisper.

"Right. Got it," she said with a smile. "Again, I ask you, what is the question?"

"Do you like children?"

"I do. *Especially* you two."

"You may pass," he said, stretching out his arm toward the beach behind him and smiling at her for the first time.

She hesitated, not wanting to leave the children alone, but then saw Anya rise up out of the bushes and move toward them.

"I'm off then!" she said. The map's path wound around the beach. Occasionally she stopped to look up into the thick foliage of the island, sure that someone trailed her high above. The map led her on a path around the south side of the island, stopping at a place where another spring led out to sea. To cross what the map showed as "Gambler's Ravine," Christina was faced with the choice of wading across waist-deep water and climbing a ten-foot lava rock cliff, or grabbing a nearby rope and swinging across, Tarzan-style. The map seemed to indicate that the rope was the way to go. "Well, glad I'm not as afraid of heights as I am of sharks," she muttered, testing the strength of the rope. Gripping it, she swept across the narrow chasm and landed safely on the other side. Hans emerged from the foliage, applauding, and took the rope from her hands. "Well done, map-quester."

She smiled up at him, thoroughly enjoying the game now. "What is your question, gatekeeper?"

"Will you continue to face adventure and danger courageously as the newest partner to Treasure Seekers?" he asked solemnly.

"The adventure I can take. I'd rather avoid the danger. Especially if it involves Hobard. Or sharks. Or booby-trapped shafts."

His jaw muscle twitched. "Truth be told, fair maiden, we could use someone to keep us out of trouble. You may pass." He bowed, showing her the way to continue.

On the map it was labeled "Playa Negro," and eventually the white granules beneath her feet gave way to a black sand beach. Christina paused, watching and listening to the rush-wash-hiss of the water as gentle waves swept upward and then back out to sea. Walking on, she followed a series of white-rock-and-seashell arrows to a place the map called "The Island's Inquiry." She paused at the spelled-out question, marveling at how much time all of this would take: Whom do you love?

The very island seemed to be asking her of it, so she answered in kind. "I love Mitch Crawford!" she cried.

Talle popped up from the brush, inadvertently scaring her. "You may pass," she said with a shy grin, as Christina covered her rapidly beating heart with a hand and laughed.

The path led upward, back toward the stream and the lava rock cliffs. Christina found herself on the opposite side of the island, farther than Mitch had ever taken her on their walks. The stream curved and wound crazily among the rocks, until she reached the next pass.

There Nora stood, like a sedate island princess in the midst of paradise, a crown of flowers about her head, a long skirt waving about her long, olive-skinned legs. She silently waited, watching the babbling water as it made its way past in pursuit of its oceanic goal.

"Hello, Nora. What is your question?"

She gestured toward the water. "Watch how the water moves, and consider this: Would you stay with your love, through the winding turns and twists of your lives, never allowing them to tear you apart?"

Christina's face softened.

"Yes. I hope I would. I pray it would be so."

"You may pass," Nora said softly, touching Christina's shoulder as if in benediction.

Christina resumed her climb, pausing on a steep rise to grab a handhold in the rock and a foothold on a ledge. She looked up for her next handhold and saw Mitch, reaching down for her. Smiling, he swiftly pulled her the rest of the way up and into his arms. They stood atop the lava cliff, looking out past the stream, over the cove below, and out to sea.

The scenery was beautiful, but it felt far more glorious to Christina to be tucked firmly in his arms at last.

"I followed you as you made your way and heard each of your answers. I could not be happier that you chose me to love. Because Christina Alvarez, I am so in love with you, I can never imagine parting from you again." From his pocket, he withdrew a band of gold, embedded with emeralds, and knelt before her.

Her eyes went wide. The gold was the color of doubloons, and the emeralds were undoubtedly part of Robert's bounty. She looked into his eyes, waiting, hoping.

"No promise of treasure could ever match the value of your love, Christina. You, my love, are God's most precious gift to me. Please," he said, taking her hand, "say you'll be my bride."

Overwhelmed with love, Christina's eyes filled with tears. "Yes," she nodded. "Yes, Mitch. I will be yours. And you will be mine."

"Sheesh, so assuming, so *grabby*," he teased, rising to pull her into his arms and kiss her, again and again. "Just like a true treasure hunter."

EPILOGUE

Three months later

Mitch couldn't resist his new wife's request to go to Mexico and "do a little diving" on their honeymoon, especially after news reached them that the FBI had managed to capture Tate Hobard. Now, knowing his bride was safe, Mitch relaxed on the deck of their small inn, watching as the deep blue water splashed against the bleached rocks below.

Christina, wrapped in a fluffy white robe, exited their room and came to wrap her arms around him from behind. "It's another ugly day in the Caribbean," she said.

"Yeah," he said, pretending to sound burdened. "We'll just have to muddle our way through. But first, breakfast?"

"Breakfast," she affirmed. "I'm starving."

He turned in her arms and gave her a kiss on the forehead before cradling her close. Despite her professed hunger, they stood there for a while, looking out to sea. "Think *La Canción* is out there?"

"It's not up north, or Hobard would've likely found her

before he was captured."

"Yeah, there would've been signs of their excavation," she said. They'd had this conversation several times before, but she found it assuring. There was still a chance...

"But even if it *is* here," Mitch reminded her, "we kinda have our hands full with Four Fathoms, as well as seeing to the treasure auction."

"I know. And the kids." She gave him a final squeeze and then sat down at the small deck table and poured a cup of coffee. Between them was a plate piled high with fresh pastries, bananas and pineapple. "I'm missing them."

"So am I," he said, pouring his second cup. "Glad this is a quick trip, but I think it's good we took the time. I needed time with my *wife* alone."

"And I needed time with my *husband*," she returned. "I'm still not used to saying that word."

"No?" he said, cocking a brow. "Well, I love hearing it. I'm a lucky, lucky man."

"Yes, you are," she said, clinking her cup to his in a cheeky "cheers."

"You know, *La Canción* has remained buried for all this time," he said. "Don't you think she can stay buried until we're ready to go hunting again?"

"I don't know. The wreck at Four Fathoms was buried for hundreds of years until I bumped up against the coral that covered her cannon. It only takes a bit to begin a widening chasm..." She looked out to sea, twisting the coffee cup in her hands. "But even if we never find her, or someone else does, I'm content. I have you, the kids. Work to fill the coming years. I'm trying to trust God with the rest. I don't want to be one of those people who is always thinking about what she wants or doesn't have, rather than seeing, really seeing what she already has. I'm a rich woman," she said, staring into his eyes, "and the treasure we've uncovered is just a small part of that."

He smiled at her, love filling his eyes. "And that, right there, is a big part of why I fell in love with you. You're a wise woman, Christina Crawford."

"I married you, right?"

"Clearly your wisest move ever," he said with a wink, raising his cup again to clink against hers.

—⚬⚬⚬—

Christina and Mitch carried their equipment aboard. They settled in, and the captain raced out of the harbor to where the best diving was to be found. The reefs.

They rose and went to the front when the captain slowed the boat, then threw the anchor. It dragged and caught, pulling the vessel to a halt.

They geared up, wearing full wet suits so they could remain under longer. Flashing an okay sign to each another, they rolled backward into the water. Inwardly Christina sighed as she looked about. Being underwater always gave her a restful, peaceful feeling. *Diving feels a lot like flying,* she decided.

Mitch gave her the okay sign again, then moved toward the elegant colonies of brain coral directly below them. She followed, careful not to touch the delicate formations, but already distracted by the wealth of marine life around her.

She giggled as a spiny lobster scuttled toward safety under a rock when she discovered him under the ledge of another. She followed a queen angelfish for a while, darting after the brightly colored blue-gold-and-pink creation as if it were a game. A bright yellow-and-red Spanish hogfish distracted her soon after though, and she followed it back to where Mitch studied a huge Nassau grouper, which oddly kept butting up against his mask, as if it wanted in.

Together they swam away from the grouper and entered a deep, turbulent chasm with a sandy bottom and steep cliffs of coral on either side and a school of golden fish moving below them. *A living yellow brick road*, Christina thought. This was what she loved about diving: the unexpected, the unseen, the undiscovered.

All except for the sharks. When three gray reef sharks entered the chasm and swam toward them, Mitch rose up and grabbed her hand. She edged behind him, feeling like a coward but needing a sense of protection. The sharks swam past, uninterested in the human invaders, and Mitch turned to look at Christina. *Are you okay?* his eyes asked her.

She nodded, willing her heart to cease pounding and her lungs to breathe normally as Mitch calmly stroked her hand. With another nod, she moved forward, in the lead this time. At the next corner, a group of amazing basket sponges garnished the sides of the cliffs, each measuring at least four feet wide and six feet tall. The tiny microorganisms rushing by on the current often caused the monsters to grow large, but Christina had never seen any of this size.

They meandered on, loving the thrill of exploring a new place together, loving the chance just to be together. She considered the name, El Puerto de Muerte, and thought it all wrong. Because this was a harbor rife with life, not death, Christina decided. She watched her husband coax a tiny octopus from its coral cave, and beyond him, rays of sunlight cascaded down through the azure waters.

A huge southern stingray rustled in a sand channel twenty feet away. Christina turned and moved to follow him as he left his nest beneath a coral ledge. Mitch joined her. The ray slowly built up speed using his wide wings. Behind him, the sand billowed up in a wild cloud.

So taken was she by the stingray, she almost missed it. But something briefly sparkled in the sunlight, before the sand filtered down again to cover it. Christina grabbed Mitch's hand and motioned toward the coral ledge. She swept away the sand and then pulled back, wondering if she was really seeing what she thought she was seeing.

Was this it? Treasure from *La Canción*? She picked up the nearest coin and saw the marking, identifying it as originating in Potosí. It was possible. It really was possible.

With a grin, Mitch pulled her into his arms—their bulky gear making it awkward—and gestured to the surface. Christina took hold of a coin in each hand and followed him upward. They would whoop and holler and kiss and make plans now, to record, excavate and salvage the site, whether it was her ancestor's ship or another.

Regardless, she was thankful, so thankful, to have Mitch at her side. The kids awaiting them. Hans and Nora, Talle, back on Robert's Foe. Because no matter what treasure they found—or didn't—in the future, she knew that all these people were her greatest find of all.

Dear Reader:

I was sitting on an airplane reading a magazine when I came across the article on a treasure hunter in the Caribbean. What a perfect hero! I could see Mitch almost from the start: cocky, arrogant, and yet a good man underneath. He just needed the right woman to teach him a lesson in love. Enter Christina. Smart, beautiful, determined. And those darling kids. Mitch had no choice but to see what he really should treasure in life: God and family.

I had a great deal of fun writing this novel the first time—I loved the adventure, the intrigue, and the highly romantic setting of a private island in the middle of the Caribbean. At the time, I'd never been to the islands, but I loved fantasizing about it. We were poor newlyweds, dreaming about one day traveling. Happily, those dreams were realized twenty years later, and now, rewriting this novel brings back All the Feels for my beloved Caribbean. (Yes, it's mine. But I'll share it with you if you ever get to see it for yourself.)

I love hearing from readers. If you care to, connect with me via email at Lisa@bergrencreativegroup.com, on Facebook.com/LisaTawnBergren or Instagram @LisaTBergren. I deeply appreciate your support. May you always store up your treasures in heaven.

Every blessing,

Lisa

ACKNOWLEDGMENTS

Many thanks to my readers who helped me get this twenty-five-year-old book into updated shape! All I remembered was that I loved this action-packed novel; little did I know how much work it would take to revise. These dedicated readers helped me by giving me their candid feedback and did a great job proofing: Mary Esque, Lilly Alison, Kiah Oosterbeek, Lisa Maddox, Kelly Norman, Carrie Henderson Weston, Bethany Hisada, Bettie Boswell, Bonnie Forte, Melanie Stroud, Karen Birkenholz, Shirley Miller, Shaina Hawkins, Shannon Talbot, Margaret Nelson, Mindy Houng, and Sharon Miles. I am forever grateful to each of them.

ONCE UPON A SUMMER...

Did you enjoy *Once Upon an Caribbean Summer*? Be sure to look for these other contemporary love stories set in other romantic settings...

Once Upon a Montana Summer

Once Upon a Alaskan Summer

Once Upon an Irish Summer (2020)

Once Upon a Hawaiian Summer (TBD)

WANT TO CONNECT WITH ME?

Visit my web site, www.LisaTBergren.com, and subscribe to my enewsletter. I promise not to overwhelm your in-box, and you can get a free e-book!

You can also connect with me via:
Facebook.com/LisaTawnBergren
Instagram and Twitter: @LisaTBergren

—◊◊—

Did you enjoy this book?

Reader reviews make a huge difference for authors, because it helps us sell books (and therefore, keep writing). Please consider adding your honest response on the retailer's site where you purchased this novel. You don't need to summarize the book—just a line or two about what you liked best works really well. (And if you want to get *extra* credit—virtual gold, shiny stars and heart-eyes from me—copy and paste that review on Bookbub.com and goodreads.com.) Thank you so much!

Also by Lisa T. Bergren

Breathe
Sing
Claim

Glamorous Illusions
Glittering Promises
Grave Consequences

Waterfall
Cascade
Torrent
Bourne & Tributary
Deluge

Remnants: Season of Wonder
Season of Fire
Season of Glory

Keturah
Verity
Selah

Lisa T. Bergren is the author of over sixty books, with a total of more than three million books sold. She writes in many genres, from romance to women's fiction, from supernatural suspense and time travel YA to children's picture books. Lisa and her husband, Tim, have three big kids and one little, white, fluffy dog. She lives in Colorado but loves to travel and is always thinking about where she needs to research her next novel. In the coming year, she hopes to get to Hawaii and Ireland. To find out more, visit LisaTBergren.com.